A WORLD EMBATTLED

The planet Nelding. Settled by a religious colony
from Earth in the twenty-first century. Slowly, the
laws of Nelding took hold, and a race of mutants—
oddly resembling the dirad, a monstrous beast native
to the planet—was born.

For years, First Fathers—still-human descendants of
the original settlers—and mock dirads maintained an
uneasy truce within their respective domains. For the
puritanical Fathers, life was a fearful, joyless mo-
notony. And for the exiled mock dirads, life was
savage, precarious, simmering with explosive rebel-
lions.

Nelding awaited its savior.

Its **STARMOTHER**

STARMOTHER

SYDNEY J. VAN SCYOC

BERKLEY BOOKS, NEW YORK

STARMOTHER

A Berkley Book / published by arrangement with
the author's agent

PRINTING HISTORY
Berkley Medallion edition / March 1977
Berkley edition / February 1984

ISBN: 0-425-06467-0

A BERKLEY BOOK ® TM 757,375
Berkley Books are published by The Berkley Publishing Group,
200 Madison Avenue, New York, New York 10016.
The name "BERKLEY" and the stylized "B" with design
are trademarks belonging to Berkley Publishing Corporation.

To Jim

Chapter One

FACE PRESSED to the single port, Jahna peered down at the emergent face of Nelding. It appeared through cloud cover in brief snatches, gray-green, dull. Then the shuttlecraft arced down into thick cloud and the port was a blinded eye. Droplets of moisture zipped across its outer surface, urgent, wind-driven, as nerve-frantic as the insistent questions that ragtailed through Jahna's mind. She pulled back from the port to confront those questions again.

Why? Why had the Service Corps disrupted her educational program to dispatch her here by first trader to care for a handful of mutant infants? Jahna's training had not been focused on any physical phase of child care. True, once her program of training was complete, once she was fully certified as general situational counselor, she would be qualified to advise parents on broad questions of child management. But she would be in no way considered a specialist in the actual physical delivery of care, particularly to atypical infants. Nor would she be qualified to educate parents in the delivery of that care, her secondary duty here.

Here. And now she was here, here to begin. Or here to fail. She weighed that last word reluctantly. Troubled, she glanced down again and found they had broken cloud cover. Land lay directly below, dark, wet, uninviting. She peered across the sodden landscape. Squinting, she distinguished a narrow strand of dirt roadway, a meager clutter of cabins, the combed furrows of cultivated fields. Quickly she reeled her glance into the cabin again, the contrast of Nelding with her own golden Peace, bright

1

beneath vivid skies and a warming sun, suddenly too painful.

The cabin comm cleared its metal throat. "Strap for final descent, Cadet." Jahna smiled faintly. Pilot Darr's Nebulese lilt defied even the comm's metal vocal apparatus. Abandoning port, she strapped into her seat. Involuntarily she glanced over the other seats, austerely vacant of human reassurance. Her hands tightened on her armrest, her mind possessed again by obsessive doubt. Even Major Holmes had not known why Jahna had been selected. Commander Dublin herself had not known. Only the men who had summoned her, the First Fathers of Nelding, held that answer.

Abruptly the shuttle nosed down and slammed through the damp air. Breath sharply caught, Jahna was crushed against her seat back. Then they returned to the horizontal and touched ground with a grinding bump. Jahna craned forward toward the port. But Nelding rocked by too swiftly, too violently, for her to form a coherent first impression.

The shuttle slowed, halted. "Nelding Field," the comm informed her. "Emphasize: *field*."

Jahna released her straps shakily and stood. The view from the port consisted now of mud, tangling vines, and a distant cluster of trees, dark and musty. Chill air rolled in to greet her when the cabin door swung. Beyond, a swath of mud stretched a hundred feet to a crude log structure. A dark figure hovered in shadow at the corner of the structure.

"Your host, Humble Nodd," Pilot Darr explained, folding down the steps. His brows arched quizzically. "You're truly sked for two years on this wet place?"

"Looks like it," Jahna agreed dispiritedly. She took the four metal steps slowly and, dismayed, found herself poised on the brink of mud. "Isn't there a portable walkway?"

Darr grinned. "Now, on Nelding you wade, Cadet. And the door, you notice, is on the roundabout side of the shed. Will you give me your hand?"

2

Jahna stiffened. "I can manage."

"Then I will check your bags from the hold, Cadet, and follow you," Darr answered cheerfully, hopping easily away through the mud.

At first contact, Nelding squelched liquidly over the toe of Jahna's boot. Cautiously she waded the sucking mud until the dark figure at the corner of the log structure clarified into a lean man in sagging trousers and rough-spun shirt. His beard was long, trimmed square, and his dark hair was pulled into a tight knot over his left ear. Humble Nodd regarded her steadily, expressionlessly, from deep eyes. His features appeared to have hardened into rock some years before.

"I'm Jahna Swiss of the Planet Peace Service Cadet Corps," she informed him crisply, when he offered no greeting. "Reporting for duty as requested by the First Fathers of Nelding."

Although the dark eyes remained expressionless, the rock of Nodd's lower jaw crumbled. The speech that emerged was slow, strangely cadenced. "There are papers of identification I will examine before any person passes."

"Of course." The pockets of her daysuit held the necessary documents.

Nodd accepted her papers deliberately and examined them at length, dark brows drawn tight, beard motionless on his chest. He returned them with a rejective flick of his wrist. "Now there is personal luggage I will examine. For that we will turn into the inspection shed."

Jahna glanced back. Pilot Darr waded toward them. She accepted her Corps cape from him and pulled it around her shoulders.

The inspection cabin was a single chamber, long and low and dark, a place of odorous shadow. Walls and low ceiling were bearded with flowing mosses in somber greens, browns, grays. At one end of the shed a long log table stood beneath a hanging lantern. Moss swayed overhead as Humble Nodd tracked heavily across the floor.

"Now you will open up your luggage here for my

3

inspection," their host announced ungenially, planting himself behind the table. "Then you will remove your outer garments and spread them."

"Cape and boots only, Cadet," Pilot Darr interposed quickly. "Modesty remains intact on Nelding."

"Modesty is first of the felicitous virtues," Nodd affirmed, an unexpected roll of thunder from their west. "You will open up your luggage now."

A quarter hour later Jahna and Darr emerged from the inspection shed, Jahna huddled grim in her cape. A dark grove grew to their left, limbs spreading low to the ground, sheltering shadow-phantoms and long swaths of hanging moss. To their right a rutted mud track wound away into a field of vines. Jahna studied the prospect bleakly, Humble Nodd's stony words, his deliberately disrespectful handling of her personals still in mind. "Have you any idea what's next on the agenda?" she asked the pilot.

"Our host is fetching his wagon to drive you to your accommodations. From here it is four kilometers to Forgiven, a community of several hundred souls. I assume you will quarter there for the night, Cadet."

Jahna studied the pilot's cheerful face, wishing she could tap his bland good spirits for her own benefit. "Have you—have you spent much time on Nelding?"

"Myself?" Darr flexed back upon his heels, hands clasped behind. "Now, one time I did find me stranded in Forgiven for a long four days. These settlers trade the hair of mo-sheep, you know, and the shearing came late." His smile grew pensive. "Four days, Cadet, in a chill un-chinked cabin eating myself dull on barley and bits of beef so big I couldn't find them. Once, you understand, I thought I had one but it crawled off my spoon and flew away. An insect it proved to be. Those we do not have on Nebulon."

Jahna sighed, unable to share his whimsy. "Did you see any mutants that visit?"

The pilot's brows arced up. "Mutants here? On Nelding?"

"That's what I'm delegated for," she said sharply. "To care for a group of mutant infants."

"Ah. . . ." Darr absorbed the information with patent interest, rocking. *"Ah."* He shook his head slowly. "No, Cadet, I did not see even one mutant, although I saw some very sour faces and some very bony bodies. Some very stunted spirits too, living under these Fathers—like Humble Nodd coming."

Jahna's head turned. Their host appeared around the far corner of the shed leading a gargantuan horse with broad muddy hooves and a prodigious mane that grew the length of its spine. Dun sheaths of hair swayed as the animal paced the sucking mud. An open wooden wagon rattled behind the animal.

Jahna turned urgently back to the pilot. "But you saw no mutants at all?"

"Cadet, I saw three hairy moles, a crooked nose or two—but not so much as a port wine stain upon any face or hand, if you want to call that a mu-sign, which I don't. And I have traveled abby circuit, Xetetter, Coronel, Smith's World—all the mutating heavens I have covered in my travels. I know a mu when I see one."

Jahna studied his bland face. "Then it must be a cluster crisis," she speculated. "Some isolated mutagen that has just been turned up after all these years." Nelding had been colonized, she knew, three hundred years ago by an Earth-party of firm religious persuasion and very little capital backing.

"A newly dug well," the pilot suggested. "That is how it began on Coronel, first one deep well drilled down into radioactive layers, then another, then a third. By the time the poor devils realized they were destroying their humanity with every dipper of water, it was too late. Abbies all now. No normal human left among them. Not that I disparage what they are, strange creatures. They have five sexes, you know, and their offspring are sometimes feathered—and sometimes not."

Jahna nodded impatiently. She knew about Coronel—and about the others. In the centuries since Earth Exodus

5

began, the stars had seared their mark boldly upon the human race. On some worlds the damage was more extensive than on others. In the case of Coronel it was doubtful that "damage" was the appropriate term at all. Transmogrification seemed a more fitting description of what the deep wells of Coronel had wrought.

But this was not Coronel. Neither was it Xetetter or Smith's World. It was Nelding, damp backworld where the human germ plasm had evidently remained relatively unscathed until recently. And why had she, child of equally unscathed Peace, been chosen to deal with the small victims of whatever genetic catastrophe had occurred? Was Nelding so backward that no one of their own citizens could organize care for the aberrant infants?

She lifted her head to find Humble Nodd's stony eyes on her. His dark beard twitched. "Now you will arrange yourself here for the journey," he rumbled, indicating the unpadded bed of the wagon.

Jahna stared at the weathered boards, suddenly victim of unwelcome apprehension. She touched her lips with a dry tongue. Once she climbed into this wagon, once Pilot Darr turned back to his craft, once she allowed herself to be transported away down the wet mud track by this strange and unpleasant Nodd. . . .

"You will arrange yourself here," that same Nodd reiterated, his dark eyes bitter with annoyance.

Jahna's forehead creased. "Of course," she snapped, irritation overriding apprehension.

The bed of the wagon was hostile with splinters and dried mud. When Jahna had arranged her cape on the planks, Pilot Darr tossed up her bags, his eyes momentarily serious. "I will fax back to your commander that you arrived safely, Cadet."

"Thank you," Jahna muttered, averting her eyes.

Nodd boarded his seat and took the lines. With a groan the wagon creaked forward. Jahna braced herself.

"Be sure to wash behind the ears," Darr called. "That's the first place the moss grows, Cadet. And eat no beef without being sure first it does not wish to fly away."

Soon, too soon, the landing field was lost around a curve of the road and Jahna was submerged in alien landscape. Dark vegetation lined the road. Nearby, a pair of massive-trunked trees spread broad branches to the ground, forming a dark shelter. The trunks of both trees were heavily bearded with moss. The drooping limbs claimed a large, irregular circle of soil from other vegetation. Beyond the perimeter of that barren circle, assorted vines twined. Oddly shaped melons, yellow, green, black, squatted beneath musty-looking gray-green leaves. Farther, a field of husky scarlet spears marched briefly beside the road, lancing the dull mist. Seed cones bulged from lateral pockets.

Jahna turned to study these plants in passing, curiosity stimulated. Then she leaned forward. "Have you been able to domesticate much of this native vegetation for table use?"

Humble Nodd's lean face tautened in disapproval. He did not turn. "We do not touch unfit food."

Rebuffed, Jahna shrank back, her lips tightening angrily. When the shuttlecraft exploded upward moments later, flashing high to bury itself in the underside of the gray cloud-belly, she was aware of a sharp pang of resentment. Darr had no right to abandon her to this stern and bitter Nodd. No right, no right at all.

And every right. It was her own Service Corps which was abandoning her. Quickly, almost ferociously, she ran mental inventory of available data on Nelding. Like her own Peace, it had been claimed by a Terran group late in the twenty-first century. Like Peace, it was classified Earth-Normal in gravity, atmospheric makeup, and general surface composition. The original settlers had claimed a single continent of the three available. The present government, Nelding's First Fathers, evinced no interest in expansion, geographic or economic, and so the two remaining continents were uninhabited by humans. Interest lay instead in what was termed in the informational letter "the life of the felicitous virtues." The exact nature of these virtues, however, had remained unspecified.

Sinking back against the rough side of the wagon, Jahna closed her eyes, suddenly bleak. She was prepared to deal with discomfort, with inconvenience, even—yes—with the possibility of failure. But a sky that held no sun? A horizon perpetually gray on gray? A succession of stony Nelding faces that yielded no recognition of common humanity? Nothing had prepared her for the reality of Nelding.

But she would not permit herself to sink into despair. Rousing herself, Jahna leaned forward again, pulling her chained chronom from her neckline. It seemed appropriate to make a first small adjustment to Nelding. "Can you tell me the local time?"

Humble Nodd peered up at the overcast sky. "Can't you read sky, Starhand? It approaches the midpoint between noon and darkness."

Jahna stared up at the solid-clouded sky, puzzled. "It does?"

"Does not the pattern of light inform you?" Nodd demanded shortly, staring straight ahead again.

Jahna tried to find some contrasting distribution of light and shadow aloft, found instead a uniform gray on sullen gray. She cradled the shiny chronom in her palm. "Then what time does it get dark locally?" she inquired, determined.

This time Nodd turned in his seat. His dark eyes encompassed the bright metal object in her hand. In the depths of his eyes judgment was passed. Nodd's beard twitched with profound disapproval. Silent, rejecting, he turned back and hunched over the lines.

An hour later a discouraged cluster of cabins loomed up from the tangled vines, a day-vision of comfortless exile. Windowless, weathered, each of identical dimensions, they were set at rigidly measured intervals. A system of decrepit wooden walkways connected them. Jahna roused herself, staring out bleakly. "Is this Forgiven?" This joyless squalor?

"It is."

Jahna hugged herself against chill. "And I will be living here?"

Nodd turned to face her, condemnation caustic in his deep eyes. "Never will you sleep under our roofs or share our tables, Starhand. You are not needed here."

Jahna recoiled, her face warming. "Then where am I needed?" she snapped, her voice little gentler than his.

Nodd pulled the creaking wagon to the side of the road. "Farther." Reaching near his feet, he handed down a pair of heavy coverlets. "Wait here and cover up your trousers. No person in Forgiven wants to see them."

Jahna snatched the damp coverlets and stared after him as he tramped through the mud to the wooden walkway. "Maybe civility should be considered someplace on the roster of virtues," she muttered angrily.

While she waited, mist turned to drizzle, drizzle to rain. Jahna zipped into her luggage and fetched out rain gear. Drawing it over her head, she fervently hoped she was not intended to wait much longer here.

Expect the unexpected, she reminded herself. "We know virtually nothing about present-day Nelding," Major Holmes had briefed her before departure. "It was settled three centuries ago by a group with beliefs and principles quite different from those of the group who founded our own society. Accordingly, you can expect that the evolutionary trend of their society has taken quite a different direction from our own. You will almost certainly find some conditions there that will strike you as alien, just as the people of Nelding will find some of your attitudes and assumptions strange. Don't expect the familiar, Swiss—expect the unexpected.

"I'm sorry not to have firmer information concerning your mission. The First Fathers specified only that your duties would include caring for a group of genetically damaged infants. Commander and I feel you must work not just with the infants but with the parents as well. Since your tour is only to be two years, you must try to leave the parents prepared to care for the young themselves.

9

"And I am most sorry I can offer no explanation for the fact that the Fathers passed over dozens of cadets fully qualified in infant care and insisted upon you instead, Swiss."

Now Jahna stared at the dreary log community and wondered. What could be unexpected here. Warmth? Fellowship? Humor? Huddling in the rain, she decided the most welcome unexpected event would be the premature termination of her duty tour.

Then the door of the hut Nodd had entered opened. Her host emerged, his beard a dark flag of disapproval. He carried two large baskets. A lean woman stepped to the walkway behind him. She was dressed in long heavy skirts and a coarse gray shirtwaist. Her hair was knotted tightly over her forehead. She stared out at Jahna, her gaze flat and unfriendly. Jahna shrank from a sense of malevolent contact. *Darr, did you set me down on the wrong planet?*

The wrong planet, Cadet? I've been skirting these back-worlds a dozen years and never dropped a bright-haired girl in the wrong mudhole yet.

But maybe this time, Darr?

Nodd plodded through the mud and set the baskets in the bed of the wagon. "These are for your use, Starhand," he rumbled censoriously. "Now you may eat your supper meal when hunger prompts and you may make up your bed whenever you are ready to sleep." His tone suggested that whatever times she chose to indulge her bodily needs would be morally reprehensible.

Jahna stared up at him. "You intend for me to sleep in this wagon?"

Nodd's beard switched irritably. "That is the intention. We will travel through the night."

Jahna's glance shot to the row of huts, indignation suddenly burning bright. "And what provision do you intend to make for calls of nature?"

Nodd's deep eyes turned to rock. "On this world those matters are never mentioned."

"We don't normally make social conversation on the topic on Peace either. But it's never considered in bad taste

10

to ask to be directed to the nearest bathroom.''

Muscles rippled in Nodd's jaw, labor contractions. His concession was reluctant of birth and puny. ''Beyond Forgiven I will make a stop.''

Jahna glanced pointedly at the house from which he had just emerged. Nodd made no response to her unspoken suggestion. He climbed to his seat, resumed the lines. The wagon groaned forward again.

Jahna huddled in the wagon bed as the conveyance bumped through the tiny settlement of Forgiven and into the countryside. There, in a grove of trees, Nodd made the promised stop. Incensed, Jahna dismounted and waded into the vines. By the time she had resettled herself in the bed of the wagon, mud from her boots had been transferred to her daysuit, to her cape, to her hands and face, and her spirit was distinctly sodden.

''When will we reach our destination?'' she demanded tightly when the wagon took road again.

Nodd turned in his seat, dark eyes aglitter. ''Are you that anxious to care for the animals? Do you champ to get your starhands into their spittle and dung?''

Jahna hardly trusted her words as they emerged. ''I don't believe I've ever heard anyone speak so inhumanely about deformed human infants, Citizen.''

''Human?'' The word was scraped up from the rocky bottom of Nodd's soul. ''Who told you you would be tending human infants? You will tend animals.''

''I hardly believe my government would send me this distance to tend livestock,'' Jahna snapped. ''The Service Corps is dedicated to helping the human race. In exchange for our education, we carry out public service projects and donate our services to people who require special assistance.''

''Here you will help animals!''

Jahna clenched her fists, fury-ridden, impotent to express herself adequately, to wound Humble Nodd as deeply as the moment demanded.

They passed from rain to drizzle and back to mist. Later they rattled through a second small community. Dusk

11

gathered gloomily around a dismal huddle of interconnected cabins. On a decrepit walkway, a young girl stood frozen, starveling eyes huge, caught, helpless to break contact with Jahna's as she bumped past. Jahna was just as helpless, riveted by the girl's unexpected fear. *That could be me, if my ancestors had settled Nelding*, she realized starkly. Then the girl clasped her swollen abdomen, her mouth open in a silent gasp of pain. And dusk separated them. *That could be me, pregnant, trapped, swollen with dread.*

Of what?

Later Jahna poked into the basket Nodd had brought. It yielded a charred loaflet of bread and a pale ball that could only be cheese. She sniffed the cheese, found its odor as untempting as the charcoaled crust of the bread. Discouraged, she returned both items to the basket.

When dark came, she spread mats from the basket and arranged herself beneath layers of rain gear, coverlets, and coarse blanketing. Lying down wet and hungry, tired and disgruntled, Jahna stared at the weathered wood of the wagonside until its coarse grain imprinted itself upon her consciousness.

Chapter Two

IN THE dusk-chill of the granary, Piety measured barley groats with a quivering hand, conscious at once of Sister Nair's sharp eye and of the dried smear at the left corner of her mouth. Darting, her tongue moistened it, but when she turned her head to secretly tongue it away, her arm jerked and grain rattled across the table.

"Sister!" Nair's vigilant hands were upon the disorder in a twitch. She swept the grain into a pile and snatched the scoop from Piety's hand. Seizing Piety's portion bag, she rattled the spilled grain into it. Impatiently she dug into the grain barrel and topped off the bag. "Where do you keep your eyes, Hand?" she demanded, thrusting the filled bag back at Piety.

"I—" Piety's lips trembled. "I felt pang," she pleaded untruthfully, her voice rising. Eyes averted, hands trembling, she strung the bag shut. But her fingers were as stiff as her mind. The tied bag slipped and rattled to the floor.

"Pang?" Sister Nair was around the table in a flap of black skirts, slapping one hand to Piety's belly. "Pang, Sister?"

"It—it's gone now!" Piety pleaded, helpless tears turning her eyes liquid.

The wiry hands continued to press. "Oh, is it?" One hand caught Piety under the chin and twitched her head up for sharp scrutiny. "Was it the first today?"

Piety's lips numbed. "It—*yes*," she gasped. "The *first*." Desperately she pulled her chin from Nair's pinching fingers and bent for her portion bag.

13

When she straightened, Nair had stepped back. But her eyes were just as sharp, just as ready to pounce. "Then you'd better take yourself to Sister Cree and tell her to ready the bed, Hand."

"I—l-later, Sister," Piety promised. "If there—if there is another."

"Oh? Now how do you think you will extricate yourself from the present state if there is not, Hand? These matters are seldom resolved with a single pang."

Piety backed away, her thoughts fervent upon the door. "I—*yes*. I'll take myself. I'll—but first, my Father Hoock's supper meal. Then I'll—I'll—"

Stumbling, she managed to escape the granary. Her last view of Sister Nair was of a vinegary face and two bitter-bright, knowing eyes.

Outside, desperately, Piety wet her skirttail and scrubbed lips and chin. But how could Sister guess? Surely no other sister had ever done the filthy thing Piety had done today when she straggled behind the work crew and seized out in her terrible hunger. . . .

Terrible hunger. Shuddering, she could feel the filthy melon between her teeth again, tough skin torn aside by her teeth, yellow fruit firm and resistant, vaguely sweet, dry. But not so dry it did not ooze and smear. She dropped her skirt helplessly, her flesh still host to the filthy feel of the melon, her teeth still feeling it too, firm but yielding, sweet. . . .

Desperately she wrenched her thoughts from the melon and hurried down the walkway. She had reached her own cabin door when she heard the rattle of a wagon in the road. With no thought she turned her head.

And she was smitten by twin harbingers of disaster. It was Father Nodd's wagon that clattered the road. He was carrying Father Lord's starhand to Pengalen to tend the monster-babes. And as the offworld woman rode by, she captured Piety's eyes with her own pale orbs. Piety could not turn her head.

It was an omen, an omen underscored by the sudden pain that twisted Piety's face and made her suck a harsh

14

breath. She grasped at her abdomen, exhaling a single silent plea.

No!

But the omen, the star woman passing at this moment on her way to the monster-babes, was clear. Piety stared, stunned, as Humble Nodd's wagon disappeared into dusk, the starhand's vivid garment slowly merging with the end of day. When the wagon was gone, Piety seized at the door for support, her legs suddenly weak with terrible certainty. She had eaten filth only twice in her life, one of those times today, but plainly she had thereby incorporated corruption not only into herself, where it would give no clearly observable sign, but into the babe she carried. And now that babe. . . .

That babe would be no babe but a monster. Piety stumbled into the cabin, eyes large in her face, staring at a near and agonizing event. Tonight or tomorrow a monster would struggle from her bowels. Within hours she would expulse horror. And there would be no hiding it. Sister Cree, Sister Nair, Sister Elms—weakly she imagined those stern faces when she delivered her guilt under their attending gaze. Beside their faces she counterposed Father Hoock's when Nair told him how his new young wife had corrupted their firstborn.

With an agonized moan, Piety threw herself against the plank wall. Father Hoock's first wife had kept herself clean and had given him two clean daughters. Now Piety was about to present him a beast.

Never. Desperately she vowed it. When the pang returned, she would close herself and refuse the monster passage to the world. It would smother inside her. Father Hoock would never know. He would never clutch her arm, his eyes bulging, his rocky jaw measuring out the harsh syllables of condemnation. The bag of barley groats slipped from her fingers as she staggered across the room to the cookpot. *Never.*

When she had the fire lit and the cold porridge warming, the second pang struck. Piety caught her lip in her teeth, refusing to gasp or moan. In a sweat of dread she prepared

Father Hoock's supper meal. Twice more pangs struck and she fought to deny them.

Then Father Hoock came with a grumble and sat himself. As she ladled hot porridge for him, a fifth pang took her, deeper than the others, harder. Involuntarily she sucked breath. Father Hoock glowered up at her. "Sister?" His brows were dark tangles, his eyes fierce gods.

"It—I burned my thumb," she gabbled, her voice senseless with dread.

Grunting, he turned back to his porridge.

When the pang had passed, she huddled by her bed watching Father Hoock's jaws work and struggling to close down the passageway of birth. But the process refused to be denied. By the time Father Hoock grumbled up from the table and extinguished the lantern for night, sweat was on Piety's face and fear wild in her heart. *She could not stop the birth.*

She fought it for longer, anyway, listening to Father Hoock's heavy snore, huddling around her misery.

Finally she knew she must go to Sister Cree. The longer she delayed, the closer the questioning the Sisters would inflict upon her later, the shrewder their guesses into the state of her mind regarding the approaching birth. Shivering, dreading, she bundled herself up from her bed. The door opened with a squawk, but Father Hoock did not stir. Then she stood on the walkway. She doubled over with a sharp pang, gasping.

When it passed, she tottered unsteadily across the walkway to Sister Cree's door. There she huddled against the wall. *No!* her mind kept crying. *No!*

Her hand raised to rap and then trembled away. She could not face Sister. She could not deliver her monster-babe under those attending eyes. She would die first.

Die she might, from the solution that came to mind. But sooner die alone in the wilds than attended by the Sister-furies! With desperate resolution she turned and crept the length of the walkway to the path that led to the road. There, with a single tortured glance back at her home, dark and desolate under the sullen night sky, she took foot

16

down the mud track. When she had rounded the first bend, slipping twice, almost falling, she cut out into the vines.

Once her ankle was strangled by a wiry stem and she sprawled. Before she could fight erect again, pang took her. With a terrible groan she rolled in the vines, fighting to keep from screaming. Then it passed. Clumsily she regained her feet.

She fell again, twice, and once she threw herself down and bit her knuckles in agony. Then she reached a small grove. Panting, she crept beneath its tenting limbs and toppled onto the bed of leaves beneath it. But when she regained her breath, she realized she was too near fields that would be tended tomorrow. If the birth were prolonged, it was all too likely she would be discovered and carried back to Sister Cree. Desperate, she scrambled up from the bed of leaves and took foot again, determined to run as far from the settlement as possible before necessity halted her.

Desperation drove her across the fields. With every pang her direction changed, until she began to fear she had run full circle and would soon emerge at Forgiven again. But the fields she ran now, she realized dimly, were not cultivated. These fields were wild with vine and native growth, untouched by hand or blade.

Finally she fell to the ground again beneath the protective arms of the trees and struggled with that blind animal, birth. It was faceless, dark, cruel. It played with her, it tore at her, it twisted and terrorized her. Then it stalked broad circles around her, preparing to fall upon its gasping victim again and inflict still another, deeper pang, to draw still another, hoarser cry.

Then, when dawn drew its pale circle around her place of struggle, the animal fell upon her a final time and in a great convulsion, her babe was born. And although the animal stalked away then, growling, chortling, she was not alone. For beside her, when she had done everything she must, when she could spare a look, beside her. . . .

But one cringing look was all. It confirmed her worst fears. She could not look at the babe again, not now. For if

17

she did, she would never live the day. The birth process had drained her physical strength. To sacrifice spirit-strength too by looking on the end result of her terrible transgression would be invitation to death. And she must not die now. For she found that even though she could not bear to look at her poor babe, she could not desert it either, could not leave it here motherless and cold. Her eyes shut tight, she drew it near and bared the fount of nourishment to it. And she slept with the babe at her breast, slept to build strength to feed the very babe she could not bear to see.

Piety woke near dusk and lay on the bed of leaves, careful not to let her eyes stray to the babe. His dawn-image still haunted her. Even with eyes shut she saw him waxy and wet from birth, limp and small, his purple-veined flesh stretched tight over his—

But she would not think about his limbs again. Or about his head. Or about the weak disinterest he showed in nursing. That could be due to her own clumsiness or to her physical and moral depletion. She had not taken cover here prepared to nurse, after all—only to deliver. How could she have guessed that a mother's concern could extend even to a monster?

But what now? She touched her babe's bare shoulder and faced an agony greater than she had known in the night. If she had given birth under Sister Cree's eye, the matter would have been resolved before she ever looked on her new babe. She would, in fact, never have seen him at all. Her eyes would have been covered for the birth. His first weak cry would have been all she ever had to remember. But she had taken herself beyond range of that easy solution. Now she must make her own decision and her own disposition. Weak tears ran from her eyes as she considered her alternatives. She could abandon him here, her little monster-son. Or she could—

Could what? Was there any other alternative? Her mind labored. If she left him here, there were two possibilities, the greater that he would perish, the lesser that he would be retrieved and carried to the fortress, the same fortress

18

where Humble Nodd had wagoned the starhand.

The fortress! There was a second alternative, she realized in a flash. She could carry him to the fortress herself. Shaking, she half-sat. She could not do it tonight, certainly. She had so little strength. But tomorrow night, if she were strong, she could walk that way with him. Even if she could not carry him the entire distance, she could at least abandon him nearer Pengalen, where the likelihood of his being claimed by some madman or monster-grown was greater than here. Was that so little to do for a monster-son?

But to do even that, she must have strength, and that meant she must eat. A quiver moved up her spine. *Eat.* Her gaze traveled beyond tenting branches to the vinelands. Without straining, she could see piebald melons, yellow, green, black, sheltering along their mother vines, round, ready, enticing.

Forbidden.

Quickly she snatched her gaze back to cover. She would not make that mistake again. She would eat clean, even though it meant pulling barley shoots and digging green tubers with her bare hands. Sitting erect, she laid hand on her babe's smooth back and vowed that.

She waited in the grove until dark. Then she bundled her babe in her arms and crept out to move through the vines. It was a distance to the barley fields, but there would be plenty there to feed her. As she moved, she carefully did not permit herself access to the dozen distressing thoughts that could have occupied her—Father Hoock's anger, the perils she faced on the road to Pengalen, the censure she would meet upon return home. All those realities she would have to deal with in time. But not tonight, not with her babe in her arms and her stomach a hard emptiness. Silently, cautiously, she took her path through the vines.

She stopped twice to rest and then she stopped again. The fields were still a distance and her small strength was waning at an alarming rate. Despairing, sucking deep breaths that did nothing to replenish her, she rested her babe on her lap and her head on her knees.

And there was a sound in the vines. It was not distant, but near, like a question, but from no human throat. Piety's head snapped erect. Searching, she found a moving shadow scant meters away. It humped toward her, upright, dark. With a gasp, she clutched her babe tight. "Who is it?"

For answer she received a croak, a bark, a gargle, a cry.

Electrified, she jumped up. Before she could run, the dark body was opposite her. She could see the massive lines of its torso, could see its inhuman face. "No," she gasped, stumbling backward.

The creature was not cowed by her wispy plea. It flexed elastically before her, knees bending, torso bobbing. From its throat came a series of utterances, inane in their irrelevancy under any other circumstance, terrifying here and now.

"No," she begged again. What would dirad do to her? Desperately she turned and plunged away across the vines.

Dirad was not hindered by frail human limbs or by woman's skirts. With two bounds, it was ahead of her, cutting her off. She dodged, panting, sobbing. It was ahead of her again, blocking her. Her breath was frantic, a whimper of fear. Dirad bounded, barking. She could smell dirad now, wild and strong.

Again she wheeled and tried to run. This time a vine caught her ankle and she sprawled in the vines, her babe tumbling from her arms. She shrilled, scrambling awkwardly to her feet.

But by then dirad was leaping backward away from her. And in its arms, hastily scooped from the vines—her babe! A terrible weakness claimed her limbs. *"No!* He's just a little—a little—" Monster? She could not utter it with him in dirad's arms.

With a gabble dirad retreated, hopping backward easily, the babe flopping in its grasp. Piety ran after it, crying, stumbling, until she fell again. Then dirad uttered a last sharp bark and bounded away across the vines. By the time she regained her feet, dirad had merged into the night.

She stumbled in the direction she thought it had taken,

hopeless, trembling. But dirad traveled fast and she did not, not tonight, her legs weak, her heart shattered. After a while she threw herself down, even sobbing beyond her. She had only one consolation in her grief. Not once had her babe wakened and cried as dirad bounded away with him flopping in its arms. Not once.

Chapter Three

THE WAGON jolted and clattered as the big horse paced the endless hours of night. Jahna dozed, waking each time to find Nodd slumped on his seat, chin on chest. Once the clouds cleared and a small yellow moon was visible overhead. She peered up at it until it was lost again in gloom.

Her next waking was abrupt. Her eyes sprang open at a touch on her cheek and she stared up into the grimiest face she had ever seen. Night-darkened eyes met her own. The features that comprised the face were young, hard. Thin lips parted exposing sharp even teeth.

Jahna gasped and exhaled a startled cry. Immediately the person who bent over her leaped back, poised like a bird of prey. She was only a girl, Jahna saw, startled, a bare-breasted girl in loincloth and mud. But her eyes were terrible to see, her face was twisted, and her hands were claws thirsting.

Then, at Nodd's waking bellow, the girl sprang lithely from the wagon bed into the mud track. Jahna sat, staring out at her, their eyes meshing in wordless communion.

"Garbage!" Nodd roared, rising up from his seat like some primitive night-god.

The girl flung back an incomprehensible rebuttal and darted away into the vines. As Jahna watched, her mud-smeared figure merged with night. A moment and the fierce young she-apparition was gone. Jahna turned, breathless. "Who—"

Nodd glowered into the vinefield, his face visibly engorged. "Garbage! I will disinfect my wagon of her when I return to Forgiven—just as I will disinfect it of

you!'' His beard jutted at Jahna, his eyes wells of righteous anger.

Jahna clutched her covers, too startled to answer his
unexpected denunciation. ''*No*, that girl—'' A half-naked
girl running the night on the same road driven by Humble
Nodd? Who did not like even to hear of calls of nature?

Nodd whipped himself back stiffly and sat. Seizing the
lines, he snapped them angrily over the huge horse's back.
That placid beast bowed its head and strained forward
again.

''That girl—'' Jahna began again.

Nodd did not hear her. As the wagon groaned forward,
his outrage spilled from him in a muttering monologue,
fierce and condemnatory. Helplessly Jahna listened to his
words, unable to comprehend more than random phrases
from the verbal spew of indignation. Finally she understood enough to realize that the girl had mysteriously
soiled not just the wagon but the roadway and adjoining
fields for a radius of miles.

Powerful medicine, Jahna mused. Slumping back, she
called up a visual image of the girl. Her mind dwelt on the
rough hair, the twisted features, the fierce eyes, the taut
lips, the sharp teeth. Younger than me, Jahna decided.
Certainly wirier and faster. And for some reason she hated
me on sight.

Or perhaps she hates everyone on sight. Obviously an
outcast. An incorrigible. Perhaps even in some dark Nelding way a witch. Who besides a witch would have power
to soil and despoil simply by imposing her physical
presence?

Who indeed? Jahna pulled her covers around her and
stared up at the night sky, body tense. Gradually Nodd's
diatribe became a troll's lullaby, monotonous, meaning-
less, finally merging harmlessly into the Nelding night.

Jahna dozed again. Much later she wakened to find
Nodd erect in his seat, the sky pale gray, and the horse
pacing as steadily, as unenthusiastically as before. She sat
up and found that they still forded mud between banks of
tangling vines. Did I wake at all? she wondered. Or was

the girl a nightmare visitation? But, stretching her stiff muscles, touching her rumpled hair, Jahna knew well what she had seen in the night—and what she had heard. Which, she reflected, spoke nothing to her ability to interpret events. Only to record them.

An hour later she replaced cheese and bread in their basket, brushed crumbs from her daysuit, and ventured a considered question at her host. "Are there many local fauna you've been able to use for food, Citizen?"

Humble Nodd did not turn. His beard twitched disapprovingly. "We do not touch unfit food."

Today the arbitrary reply presented challenge. Rested, fed, Jahna was ready to learn more about life on Nelding. And Nodd was the only available instructor. "Now by that do you mean that local game actually is not edible? Or that there is simply some social stricture against using it?" she demanded, scooting forward.

This time Nodd did turn. His dark eyes were intense. "On your world, can a substance be declared unfit and still be considered edible?"

Jahna's brows rose. "Actually I don't believe there is anything on our world we would declare categorically unfit to eat, unless it happened to be poisonous. In those cases we designate the substance unsafe—not unfit."

Distaste was plain on Nodd's bearded face. "You devour everything then? Clean and unclean alike?"

"No, we simply do not classify things that way," Jahna explained patiently. "Oh, we wouldn't eat our dogs or cats or pet garna. Not unless a state of famine existed. But if that did happen, we wouldn't consider anything that could support human life unclean." Tactfully she added, "However, I studied comparative cultures last session, so I appreciate that in some societies things are managed differently." How differently she intended to find out now. Nelding, backward and uncommunicative, had not been included in her study format.

Nodd's dark eyes seemed to grow implacably, damning her from their deep sockets. "In some societies it is permitted to eat offal and garbage. And in those places the human race has become something else. Something lower than man or beast.'' His pale lips snapped shut on this pronouncement. Stiffly he turned, presenting his back.

Startled, Jahna required a moment to regroup mental forces. ''Of course I know that on a few worlds there have been mutagens that have—''

''I will not discuss it,'' Nodd growled, whipping lines across the big horse's back. ''You have been given clean bread and clean dairy. From us you will receive nothing other because we permit nothing other. Later, when you have arrived, you may eat whatever you please, and the curse upon you.''

Jahna stared at the back of Nodd's neck, grim lines slowly transforming her face. ''I don't mean to be tactless—''

''Then be silent!''

Jahna's eyes flared. Teeth snapping shut, she retreated to the rear of the wagon. Conversation turned grim quickly on Nelding, she reflected angrily. As grim as the weather, as grim as the landscape.

As grim as life? Nelding life?

Half an hour later they passed through another log village. It was laid out on the same plan as previous ones, windowless cabins spaced at rigidly measured intervals, rickety walkways connecting them. Today, peering out, Jahna saw women on the walkways. They were ageless, lean, hair knotted tight, dark skirts hanging to their ankles. The faces they turned to the passing wagon were closed, expressing nothing. On their bowed shoulders they bore large, untidy bundles. When the settlement was behind, Jahna ventured another question at Humble Nodd. ''Are work roles assigned according to sex in your communities?''

Nodd turned. ''They are not on Peace?''

Involuntarily Jahna bristled. ''There are some categories of work that involve more women than men of course—and vice versa. But no field is closed to either sex.''

"Ah? So women on Peace are allowed to impregnate their men? And men are allowed to bear these children and feed them at breast?" Nodd's dark eyes glittered scornfully.

It was impossible to talk to the man. Jahna's jaw crackled shut.

Her discomfiture delighted Nodd. "Ha!" he snorted, his mouth snaking into a bitter line. "You have brought a lot of questions from the stars! Shall I answer others for you?"

"If you wish."

"Ha! Then I will show you something you would do well to learn—how the people of this world produce food fit to be eaten by humans. And in that category I include even women." He yanked at the lines. The big horse moved perceptibly faster until they reached a narrow side road. With a flick of reins, Nodd took beast and wagon down the side road.

Jahna clung to the side of the jolting wagon. Soon tangled vegetation gave way to cultivated fields of tender seedlings. In the distance a scatter of Neldings bent at work. Gazing intently, Jahna saw that a single supervisor hulked over them, a stocky man with square-cut beard and knotted hair.

Nodd pulled the wagon to a halt and dismounted. "Now you will see how our bread lines are kept clean." He strode to the first row of seedlings, yanked at a stalk faintly streaked with scarlet. Scornfully he thrust it into the wagon. "You see the unfit texture of the leaf? The unclean color?"

Jahna accepted the plant and peered into the field for comparison. "I can see it's slightly different," she admitted, "though it's obviously of the same species as the rest of the crop." The variation of color and texture was minor, almost imperceptible.

The Nelding nodded emphatically. "Even though the seed are triple-sorted, this garbage appears in our wheat. And so we come to the fields and we rip it out and destroy it by fire." He indicated the opposite side of the road, where a single melancholy vine straggled past the cultivated crop, yellow and black melons sheltering at intervals beneath its dull leaves. "Once that species was human food. Now it has degenerated and it grows wild everywhere. You saw it. There is no specimen fit for human consumption on Nelding."

Jahna's gaze shot to the piebald melons. "That isn't a native species?" she asked, surprised.

"Native to this place? No. Once it was one of the clean lines that came here with our party, but it is clean no longer."

"You mean the melon has mutated and become poisonous?" Jahna asked, struggling to grasp the situation.

"It has become degenerate. It is corrupt."

Jahna stared into the rigid face, puzzled. "But is it actually poisonous to eat? Or is there simply a social stricture against using it?"

Nodd's eyes flared fiercely. "It has become unclean!" Angrily his arms swept to include the fields around them. "So will the wheat become unclean if we permit. And the barley and the tubers and the leafage. Do your own food lines breed pure without the necessity of constant intervention?"

Evidently there was more than a cluster crisis involved here after all. Jahna considered her answer carefully. "If by pure, you mean unmutated—no. The foods our original settling party brought were laboratory-bred to flourish and hopefully to remain stable under Peace conditions, but they've been affected to some degree. Our domestic animals show changes too, though of course not so markedly."

Nodd's eyes were fiercely incredulous. "And you permit mutation? Of your field crops? Of your domestics?"

"I don't see what else we could do. As I understand it, unfit mutations tend to die out by themselves and favorable mutations increase the yield. With stock animals, if an unfavorable mutation appears, the animal is marked for table use only and never bred, of course."

Nodd shook his head slowly, damningly. "On this

world domestic monsters are destroyed at birth and their carcasses burned." He stalked back to the wagon. "May you rejoice in your destination."

Jahna studied him, troubled. "Citizen, has there been much problem with human mutation before this—" She hesitated, uncertain now whether the settlers confronted a cluster crisis or a larger problem.

Humble Nodd's eyes glazed. "I will not discuss it."

"Citizen Nodd—"

"My proper title is Father Nodd," the Nelding said viciously, "and you will be silent. There is nothing more to be discussed between us."

Jahna catalogued his bone-white face, his taut lips, his rigid neck. "All right," she agreed stiffly. Indeed, it seemed fruitless to attempt to draw objective information from this man. And on Nelding was she going to encounter any other kind of man? Jahna settled back against her luggage, thoughtful.

They turned back into the main road. Half an hour later they passed a field where a dozen bulky animals grazed on sparse grasses. "Now, these beasts are clean," Nodd pronounced stiffly, not turning.

Jahna examined the animals in passing. Their coats were thick, curly, and gray, their legs stocky, ending in broad hooves. "They're quite unlike our cattle," she observed levelly.

Nodd's voice was implacable. "That is because you have permitted corruption."

"No, that is because our cattle were bred for conditions on Peace and your cattle were bred for conditions on Nelding," Jahna informed him evenly. "And both strains evolved originally from primitive Earth range cattle, with some human help. Man selected mutations he considered valuable and bred to them."

Hair bristled on Nodd's lean neck. "There is no mutation in these bloodlines. We have photographic proof that these are the same clean cattle brought from Earth three hundred years ago."

"Of course they are if you've destroyed the variants.

28

But this line of cattle could never have been bred in the first place if it hadn't been for mutations. And the special seed you brought from Earth couldn't have been perfected if seed labs hadn't induced mutations and taken advantage of them. We wouldn't be here ourselves walking on our hind legs and speaking Universal if it hadn't been for mutation. We would be sitting in a tree somewhere picking parasites.''

"If that is how you regard your own ancestors,'' Nodd muttered ferociously, glaring at the road.

Jahna huddled, face creased in exasperation. They rode the gray morning hours in silence. Several times they passed cultivated fields where women and children worked, silent, lean, dour, supervised by stern patriarchal figures. Occasionally younger men, too, stooped at labor. Myriad questions took form in Jahna's mind. Were the children schooled formally? Were there systems of social caste, other than the obvious divisions along sex and age lines? Was the land under family or communal ownership? Were there no farm machines? Why were the children so stiff and joyless, the women so gaunt?

Most haunting of all, how would she herself react if she were a young girl growing into one of these lean women? Staring at the toes of her boots, she remembered the girl of the night before. Would she rebel too? Turn half-savage, running the countryside by night, hiding in some dark place by day, eating whatever came to hand? Or would she capitulate? Stoop there in the field under the basilisk eye of some Father Nodd, all rebellion turned poisonously inward?

Were these questions even rhetorical? She was assigned to this world for a two-year duty tour. For that period she would necessarily function within the prevailing Nelding social circumstance. She frowned at the back of Nodd's neck, scrawny, abristle with coarse hair.

Later, she ate again. Then, looking ahead, she saw that they approached a looming fortress which appeared to be built directly across the road. She sat straight, straining for a better look.

"Your destination," Nodd pronounced darkly. "The madhouse of Pengalen."

Startled, Jahna popped to her knees. As they came near, the structure defined itself, tall, dark, built of massive logs half-rotted with age and heavily mossed. "You can't keep your disturbed this far from any settlement," situational counselor Swiss protested. "There's no one out here to treat them." It had been more than an hour since they had last passed a cluster of cabins.

"Now there is you, Starhand," Nodd said with satisfaction, urging the horse into a cumbrous half-trot.

They halted before the big log face of Pengalen. It swallowed the road in its mouth, an archway no taller and no wider than would admit two adults side by side. Nodd turned in his seat, savoring Jahna's consternation. "Two years from this day I will return for you. Learn what you will—or learn nothing."

Clumsily Jahna climbed down and reached out her luggage. She stared up at the log walls that faced her, intimidated—a fact she did not intend to betray to Nodd. "I would like the name of the individual I am to report to," she stated briskly.

Humble Nodd shrugged carelessly. "I do not bother with names where these garbage are concerned." With a smirk, he took the lines and flicked the big horse into motion.

Jahna watched the wagon groan away into the viny landscape. Then she turned and confronted Pengalen again, limbs weakening. If this were where the disturbed were segregated and Humble Nodd had just driven away a free man. . . . Obviously the standards of social adjustment were quite different on Nelding. Composing her face, Jahna hoisted her cases and passed through the arch into Pengalen.

Emerging from the long dark entry arch, she found herself in the courtyard of a three-story log quadrangle. Underfoot, mud oozed up through a decomposing layer of moss. Vivid, velvety live moss grew in haphazard patches across the rectangular yard. The log walls of the apartments lining three of the four sides of the quadrangle had been patched and chinked with a mosaic of materials. Rows of bleak slit windows marched the length of each wall. Turning, Jahna saw that the interior face of the fourth wall, the wall containing the entry arch, had been permitted to deteriorate, giving view into a series of narrow cells. Moss hung dense from rotting ceilings.

Alarmed, Jahna spun at a grotesque burst of sound behind her. A muddy wad of fur bounded across the courtyard and danced before her, uttering a series of painful croaks.

"Tetz! Back!" A tall, broad-shouldered figure in skirts emerged from shadow to her right. Her face was arresting, strong jaw and brows forming a protective framework around oddly dished cheekbones and deep eyes. She wore her hair caught with a tie at the nape of her neck. "You are from Peace?" Her voice was deep, masculine in timbre.

The little dog hurtled away. Jahna's breath was short as she replied, "I am Jahna Swiss of the Planet Peace Service Cadet Corps—reporting as requested by the First Fathers of Nelding."

The tall woman nodded, her dark eyes absorbing Jahna. "And I am Valor. Were you given to eat by Humble Nodd?"

Jahna's stomach knotted queasily. "I—yes."

"Good. Then I will show you the quarters, Jahna Swiss."

They entered the rank of apartments to their right. The tall woman conducted Jahna up a single flight of stairs and down a dark second-story hallway. They entered a narrow doorway. The Nelding woman moved across the dim room and touched the light cube that stood on the rough dresser.

The room was small, ventilated by a single slit window. A heavy plank bedframe supported a deep puffy mattress, and half a dozen wooden pegs lined one wall. The tall woman rested a caressing hand on the light cube. "This we traded from Peace for your use." Across the hall, in a windowless cell, crude bath facilities had been arranged.

"This is yours alone," Valor explained. "We have provided ourselves with another. We have here, you see, a superfluity of small chambers."

And a shortage of occupants? Jahna stepped back into the hallway and peered its length. Although moss had been cleared from ceiling and walls at this end, it grew in thick billows farther down, evidently undisturbed by human passage for a very long time. "I was told that this was an institution for the emotionally disturbed," she said hesitantly.

"It is no longer." Shyness, reluctance, passed across the Nelding woman's face. "When you are ready to eat, please come to my door. It is first when you pass the staircase. If I am not there, please step into my kitchen and find food and drink. What I have is yours." With a formal nod, she slipped into the murk of the hallway.

Tense muscles relaxing, Jahna turned back to her bedroom. Her eyes moved about it in slow circuit. Bedframe, dresser, puffy mattress—she tried to establish rapport with these homely furnishings, obviously created with much greater human effort than the furnishings of any room she had ever occupied on Peace. Jahna flipped the smaller of her cases onto the bed. In this room, on this afternoon, even the plaston fastener seemed a miracle of convenience.

When the first case was unpacked, Jahna crossed the hall and splashed her face. Then she returned and stretched back on the fluffy mattress. Despite its musty odor, it moved up around her welcomely, swallowing her in a big tender maw. She stared at the dark ceiling, scourging herself with thoughts of personals still folded in her second case. Despite her efforts, her body relaxed.

She wondered briefly if the dresser held blankets. But before she could rouse herself to investigate, the puffy mattress became a cloud that gently lofted her and carried her elsewhere.

Chapter Four

ZUNIIN RAN through the vines, her breath a harsh rattle in her throat, fury driving her like a scourging demon. Five days she had been gone from the grove, a lifetime now, for this afternoon StarMother had claimed Pengalen. Hard legs apound, Zuniin called back savage images of Star-Mother, her mind fastening tight on StarMother's first arrival on Nelding yesterday.

Zuniin had burrowed feet and ankles into the cold mud beyond Humble Nodd's inspectcabin at first dawn and covered herself with vines. She had remained there until at last her ears detected the bug-buzz in the sky. Then she raised her head and arched her neck. Her eyes, seeking, found the shuttlecraft lancing distant cloud. So high, so swift it came, like a manic metal insect, now losing itself in cloud, now finding itself, small but growing. Coming. Bringing StarMother down, bearing her to Becklord, Hurak, the others.

Bringing her to steal away the future. Pale and powerful she would be, her hands white, her hair yellow as the sun Zuniin had last seen two weeks ago, her eyes blue as halma was white, blue as morning mist rising from hot mud sinks. That blue.

Zuniin bared her teeth, her lips falling back like flesh-veils to reveal menace, her face twisted hard beneath the sulphur mud she had smeared across it. The little bug was bigger now, a flash across near skies, and then it was a terrible sound, a loud and rending sound, whine turned roar to ravage the ears and shatter the mind. The roar wrenched Zuniin back into the mud, breath caught, ears slammed hard with muddy palms, teeth gritted against the howl she wanted to loose to join with the terrible tearing violence of sound, to appease it.

Then the sound died, moaning, guttural, in the clearing. Zuniin raised her head and peered over the vines, flower of mud blooming warily. Grounded, rolling, the insect was a clever contrivance, metal bright with orange witch-marks painted on its side—in warning perhaps, or as safety-blessing. Quickly Zuniin ripped off a large flat leaf of vine, slapped it against mud to coat it, and jaggedly reproduced the witchmarkings in the mud with her forefinger. N72Z NEBULON TRANSPORT CORPS. She checked her effort against the original, found it good.

Good—and powerful. Her chest rose. Clearly this witchpattern was more than safety-blessing. Did not it have to be to carry StarMother under its influence? Impatiently Zuniin flapped the leaf to dry it.

The metal insect stopped, brooded momentarily, then popped out its belly and gave birth. First child was a male in dark suiting, a male hardly different from any huttown male except that his face was Beck-bare and his hair was cropped off short. Hunching up on her elbows, Zuniin stared avidly. With Becklord, bareness of cheek and jowl was no admission of weakness. So with this star male, who knew what lack of beard and hair signified?

What indeed? There was no time to puzzle it because the ship was birthing again. The male popped at another section of metal belly. Steps folded down. The male's naked lips, strangely pink in his bare tan face, spoke something up into the laboring belly.

And StarMother emerged.

There was no mistaking her as she put foot to stair. She was the one Becklord had spoken in word picture. She wore a wondergarment that covered her all, eloquently molding the lines of body, leg, and arm, leaving only hands and head bare. The garment was loomed of brightest blue, clearest blue, boldest and most dazzling blue. Zuniin's pupils widened to accommodate the vivid richness.

34

StarMother's feet were shod with black, and upon her head, ah, there she bore her true glory. Zuniin's mouth drew tight at sight of it. For StarMother carried her glory-hair upon her like some rare and precious crown of mo-pelt, like some sleek animal coiled and looped upon her head, some regal animal of golden yellow, every separate hair catching light from nowhere and magnifying it, making of it still richer glory to crown StarMother's head.

Golden StarMother. With an angry rake, Zuniin seized at her own coarse hair and yanked. She bared her teeth against the pain and stared ferociously at the dirty brown hank that came free in her fingers. No gold on her head. No yellow. No glimmer of light to make her bright and royal. Angrily she flicked the hair of her own head into the mud and snatched a second time, at her waistlet. But the garment did not rip. It was sturdy.

Sturdy and rough, thick with mud. A coarse garment, ugly, abrasive, a punishment to wear after glimpse of StarMother's garment.

So, what of the person it covered? Zuniin glowered from her hiding place as StarMother progressed down the metal steps to set first foot to mud. Was the body Zuniin's waistlet covered any less than the one StarMother's bright garment hid? Zuniin raked a hand down her thigh. She pounded a fist against hard muscle of hip, thigh, and calf. She bared her teeth again.

It *was* no less, and this body of hers was strong. Could StarMother say as much? Lashing out, Zuniin grappled a vinesystem up by the roots, demonstrating her power. So are you this strong, StarMother? This strong to steal our she-babes and make them your own? This strong to take Becklord and make him yours too? This strong to have mockdirad dance to you and seat you on ceremonial furs and bow down and kiss your aura, humbling themselves?

And this strong, to nurse fat babes with potent blue white milk, stuff of life? Zuniin grasped one supple young breast and brandished it at StarMother's back, taunting. So, if you are this strong, why do you mince your way across the mud to Humble Nodd's inspectcabin? Why don't you set foot squarely into the mud and stride? Ha! No more will you be able to nurse babes on your flaccid breast.

But now StarMother had turned the corner of the inspectcabin and passed from sight. So had her accompanying male, and so had Humble Nodd, who had hovered briefly at the corner of the cabin, eyes aglitter, square beard black on his chest. They were gone into the cabin, all three of them.

Zuniin sprang to her feet, lithe and strong, legs muscled hard. With a growl, she seized both breasts and flaunted them at the cabin, a boast, a taunt. Even the discredited left breast, with the slash of matted scarlet on its globular underside—even that one was better than anything Star-Mother could offer.

But when both breasts bobbed free again, when Zuniin's hard young legs carried her across the tangle of mud and vine to secrete herself along the road to Forgiven, it was of her hair that Zuniin was most conscious. Her mud-coarse tawdry brown hair, her no-color, no-glory hair that hung down her back like a shameful mockery now that she had seen StarMother's golden beauty. She had wagged her head savagely and plunged across the vinescape, a strong young figure, hatred twisting her face, gaudy anger lighting her heart.

And now, today. . . .

Now, today, StarMother had taken the fortress. Zuniin's mind lit with fresh images: StarMother disembarking from Humble Nodd's wagon, golden crown atilt, white hands smeared muddy, wonder-garment rumpled. For all that, StarMother advancing upon Pengalen, Star-Mother conquering, had been no less the creature of Becklord's promise, wondrous, strange, and threatening.

Threatening everything. The grove, the Mothers, the Mother-future Zuniin had rejected for herself—and was now racing home to defend. Zuniin ground her teeth savagely and called up another, more comforting image: StarMother's startled face, eyes exophthalmic, mouth stupid, when Zuniin had wakened her in the wagon the night before.

Now Zuniin cursed. Thirsty moments her nails had coiled against StarMother's cheek—and Zuniin had wakened her, nothing more. But what had Narrel said—that StarMother, coming, would carry with her a starplace witch-kit that could restore to her all things, flesh, blood, beauty, health? And Narrel said that if any person assailed StarMother, witch-kit magic would cause the minutest spatter of blood staining the assailant's flesh to sear and scar that person and to destroy him by agonizing bits. No matter how that person might rub and scrub, those traces could never be removed. StarMother's blood—Narrel said—was an eternal stain.

Witch-kit, revenge-kit—Zuniin grimaced fiercely. Why did not *she* own some hide-and-fur bag with spells to protect and avenge *her*? True, her body-blood was not on StarMother, but was not her spirit-blood there already, smearing those long white hands?

It was, and the spirit-blood of every Mother of every grove.

Zuniin's mind raced and her legs pumped, and then the grove loomed up from late-afternoon mist, dark home. Her legs slowed. She sucked breath and swore one fervent vow. StarMother *would* be stopped. But that was not the vow. The vow was that although Zuniin might incite and inflame, direct and ultimately destroy, never would she permit one drop of StarMother's blood to stain her own flesh. Nor would any golden hair sweep against her own hand. Nor would she permit StarMother's saliva to fall upon her or, if terminal fright were expulsive, would Zuniin commit the error of stepping in StarMother's water or on her dung. Protect her destiny Zuniin must, but she must first protect body and soul.

The vines thinned. Zuniin leaped twin hummocks of stiffgrass and skirted a small mud sink, pausing only to sweep up three fingers of yellow foam from the rim of the bubbling pool and smear it across either cheek. Then she rustled through a stand of redspear and she was within first shadowrim of the grove. Mammoth trunks rose up from the moist soil, brown, stalwart. Broad branches swept low, creating tenting shelters at their bases. Within the arms of the grove, Zuniin was greeted by sounds and smells of home: brindle mush bubbling, bed moss drying over low fires, chitterlings aroast on pointed stakes, damp reedcloth steaming with human body heat.

Zuniin pattered quickly past mockdirad compound. Behind its log walls some mockdirad—Narrel? Kardon? —was coursing raucously through an evensong. Whoever, his voice was young and deep and it was answered by infantile gibberish, the babble-song of mockdirad babe. Zuniin glared bitterly at the log wall of mockdirad compound. So, what was it to mockdirad that StarMother had come? Loss? Indignity? Death?

Never! Mockdirad would celebrate tonight. Mockdirad, after all, had conspired with Becklord to bring her here. Hurak, Tirammer, Carock, Narrd—all the old pelts, all the powerful pelts, would lead their groves in cry tonight.

Ancient resentments scorched Zuniin's soul. *Pelts.* She pinched her own bare skin. *So where is my pelt? When does my fur grow?*

Never, answered a still voice from the center of her soul. Your skin is bare and always will be. Rant, fight, scream—it will never motivate fur to spring out of your pores or a flexing cylinder to open at the base of your throat. *Never, Zuniin.* Never, never. She mouthed the word, letting it jab her viscera like a thrusting wood stake, blunt, agonizing. Killing.

But Zuniin would not be killed! She had rejected her Mother-destiny. Now she reclaimed it. Better that small realm of power than none at all.

She found the grove Mothers mumbling together over the night cooking. Yuba stirred mush, her multi-breasts swaying stolidly. Sharne turned the chitterlings and poked them with a stick to make the grease ooze. Dahda caught it in a clay bowl for skin rubbing. And Ejja, Hiilo, Nana—

Zuniin halted at the perimeter of their circle, riding her emotion savagely. She despised the Mothers. Despised their menial mentalities and their smug souls. So they were molders of she-babes—and what was that? When mockdirad compound claimed an entire edge of the grove, when mockdirad took away every male molding and gave him pelt, when mockdirad made dance and song and everyone squatted, cowed, into respectful audience— what was the Mother's small power then?

And what was their image? It was as discredited as Zuniin's flawed breast now. Yuba's dozen breasts were obscene and superfluous beside StarMother's two. Sharne's bright scales were gaudy and obsolescent, Ejja's pretty face puny and sallow, Hiilo's magnificent body ridiculous on her two stumpy legs. They were all lessened by StarMother's gold-crowned arrogance.

So, was it any wonder Zuniin's words crawled out her throat in anger? *"She is here."*

Heads turned. Eyes glistened up at her, stark and startled in evening shadow. They had not seen her come.

"StarMother is at Pengalen now." Zuniin glared. And what are you going to do about it? her eyes demanded.

The answer came back from six pairs of evasive eyes, from six uneasy faces. Nothing, Zuniin. We are going to do nothing.

Nothing at all. It did not have to be spoken aloud. StarMother was come and they were going to stir mush and catch drip.

"You have been gone long," Ejja said at last, her delicate features forming up with polite interest. She was youngest of the grove Mothers. She had her first molding in her tent now.

"I saw her come and I saw her down the road," Zuniin stated aggressively. "And then I saw her step through the arch to take Pengalen. Tomorrow she will be here for your babes."

Even that blunt assertion did not rouse the grove Mothers. Their eyes oozed away from hers and consulted. Dahda, eldest, set aside her clay bowl and stood. Once,

Zuniin knew, Dahda had been magnificent. Now she sagged, an old woman, her face stained brown with years. Nevertheless she held authority. "Now, that is not true, Zu. Becklord has explained to us all, and you heard him, too."

"I heard him talk of a goddess, and now I have seen her. She came in the starbug yesterday. Today she rode a wagon to Pengalen."

Dahda's dark eyes fired scornfully. "So now you have told us three times she is at Pengalen. It was expected she would be."

Stung, Zuniin flicked her ragged hair across her shoulder. "So I say it and say it and I never see anyone hear it: *She has come to steal your babes*. She has six of them already."

Troubled eyes flicked away. Sharne bent quickly to her chitterlings. Yuba suddenly needed to stir mush again.

"And six is all," Dahda said strongly. "Becklord has explained it clearly. Six this year and six next, and then she goes away and all twelve are returned to the groves."

"So twelve years from now all twelve of them will be grown into Mothers. Who will be granted girl-babes then?" Zuniin's glance whipped wide, seeking vulnerability. "Do you think Hurak will grant you another molding, Ejja, when these twelve StarMothers are matured?"

Ejja's fragile features shuddered from confrontation. "That is a long time, Zu," she offered tremulously. "Twelve years."

"So you expect to be defaced in twelve years?"

Ejja batted round eyes and touched her cheeks, shaking her head fearfully. "No. No."

"So will you be ready to see your daughters refused daughters of their own? Will you be pleased to see your line die out of the groves?"

Ejja batted round eyes and touched her cheeks, shaking her tongue. "There will always be daughters for everyone, Zuniin. Becklord told us."

Always the same answer! *Becklord told us*. Zuniin's eyes flared. Her words crawled fiercely between her teeth.

40

"So run into Becklord's net, chitterlings! He'll roast you crisp and use your grease to rub StarMother's rump!" Her gaze swung to Yuba, kindling. "You saw him throw devil. So now you trust him, too!"

The stolid Yuba reared back from her pot, her dozen breasts quivering alert. Slowly intelligence battled across her face. "I saw him," she agreed deeply, standing up from her kettle. Her gray-puddle eyes deepened with her voice. "I was passing from halma hunt to grove again when I saw him throw himself into stiffgrass. I watched him stiffen and shout and froth and—"

"You saw Sharne throw devil once too, when I saw her cough up a bone from her throat," Dahda interrupted impatiently. "You saw Minna-small throw devil when I saw him die choked on lung-wad. You saw Rella throw devil when you are here, Yuba-bull." Big Yuba's face darkened. "You burp enough," she accused, her voice shuddering up from her deep chest like an angered beast. The stir spoon snapped in her hand.

Dahda was not intimidated. She snatched the broken spoon and tossed it away across the dirt. "Hiilo, you stir and this dumb beast will root elsewhere for her dinner." She gestured imperiously at the younger woman.

Hiilo hesitated, still too young and unsure to wear her splendid body confidently.

"Stir!" Dahda ordered. When Hiilo still did not step forward, Dahda swung her heel around and caught Yuba in the calf. Almost in the same motion, she rounded on Zuniin and slammed her flat with one open palm. "Stir, Hiilo!"

Zuniin clutched breath and scrambled up from the dirt, fierce tears blinding her, anger noising in her throat. She swiped hard at her eyes, her teeth jamming one other painfully.

"No, no talk," Dahda ordered. "First you tell us we are weak and stupid to accept our station. Now you come and try to pull us to fight for our same station. So go back to the vines, Zuniin. We are happy enough here without you."

41

Zuniin's lips trembled and snaked back, exposing her teeth. "This is my grove," she uttered, voice dangerous.

Not dangerous enough to intimidate the matriarch. "This is your grove again in three days. Until then we will not see you." Dahda planted hands on hips, face hard. "So run, Zuniin, or I will call Narrel to whip your belly again. He won't mind interrupting his song for that."

Zuniin jumped back, calf muscles twitching spasmodically. Her face, twisting, failed to express her bitter emotion. There were no words for it, either. There were only jagged nails, sharp teeth, and hard fists.

Which she knew better than to use. Narrel was Dahda's birth-born and he used the whips with relish. With a futile snarl, Zuniin sprang back and took foot.

"Three days!" Dahda bellowed after, and then Zuniin could hear the Mother laugh raucously, as raucously as her son had sung in mockdirad compound.

Zuniin hurtled through the tented grove. Faces rose to watch her pass and became pale blurs in the darkening shadows of evening. Hate words ran vicious circle in Zuniin's mind, stomping heavy rhythm: *bitches, bitches, she-bulls; witches, witches, hags!*

It was dark over the vines when she finally threw herself on a hummock of stiffgrass. She flung herself on the grass, crushing it. *Smash your body, StarMother!* Zuniin wallowed and twisted and yanked at the grass. *Pull out your hair!* She beat ground with her fists. *Your breasts, Star-Mother!*

Finally her anger deserted her. She lay back and stared up at the dark sky, breathing heavily. *If I had halma, I would eat it and call it your eyes, StarMother.* But there was no spirit behind the curse. Zuniin was spent.

Time passed and she slept, her half-bare body exposed to whatever god might ride the night cloud. Her legs sprawled wide. Come down and take me, they seemed to offer.

Then half-dormant senses alerted her. Footsteps through the vines—one person coming, dogs ranging wide circles around him. Instantly awake, Zuniin rolled off the hummock and burrowed down into the vines.

As the dogs ranged ahead, the steps came near. Raising her head, Zuniin distinguished a human silhouette black against the gray-black of night. Her eyes narrowed. The line of torso and shoulder she recognized, straight, long. The shape of the head she recognized, too. It was Becklord, bound Pengalen way, moving easily across the treacherous night vinescape. Zuniin ducked back into the vines, eyes squeezed tight until his footsteps were gone. Then her head popped up again. She sat, chest tight with the complex of emotions Becklord roused in her.

Not passion. Other Mothers felt that. If Becklord were a male easily gained, Sharne, Ejja, even Hiilo would be muttering against one another for him. But that was not what he stirred in Zuniin.

No. As his shoulders merged with night, Zuniin's mind filled with dark jealousy. Not only had birth denied her pelt and mockdirad brotherhood, she had been further denied the person she would have been if she had been born a man. Specifically, if she had been born the man Becklord was. Zuniin crept back to the hummock and huddled into the grass, staring bleakly in the direction Becklord had gone, imagining his homecoming. So how would it be to stride master through the archway of Pengalen? To call and have tanglings and women jump to command? To have StarMother step forward from the shadows at your summons, her star-face perfect, pale?

How? Zuniin ground her teeth in frustration. She would never know. She was trapped in a female's body, impotent, denied the destiny that might have been hers. *That would never be hers.* Her bitterness was an ulcerating wound, ugly, septic. Misery-ridden, she crept around the hummock and peered back toward the grove. Fires were lit now. She saw their flicker. There were chitterlings tender and halma crisp, redspear and hot mush. There were mockdirad dancing, there were warm bodies gathering on dry beds of moss, there were tangling males whose eyes lit with helpless ardor at sight of

Zuniin's perfect Mother's body. And she was exiled here, hungry, cold, alone.

Her hand groped into her waistlet. She found the witch-leaf, but the mud had dried and rubbed away. The leaf was powerless. She held it in her hand and her wound oozed poison into her system. Slowly her hand closed, destroying the useless leaf.

Then, on her belly, she crept back grove way. There were tents where she would be welcome even tonight. There were bodies that would not reject her despite Dahda's edict. Tonight her wounds demanded drainage or she would die of spiritual septicemia.

Chapter Five

THE ROOM was dark when Jahna's cloud returned to Pengalen. Spreading curtains of sleep, she fought her way out of bed and stroked bright the light cube on her dresser. She crossed the room unsteadily. It was dark in the courtyard except for faint light from second-story windows in the adjacent wall of the quad. Her chronom indicated approximately 7 P.M. local.

Hesitantly she ventured into the hall. With her light cube she illuminated the deserted arm of the corridor. By night the festoons of moss that depended from the ceiling were tattered lacy shadows barricading the hallway with musty whimsy, a spell cast by a destitute fairy.

When she reached Valor's door, the Nelding woman welcomed her with reticent courtesy. Jahna glanced around the room. Walls had been cut through to create a long chamber with half a dozen slit windows facing onto the courtyard. This chamber was lit by lantern. Its furnishings, chairs, chests, a single small table, had aged together to create a setting of rugged comfort. Valor motioned Jahna to a counter hung from one wall. "Your dinner will be hot quickly. Please sit."

Minutes later Valor reappeared bearing a clay bowl of yellowish mush, sweet-smelling, grainy in texture. "This is brindle squash," she volunteered formally. "You saw it along the road today, where it grows wild."

Jahna's brows arched in surprise. "The yellow and black melon?"

"Yes. It grows everywhere, wild. If you do not like it mushed, tomorrow I will fry it for you. It is our staple, you see."

The small universe of Jahna's hypothesized Nelding wobbled on its axis. She probed the mushy surface with her carved spoon. The unfit, unclean melon. "Our staple? Nodd told me this was not eaten here."

Valor's deep eyes became aloof. "It is not eaten where he lives. And that is why Humble Nodd's children are hungry tonight." Before Jahna could voice a second question, the tall woman slipped away through the doorway to return with a pitcher and mugs. "This comes from the tent tree, and so we call it tree milk. It too is unacceptable to huttown."

Tree milk was brown and thick. It flowed torpidly into Jahna's mug. Her thoughts moved more fluidly. "Then there are two groups on Nelding," she ventured. "Humble Nodd's group—"

"Huttown," Valor specified quickly.

"Huttown—and here?"

A faint smile warmed Valor's deep-set eyes. "Huttown and tentback they are called. This is Pengalen, waystation between them."

"A cultural interface," Jahna murmured thoughtfully. This grim fortress was more than a moldering madhouse then. It was a place where two ways met, two ways, she realized, that must be quite different one from the other. "But where will I be working?" she wondered immediately. "Here? On these premises?"

The dark eyes became reluctant. "You will."

Jahna squirmed impatiently, her aroused curiosity struggling against her sense of Valor's deliberate reticence. From which milieu had the mutant infants been drawn, then? "The babies—"

Uncannily her burgeoning skein of question was interrupted by a thin wail from somewhere beyond the Nelding woman's apartment. Jahna looked around quickly. Valor set the pitcher down. "One of them needs me now. So I must ask you to serve yourself. Elda has gone into tentback for the early evening, you see, and so there is only me here to attend the nursery."

Jahna jumped up. "I would be pleased to help, if you will—"

"Oh, no." Quickly Valor shook her head. "I have very specific instructions. You are not to visit the nursery until Beck has returned from tentback. He will assess you himself, you see." A rueful smile touched her lips. "He is very concerned, you see. And he does not trust my judgment entirely—although I myself do."

"But if you are here alone—"

"There are only six babes," the Nelding woman pointed out. "And if you listen you will hear that only one of them is crying. Even without Elda I can manage one crying babe. So please sit and eat. Serve yourself more from the kitchen if you wish. There is no shortage here."

But there was elsewhere? In huttown? Jahna saw the tall woman from the apartment with turbulent emotions. Suddenly she found she had two societies to reckon upon. Two societies, a waystation between them, six aberrant infants, an unknown Elda, and an equally unknown Beck, who was very concerned.

But concerned at what level? That Jahna would be inadequate to the job of child care? That her character would prove unsuitable? Even that she would in some way contaminate the six mutant infants?

Or was the cast of mind here sufficiently different from huttown to make that final question ludicrous? Jahna listened to Valor's steps on the stairs. Curious, she took herself to a window in time to see the Nelding woman cross the courtyard and enter the adjacent wing of the quad.

So now she knew that the nursery was located on the lighted second floor of the wall that faced the entry arch. She knew she was to have six charges, provided she satisfied Beck's—unstated—requirements. And she knew that the piebald melons that grew along the road were edible, that milk, brown and thick, flowed from trees.

Further, she knew that affairs on Nelding were not at all as they had first appeared. Pensively she returned to her chair and dipped spoon to mush. As she ate she held in

47

mind twin images, Humble Nodd's beard, prickly, fierce, and the girl's wind-torn hair. Although the mush was bland and filling, the tree milk nutty sweet, there was little to satisfy the void in Jahna's mind.

An hour later, in her room, Jahna moved across a dreamscape of mud and vine, lost, when the dog Tetz exploded below, shattering her sleep. His croaking was answered by several deep canine voices. Startled, Jahna struggled out of bed and trailed covers to her window.

Below, she distinguished a tall man emerging from the archway, his progress impeded by an active tangle of dogflesh. The three new animals were waisthigh, massive, but they frisked with the smaller Tetz in good-natured camaraderie. Valor appeared from the doorway below and called the smaller dog.

Tetz struggled to disentangle himself, but the three larger dogs bounded after him, engulfing him. "Guard!" the tall man commanded sharply. All four dogs turned and panted at him inquiringly. *"Guard!"* At the second command, they loped away across the courtyard and disappeared into an open door in the nursery section of the quad.

With a sweep of skirts, Valor retreated into her doorway and the tall man followed. Hurrying to her own door, Jahna heard their feet on the stairs, heard their voices in the hall. Then they entered Valor's apartment and their voices were muffled by intervening walls.

Thoughtfully Jahna returned to her bed and stared up at the ceiling. Evidently she had just caught first glimpse of Beck. But it was useless to try to infer the situation from the shadow of a single man. With deliberate effort she relaxed, allowing the big mattress to cradle her. Gradually she stroked all thought from the surface of her mind. Then sleep enveloped her almost casually.

Her waking was violent. Suddenly her head exploded with sound. The night was ajar with bellows and shrieks, whistles and calls. Cacophony was a physical thing in her room, alive, writhing, all-enveloping. Lending body to the vocal chaos was the stiff rattle and deep thunder of drums. Jahna sat, eyes wide, breath shocked from her lungs. Her hands clutched her throat as her mind groped to classify the phenomenon, to deal with it.

A noise storm—it was a hurricane of sound, a violent meteorological entity, sweeping and billowing through her room. And instead of abating, it seemed to be constantly on the swell, calls giving way to shrieks, shrieks to groans, groans to bellows, in surging waves. And now, first shock receding, lungs filling again, she was able to distinguish mechanical voices, some deep and harshly vibrant, others unbearably shrill. Desperately Jahna clasped her ears with her palms.

Without warning, her door opened and a broad apparition padded into her room. Grossly female in conformation, it wore a face hideously wattled with excess flesh. Its hair hung in untidy hanks from a patchily thatched scalp. Its body was enormous, gelatinous. Jahna's heart squeezed with primitive fear.

Working features, contorting lips, stubby fingers gesturing urgently. Finally the apparition communicated two words. ''Valor—come—Valor.''

Valor wanted her? The din permitted no debate. Stumbling, Jahna followed the waddling figure into the hall and down the stairs. Outside, the four dogs loped the perimeters of the yard, indignant voices lost in the storm of sound. As Jahna followed the wattled woman across the courtyard, dread clutched her heart.

They entered the middle section of the quad and emerged on the second floor in a large chamber lit by hanging lanterns. Rectangular wooden boxes were arranged across the floor on crude stands, six of them. Valor bent over the nearest box. Its perforated wooden lid lay on the floor. Stepping near, Jahna saw that the tall woman was stuffing a skein of soft ragging into the box—around the head and shoulders of an infant blindfolded by a heavy fabric half-mask anchored under its chin.

Jahna stared at the baby dumbly. It was tiny, naked except for the mask and a loosely fastened diaper. It flailed at the ragging with angry fists, contorting its tiny body to deliver what might, under other circumstances, have been piercing screams. Now the cries disappeared without trace into the sound that throbbed around them.

Glancing up, Valor registered Jahna's arrival. With urgent gestures she instructed the wattled woman, who took Jahna's arm and guided her across the room. She pointed to big spools of ragging. Taking one herself, she set aside the lid of the nearest box. Her hands shook as she stuffed the soft fabric around a second screaming infant.

"I'm supposed to do that? To protect them from the noise?" Jahna shouted. It seemed an overzealous approach despite the intensity of the storm.

The woman nodded wildly. And this was not the moment for argument. Hurriedly Jahna took a spool for herself.

Pulling the lid from her first box, she found a larger infant stranded on its abdomen, head wobbling furiously on its weak neck. As she turned the baby to its back, she saw with surprise that both its ears were sealed with what appeared to be vegetable gum. Hands shaking, she began padding its box. The infant objected. It struggled and writhed back onto its stomach. Jahna twisted it onto its back again. Immediately it squirmed and half-flipped its wiry little body. Desperately Jahna unreeled a length of rag and began winding it around the infant until its arms and legs were wrapped tight against its body. Then, when it was helpless, she laid it back into the box and padded its head and shoulders.

Her second infant was larger, perhaps a month older, and fought as valiantly as the first. As Jahna struggled to tame and pad it, waves of discordant sound created and broke around her. Drums throbbed. Mechanical throats bellowed.

Then, the job done, she looked around dizzily. All six boxes were lidded again. All six infants were padded. Jahna straightened, her arms quivering with fatigue. The babies she had padded appeared to be two and three months of age.

And, it struck her, *both appeared to be perfectly formed physically*. She rested a palm on one perforated lid. Could the defect in both cases lie beneath the half-mask? Were the eyes alone affected? She knew that on Smith's World only certain biologic systems were in fact affected by mutation.

But this was Nelding and there was no time for speculation. The hurricane continued. Valor motioned her to the box where she had been working when Jahna entered. Setting the lid aside, she showed Jahna what flailing infant hands had done to the padding. The rag was in disarray, the infant submerged somewhere within its folds. Quickly Valor excavated the child's face, stuffed the ragging back into place around its head and shoulders, and replaced the lid.

Before night was done, Jahna had reswaddled and repadded both her infants a dozen times. Then, as slit windows grayed with dawn, the furor suddenly ceased. Jahna straightened and stared around the nursery. Vacuum seemed to have sucked it bare. The only sound was the thready wail of aggravated infants.

"They've quit," Valor whispered.

Jahna tongued dry lips, uncertain that her own vocal organs were still functional. "What—what was it?"

"Mockdirad—that was mockdirad in cry. And we must leave the padding. They may not be gone." She saw that Jahna stared at her uncomprehendingly. She motioned to a bench beneath the windows. "Rest. If they make cry again, you will be thankful for these brief moments."

Leadenly Jahna sank to the bench, arms and shoulders aching, feet numb, "I didn't know noise could be so exhausting," she observed thinly.

Valor sat beside her, silent, forehead in hands. Only the wattled woman continued to fuss over the complaining infants. Finally she too sank to the bench. "Gone, gone, begone, dirad," she muttered, her eyes cloudy. Her wattled face glistened.

Then there was the sound of feet on the stairs, distinct, sharp-edged. The nursery door opened and a tall man entered. His jaw was taut, his face clean-shaven, his hair pulled into a knot at the nape of his neck. Dark eyes found

51

Jahna. He paused, cataloguing her intently. Then he moved across the room to the nearest box. "They are gone. So do you intend to leave these windings here now?"

Valor jumped up. "We were waiting. Now we will unpack them."

Stifling her pique, Jahna mobilized herself with Valor and the wattled woman. She fumbled over the smaller of her two infants, painfully conscious of the tall man at her elbow, evaluating her performance. The infant squirmed irritably. When padding and swaddling lay on the floor, she gently eased the plug from one small ear.

Abruptly lean hands seized hers. "Not that!" Emphatically the tall man jabbed the gum plug back into the infant's ear. "Did I tell you to remove that?"

Jahna spun and stared up into his taut face. "You intend to leave this baby's ears plugged?" she asked, incredulous.

"Didn't I say so? You do not remove the plugs—or touch the blindings—until I instruct you to."

Jahna stared back at the infant in the box. The seminaked little body seemed combative, fists clenched, knees flexed. "You—you want me to leave this baby lying here blind and deaf?"

"Did you think we blinded the eyes against mockdirad cry?"

"I—"

His critical gaze fragmented her composure. What had she thought?

"We blind the eyes because they are to be blind. We plug the ears because they are not to receive our voices. For that reason, we do not speak aloud. We whisper in this room—even you whisper until I specifically instruct you otherwise."

Staring up into his unyielding eyes, she realized with shock that he had not spoken above a whisper. Nor had Valor or the wattled woman. Only she had employed her normal tone.

"So," he commanded, "remove the windings, close

the lids, rewind the spools, and go back to your own bed. I will not assess you for contact until we have all slept."

Jahna's eyes sought Valor's, expecting support—finding none. Her glance shot back to his. "I can't do that. I can't leave this infant lying here—"

"But you will. I am Beck Lord, Father of Pengalen, and I have the authority of your own government behind my word."

Oh, did he? Angrily, Jahna turned back to the infant. "Citizen Lord, my government was founded on humanitarian principles and it has maintained itself through the years on those very same principles. My government would never condone anything like this. Peace Council—"

"Cadet Swiss, your government—Peace Council—has assigned you to work at the authority of the First Fathers of Nelding. They in turn have assigned you to work at my authority. You are therefore pledged to follow the procedures and practices I find it judicious to apply here. I have made tonight's procedure clear to you. Now you will comply with it and you will do no more."

And the whole thing was said in a whisper. Jahna glared up at him, shoulders and neck painful with indignation. "I—"

The authority of her own government? Involuntarily she sagged. Yes, he did have that.

Tonight he had it. "All right," she said, matching his taut whisper. She lifted the perforated lid, placed it firmly over the masked infant's box, and bent to gather heaped ragging. "You have made yourself clear. I understand my position." Tonight Beck Lord, Father of Pengalen, did have the authority of her own government.

But not tomorrow. Because at first light she would fax a message to Commander Dublin relating the conditions she had found here and the practices she was expected to engage in. And then?

Would she be called back to Peace? or would her government simply insist that conditions in the nursery be ameliorated? Jahna had no idea. She only knew that she would not silently tolerate present conditions.

Five minutes later she stepped into the courtyard. Her last view of the nursery was vivid in mind, six small wooden boxes in rows, lids shut, infants cut off from any possible sensory stimulus. True, Jahna held no credential in any childhood specialty. But the few courses of pediatric study she had mastered had taught her one thing. No child could grow to normal adulthood from an infancy spent under such conditions. The mental capacity would be permanently, irrevocably impaired.

How could Beck Lord fail to know that? Even here, under whatever primitive conditions prevailed in huttown and tentback—and she still did not know from which milieu the six babies were drawn—how could he fail to realize that he was permanently stunting the infants' capacity to deal with life? How could Valor fail to realize that?

Valor. She certainly had received no support from Valor. Jahna took the stairs and paced her room. The sky was pale gray now. Soon it would be daylight. Where in the fortress of Pengalen, she wondered, would she find a fax unit to communicate with Peace?

Jahna halted. Slowly, unwillingly, she realized the situation was not to be so easily resolved. A fax unit at Pengalen? Improbable—extremely improbable. It seemed equally improbable that she would find one in any of the log villages she had passed through on the road to Pengalen. The nearest most probably was located in the vicinity of the landing field. And could the man who commanded this outpost be expected to dispatch her to the landing field with his blessing? More importantly, with his horse and wagon? Jahna ran to her window and stared down into the courtyard. There was nothing below to indicate that Beck Lord was master of any mode of transportation other than his own two feet.

Well, I've done some distance hiking in my time, she reminded herself grimly.

In mud?

With a moan she sat on the edge of her bed. It could take

days to reach Forgiven afoot and she had received no briefing whatsoever on native life forms. There might—or might not—be dangerous carnivores. She had no idea. Certainly there had been *something* outside the walls not an hour ago. Helplessly Jahna dropped her forehead into her hands. There were six babies in the nursery. Six babies blindfolded and deafened with gum plugs. How would she benefit them by venturing down the road and perishing? Or vanishing?

Was she perhaps oversubscribing to the possible dangers that prevailed beyond Pengalen? Her only rational choice, she decided finally, reluctantly, was to remain here long enough to evaluate the situation more fully. Then perhaps she would find that it was safe to venture afoot toward Forgiven.

She lay back. Perhaps, even, she faced no problem at all. Perhaps when Beck Lord interviewed her later today he would find her entirely unsuitable to work in his nursery. If she expressed her disapproval of his methods strongly enough, that in itself might disqualify her. Then it would be his problem to communicate with Peace and arrange her passage home.

And when she reached home, she would report fully on what she had learned. It would become a matter for Peace Council whether they dispatched another cadet to Nelding and under what conditions.

Jahna closed her eyes. Immediately the nursery was with her in a series of dark images, a row of small boxes, closed. The tall Nelding's whisper was with her too, cutting. *"We blind their eyes because they are to be blind."* But she was not helpless to ameliorate the situation. Not entirely.

Chapter Six

JAHNA TWISTED and moaned in protest, but the new garble of sound refused to retreat into dream. It remained solidly in the waking world, not a storm of sound this time, but a series of abrupt individual utterances: whistles, shrieks, groans, calls. And it issued from the courtyard. Finally, pulling coverlets around her shoulders, Jahna staggered to the window.

Below, an animal danced across the courtyard, brown-furry, muscular, mansize, with a long face totally alien in conformation. The creature had six limbs, two upon which it supported itself, two located midway on its massive torso, and two situated and used as arms. Under one of these it carried something that looked like a misshapen doll, a doll whose limbs flopped grotesquely in rhythm with the creature's movements. But the doll, Jahna realized with horror, was a limp, misshapen human infant, arms and legs twisted, head no more than a stumpish extension of its neck.

She was down the stairs in a moment, poised in the doorway. The dogs, Tetz and three lumbering blacks alike, were cowed, crouching tight to the ground, ears flat. Before Jahna could launch herself at the antic brown creature, Valor appeared from the middle rank of apartments. She moved quickly across the yard. "Dirad," she commanded sharply, her deep voice imperative, "give to me. Come! Give!"

The creature brayed, yelped, and abandoned its random path to orbit Valor. Circling, teasing, it threw itself back onto its midarms, sprang up and down elastically, then jumped forward again, agile for all its muscular solidity. The limp infant bounced against its furry chest.

Jahna tensed with helpless dismay. Valor caught her eye. "Run to the counter in my parlor. There is a platter of cakes. Bring them here—all of them." She moved as she spoke, turning to keep her arms stretched to the animal. "Give me, dirad. Give me now, so you can eat," she coaxed, but without apparent result.

Jahna retreated, taking the dark stairs by twos. In Valor's apartment she found a big platter of yellow cakes. She hurried back to the courtyard.

The dancing animal spotted the platter instantly and bounded toward Jahna. Landing with a solid slap of feet, it edited its output of vocal garble to a deep insistent bark. Jahna jumped back in alarm but the animal followed, slapping its feet to the ground insistently.

"No!" Valor insisted sharply. "Give me first, dirad."

The creature's head spun. It took her words as affront. It danced away yapping shrilly, alien features contorting.

"No. Give me. Then you can eat." Valor planted herself firmly beside Jahna, presenting her empty hands to the barking animal again.

Confronted with Valor's firmness of intention, the creature became indecisive. It shuffled, hopped, slid—and abruptly leaped to place the limp infant in Valor's hands. Immediately it grasped the platter of cakes. Jahna yielded and the animal flopped down on a patch of vivid green moss and with all six limbs began to systematically stuff the cakes into an orifice that appeared in its upper neck.

Jahna stared as a flexing cylinder of horny teeth ground the mealy yellow cakes. Then, remembering the infant, she turned. It looked no better now that its macabre dance had been terminated. It was pitifully small, its flesh purple-gray and fragile. Its arms hung from its bare chest like twisted abortions of flesh, ending in limp flaps, boneless hands. Its legs and feet were similarly malformed. Its head was no head, although there was a constellation of pinched features at the end of the neckstump. "Is it alive?" Could it be?

57

"Come in with me," Valor urged. "We must examine it."

In her apartment Valor placed the small body on the seat of a chair. It sprawled limp, no stir of life in torso or limbs. Quickly she laid her ear against its chest, moved its twisted limbs, opened one thin eyelid. She stood, her face grave. "It is alive." Her expression completed the statement for her.

It was alive for now. Alive today. Jahna stared down at the limp infant, emotions painfully engaged. "But where did it come from? Did the animal steal it?"

Valor shook her head. "No, it came from the tangles. Now we will put it away for a while. Perhaps it will revive with warmth. And perhaps it will not." She moved across the room to a chest and pulled a small coverlet from a lower drawer. She wrapped the small body deftly.

Jahna watched, appalled. One small life, a promise about to be rescinded. But with those feckless limbs, those useless hands and feet, like empty gloves, that vestigial head, what promise had life ever held?

Valor cradled the bundled infant. "Come and you will see our second nursery."

Jahna followed her down the hall to a small bleak room. Half a dozen wooden boxes were stacked against a wall. Stands were pyramided in the corner. Quickly Jahna fetched stand and box, combined them. A thin pad covered the bottom of the box. Valor placed the infant in the box and stepped back. "It may be that there is no true brain function, you see," she explained softly.

"Yes, I—yes." Jahna stared at the unmoving child. It certainly appeared little more than a blank slate of flesh.

"However, even in that case it may be able to nurse. So I will check it at intervals to determine."

Reluctantly Jahna followed the Nelding woman from the room. "But its parents—"

"They are not concerned," Valor said firmly. "So now that dirad has eaten your dinner, I will fry you squash. However, there is time to wash and dress, if you want."

"I—yes. Thank you," Jahna agreed gratefully. Avert-

58

ing her eyes, she hurried to her room. From her window she saw that the animal in the courtyard wore the empty platter on its head, midlimbs and legs wrestling with one another playfully. Jahna sat on her bed, eyes closed, until she had regained composure. Then she dressed and crossed the hall to splash her face.

As she approached Valor's door, she met the Nelding woman coming up the stairs, empty platter in hand. "Is he gone?"

"I was able to send him along—fortunately. Dirad sometimes want to stay and talk. And dirad conversation, as you heard, can be painful to the ear."

Jahna followed the tall woman into her apartment. "So dirad was what we heard outside the walls last night," she ventured.

Valor's dark brows arched. "Ah, no. Last night was mockdirad, Jahna, from the groves of tentback. True dirad, our friend with the hundred teeth, moves alone. And he carries no horn or drum. He is satisfied to be only as loud as he already is."

Jahna frowned, baffled. No sooner had she grasped understanding than it dissolved in her hand. "But, then, what is mockdirad? Some other kind of animal?" A more intelligent species, evidently, if he carried drums and instruments.

Valor shrugged. "Mockdirad gathers in tentback and moves through the tangles on two feet like man—for the most part, at least. He carries a horn in his two hands, like man, usually. Then he gives cry—song, he calls it—and for the night he is dirad. With dawn he returns to tentback."

Jahna groped through utter confusion. "He—those were men out there last night? Men from tentback?"

Valor's smile was wry. "Men, more or less, come to serenade you on the eve of your arrival. But you will see mockdirad soon enough. You can decide for yourself then." She led the way to the kitchen and took a heavy metal skillet from a shelf. Within minutes brindle squash was frying light and sweet. "Tree milk and mugs are

59

already on the counter. Will you pour for me, too?"

Together they sat. Jahna attacked the fried squash, her mind a welter of confusion. It was difficult to isolate a single coherent question for consideration. But the baby they had left in the second nursery demanded first attention. "The baby—" she speculated, "it came from tentback, too?"

Valor's eyes were briefly startled. "*Never*. A tentback mother never abandons her infant, not even the most hopeless. It is the virtuous Fathers of huttown who leave helpless babes in the tangles to die."

Jahna's eyes widened with comprehension. *"We destroy monsters at birth,"* Humble Nodd had said righteously of monster offspring born to domestic stock. But when one of their own offspring was deformed. . . . "You mean one of the settler families left that child to die because it was malformed?" Jahna asked slowly, ordering her reluctant thoughts. "And the animal found it and brought it here?"

"Yes, Beck has trained that dirad and a few others to enjoy my cooking if they can find something to trade for it. Some abandoned infant."

Jahna stared at her incredulously. "But—how many children are left out there to die? There can't be so many that—the second nursery is empty now except for that one."

Valor's eyes sought concealment beneath lowered lashes. "It is empty now because Beck takes the tanglings —that is what we call babes who come from the vineland —into tentback at first opportunity. But once, you see, this entire compound was home for tanglings."

Jahna's bafflement was complete. "But I thought this was formerly a madhouse, Valor, an institution for the disturbed."

Reluctantly Valor nodded. "It was when this world was first settled. There were so many who could not face the realities of Nelding. Earth was quite different, you see— so different that many thought their God had abandoned them when they came here, and they in turn abandoned their reason. Then Pengalen was built, retreat and exile.

"Later, Pengalen became shelter for tanglings, too. That was before the Fathers decreed they be abandoned to death. The disturbed, in fact, were caretakers to the tanglings for some years. And later it was a madman's mission, roaming the vines to find these little bits of garbage, bringing them here or to the groves for salvation. And so many of them were unfit, their lives a short sad suffering." The Nelding woman stared at the rough countertop, her narrative abruptly at an end.

An unsatisfactory end. Jahna prodded her. "But when did Pengalen become—what it is now?" Whatever that was, abandoned madhouse, way station nursery, or something more significant in terms of the two societies that had evolved on Nelding.

Valor raised her eyes. Their expression was rueful. "It has been some years, Jahna Swiss. And I am not to answer your questions yet. I have those instructions from Beck. However, you notice I do forget them sometimes." Quickly she stood.

Jahna stared up at the Nelding woman, a dozen fresh questions finding foothold in her mind. "But, Valor, where are the disturbed kept now?"

The Nelding woman was not able to deny her insistence. "The descendants of those who were here are not kept now. They live in tentback. For those who occur fresh in huttown, the Fathers make their own—arrangements."

Jahna frowned, imagining the quality of those arrangements. "I see." But there were other questions, dozens of them. The next was awkward. "Then have you lived here long, Valor?"

Unexpectedly Valor smiled. "Meaning, 'Are you a tangling, Valor? Or daughter of a madman?' " Valor shook her head gently. "I was never left in the vines. No dirad or madman ever carried me this way. And I have never abandoned my reason. I came here of myself from huttown. The people who were once my family live there still."

So Valor was not one of those abandoned at birth, although her dished features and her deep voice were unusual. Speculatively Jahna ventured, "There must be a very high incidence of birth defects here. Much higher than we have on Peace."

Valor moved into the kitchen, skirts swinging. "Then surely the people of Peace are full of virtue, Jahna Swiss."

Jahna started to protest, then saw Valor's ironic smile. She acknowledged it with a nod. "We've never had a food crop mutate and move out into the wild, for instance," she went on thoughtfully. "And we've never had to take special measures to keep our stock lines from altering radically. They do occasionally produce aberrant offspring, but not to a degree anyone has ever considered threatening." Then a fresh thought, a troubling thought, claimed her mind. Rather it reclaimed her mind. "But, Valor, those babies in the first nursery don't appear defective. I didn't see so much as a strawberry mark last night."

Valor turned from her stove, her face suddenly very still.

Jahna realized from the Nelding woman's expression that she had arrived at an important point. "Where did *those* babies come from?"

Slowly Valor shook her head. "Now, that is one of the questions, Jahna."

"Valor, one of *which* questions? I'm going to be here for two years. I'll be working right here in Pengalen. You told me so last night. It's pointless to keep things from me that I'll have to know eventually anyway."

Valor gestured helplessly. "And now you see why Beck did not want me to tell you even that you would be working on these premises."

"He didn't? *Why?*"

"Because then would follow more questions, the ones you are asking now."

Jahna's forehead creased with exasperation. She abandoned the counter to frame herself in the kitchen doorway. "In that case, Valor, it's Beck who is wrong. Not you—or me. I left my family and friends and traveled twenty days on a star trader to reach here. I certainly didn't come to play games.''

Valor's gaze dropped. "These are not games, Jahna."

"No? Well, there's something much worse than games up there in the first nursery. If those babies are kept in boxes with their eyes covered and their ears sealed for very long, their mental growth will be permanently stunted. They will be mental defectives. Don't you realize that?''

"And is that the worst that can happen to a child?''

Jahna started at the sharp question behind her. Beck Lord had entered the apartment silently. "Is it?'' he demanded, challenge in his lean, clean-shaven face.

Involuntarily Jahna bristled. "I can't think of many things that can be more crippling over a lifetime than mental deficiency,'' she stated. "Especially on a world like Nelding, where you obviously require an intelligent effort to survive.''

"That is obvious?'' he demanded. "From what?''

"It's obvious from—'' Jahna faltered, frowning. It was obvious that this was a grim and gray world standing to its ankles in mud. But brindle squash grew wild in the tangles, and trees gave milk, or so she was told. "It's always desirable for citizens to possess mental capability,'' she concluded evasively. Score one for opposing counsel.

"You name intelligence first of the virtues, then?''

"*No*. I'm not talking about virtues at all,'' she protested, sensitive to his challenging tone. "I'm talking about human qualities that can make life worth living. A person whose mental abilities are limited simply cannot function adequately. He'll never be able to. In some degree he'll be dependent throughout his life. And if mental deficiency can be avoided just by taking an infant out of its crib regularly and giving it contact with its environment—''

"So. That is why you have superior intelligence, then? Because your parents took you out of your crib?''

Challenge again. "That's part of the reason,'' she said with emphasis.

"There *were* other factors, however?''

"Of course there were. Both my parents came from families inclined to superior mental efficiency. And I've had programmed schooling from the beginning. I've— But the point is, there would have been nothing for my schooling to build on if I had been kept in a box with my eyes bound as an infant."

Beck nodded, a slight inclination of his head, admitting nothing. "So that is how it was with you."

"That is how it is with human infants. It's a physiological fact. Any twelve-year-old on Peace knows as much. And aren't those human infants upstairs?"

Now the taut lips stretched into a bare smile. "They appear human."

Was he trying to deny her her point? "But you don't think the usual rules of human development apply to them? Just as they would to any other human infant?" Her eyes, flickering to Valor's face, caught an expression of startled intensity. She glanced quickly back to her opponent's face.

But Valor's expression was not mirrored there. The same taut smile stretched the tall man's lips. "Your heart is in your argument, Peace. Have you ever contested with shouts?"

"I haven't any idea what you mean," Jahna snapped, irritated to have missed something in the interchange.

"It is a practice in tentback, when two bucks want the same female. They stand on either side of her tent—and then they shout."

"And?"

"They shout and shout until finally one of them can't shout anymore. Sometimes that is two days later." He shrugged, his lips curling back into a tight smile.

Jahna's brows creased. "And the winner gets the female, obviously. But I don't see where that fits into the present argument."

His smile became mocking. "Females never practice the shout on Nelding, Peace."

Jahna's face hardened. "And did I express sexual interest in you?" she demanded. "If I'm shouting—and I'm

64

not—it's about a roomful of babies. Six by count.''

Slowly, appraisingly, the Nelding man nodded. "So. Your point, Peace." He turned to Valor. "I do not see my dinner yet."

It took Valor a moment to accommodate the abrupt change of topic. "It has already been eaten—by dirad."

Beck's eyes were suddenly intent. "It has? When?"

"Some minutes ago. You did not pass him in the vines?"

"So, would I ask if I had? Did he bring a child?"

"He did. I have already examined it and put it away for the night. I am afraid it does not appear fit."

His eyes searched her face. Abruptly he turned. His footsteps were a hasty clatter down the hallway.

Valor shrugged. "Do you wonder why I bother to examine them for him?" she asked ruefully.

Jahna made no attempt to reply. She was staring at the empty room behind her, her bold scheme of argumentation curdling and souring unexpressed. One moment Beck Lord had been fully engaged in controversy. The next he had been demanding his dinner. And now he was gone. The Father of Pengalen: high-handed, arbitrary, fickle.

The Father of Pengalen: the man she must deal with to ameliorate the condition of the six infants in the first nursery. Could she deal with him? And prevail?

Suddenly she had to have privacy to pursue a hundred clamoring thoughts, none of them thoughts she wanted to pursue on this gray world with the star trader already pressing toward some other solar system, Peace Cadet Swiss forgotten behind. She had to pursue thoughts she was afraid to take down the hall to her room, afraid to haunt her private chamber with.

She had to pursue them alone. Alone someplace in this grim compound on this sullen world.

"I am frying more squash if you are still hungry," Valor offered from the kitchen.

But Jahna had already escaped the apartment. She pattered down the stairs and found herself alone in the courtyard. One of the black dogs trotted from a doorway.

Absently Jahna offered her hand for his evaluation. Her eyes moved around the compound. The log walls seemed to offer no retreat.

"Are there carnivores out there?" she asked the dog, raising his muzzle. He regarded her steadily from clear golden eyes. "Carnivores or just madmen and tanglings?"

Slowly the dog wagged his tail.

She made her decision. "Come," she said, she hoped with authority. "We're going for a walk."

The big black animal accompanied her to the arch, an encouraging ally of muscle and sinew. But when she stepped out onto the road, he offered wag-tail regrets. Despite coaxings and commands, he refused to leave the courtyard of Pengalen.

"I wonder what you know that I don't," she mused. But she was decided, despite his desertion. She hesitated briefly, searching the sky for some indication of the hour of day. To her eyes the overcast was a uniform gray, cloud on cloud. And the road, she saw with distinct discouragement, was as much an avenue of mud as it had been yesterday.

Yesterday. A lifetime ago.

Well, the road would take her nowhere, anyway. It was an hour by wagon to the nearest huttown village and she suffered no delusion that she would find welcome if she hiked there. So instead she ventured out into the damp tangle of greenery that grew along the rotting front wall of Pengalen. Slowly, picking her way, she traversed the front wall and rounded the corner. Her new vista was more of the same, stalk and vine sprouting with damp enthusiasm from mud. In the near distance a small grove of trees, branches sweeping low, claimed a circle of soil. She stood at the corner of the compound for long minutes, assuring herself that she was the only living creature who surveyed this particular scene. No leaf or blade moved.

A scatter of rain wet her face. She peered up at the clouds. Would they open? Or were they simply threatening, trying to frighten her back into the fortress?

Determined, she set course for the grove of trees, reaching it just as rain began to pepper her hair. Ducking, she took shelter.

It was dark beneath the trees. The smell was of damp earth. She peered around. A heavy thatch of fallen leaves covered the soil. She touched the layer experimentally and sat on it. It gave like a cushion and something small chittered away, fleeing the circle of trees.

Jahna drew her knees under her chin, a hundred clamoring thoughts temporarily relegated to some back chamber of her mind, and watched rain beat the face of Nelding. It rattled against leaf and vine with hypnotic insistence, and the mud drank it down, welcome tonic. With rainfall, Nelding achieved elemental harmony, skies as dark as tree shadow, waters feeding slippery mud and glossy vine with drenching generosity.

And then, somehow, it was dark. Dark within the tenting trees, dark without. Sometime during the rainfall dusk had come across the land.

Jahna ventured warily from the perimeter of the trees. Pengalen was a vague shadow against an almost indistinguishable horizon. Between the grove and the compound stretched a sea of mud, well laced with things that go bump in the night. She studied alternatives with scant enthusiasm. If mockdirad were abroad, were they dangerous as well as discordant? Would she be missed in the compound? Would Beck come with a lantern and dogs to find her and conduct her back?

Her jaw set. Now that he would not. When foot follows foot, distance can be covered, even treacherous distance, in the sullen dark of a Nelding night. She set the first foot beyond the cushioning leaves and followed it with the second.

She fell only twice. By the time she reached the archway, she was no more than half covered with mud. Dogs ran to greet her, bounding around her happily. Tetz croaked joyfully. Jahna stumbled through the archway and drew a deep, musty breath. The compound was as it had been the evening before, lights in second-story windows, some flickering and dim, one, the light cube Valor had traded from Peace, steadily incandescent, welcoming.

The dogs' alarm had brought no one to witness her entrace. Relieved, she staggered across the courtyard and up the stairs. She secreted herself in her room, bedraggled, muddy—miserable? She stood in the middle of the floor, undecided. She had, after all, extricated herself from the situation. There remained only the matter of extricating herself from the mud.

Taking herself in hand, she proceeded to do so. Half an hour later, mud scrubbed away in a wooden tub, she was dressed again. She brushed out her hair and confronted her empty room. Bedtime again? With her hundred thoughts still unconfronted?

Wearily, dutifully, she sat on the bed and confronted them. But instead of receding as they were dealt with— unsatisfactorily, she admitted—they continued to clamor at the forefront of her mind. Jahna dropped her forehead into her palms and stared at the plank floor. *Why* had Beck Lord brought her here? Why send all the way to Peace for someone to care for the six babies in the nursery when he had Valor, the wattled woman, surely other equally capable women available? What would she find if she removed the half-masks from the babies? Why had Valor been instructed to tell her virtually nothing?

Valor. She seized at Valor. Whatever was being done here seemed to violate none of Valor's principles. Or did it? Nelding appeared, after all, a heavily male-dominant world. Under those circumstances a woman might acquiese to deeds she would never permit if she considered the major decisions her own responsibility. Jahna sighed. After two days at Pengalen she trusted Valor's instincts— but not necessarily her actions. Not with Beck Lord standing behind her determining what those actions were to be.

But it was possible she was letting the atmosphere of Pengalen influence her judgment. If Nelding were a bright, sunny world, if there were rugs on her floor, if the babies were lying in a whitewashed nursery in plaston cribettes with clean sheets beneath them and coordination equipment dangling near—what would she think then?

She would think something was very wrong. Babies in such nurseries were never kept blindfolded.

She stiffened at the sound of footsteps in the hall. There was a rapping at her door.

Valor hovered in the hall, deep eyes concerned. "I am leaving hot mush and tree milk ready in my apartment, if you need them to warm you after your—if you need them. Please enter and serve yourself, because I must go now to the nursery so that Elda can rest."

Two discrete bits of data reached Jahna. Valor *had* known of her venture into the mud. And Elda, presumably the wattled woman, was about to be freed from nursery duty for the evening. Quickly Jahna dismissed the first bit of data and focused on the second. "Won't I disturb Elda if I go into your apartment?"

"It is no worry," Valor assured her quickly. "Her bed is on the nursery floor, next to the nursery itself."

Dampened, Jahna returned to her bed. For one brief moment it had seemed possible she might slip into Valor's apartment and, in her absence, quiz the other Nelding woman. Not, she reflected, that Elda seemed particularly bright. Neither, at the moment, did Jahna.

That small scheme undone, she paced her floor and finally decided to avail herself of Valor's offer. And so her second evening at Pengalen passed into uneventfulness.

Chapter Seven

Waking slowly, Jahna lay astraddle her cloud, taking inventory of her situation. Beyond her window the sky had the dense frowning look of very early morning. Before she could reach decision about the disposition of the next half hour, the dogs let cry in the courtyard, three booming, one croaking excitedly. Mobilized, Jahna struggled out of bed and stumbled to her window.

Two men in dark trousers stood at bay in the mouth of the archway. They were huttown men, lean, dark beards squarecut, dark hair knotted tight. "Lord!" the shorter bawled up the walls of the quad, fists clenched at his sides. "Lord! Come down!"

The three black dogs wheeled and addressed their own voices in the same direction, but Tetz continued to harass the intruders. Quickly Jahna shed her blanket and tugged her brown daysuit from its wall peg.

By the time she reached the foot of the stair, Beck was in the courtyard. "Guard!" he commanded the racketing dogs. *"Guard!"* When they had disappeared into the middle section of the quad, Beck glared at the trespassers. "So why are you here at this hour?"

"That we will show you now," the taller man snapped. Both disappeared through the archway. A few minutes later they returned with a companion, dragging a heavy gray carcass. They tugged it into the courtyard and stood back from it, three men alike in bitterness of feature and ferocity of stance. "This is why we come here."

It was a clean heifer like Nodd had shown her, but its throat was disfigured by a wound resembling a pair of lax bloody lips. The eyes were gaping and glassy. The gray hide was smeared with mud and blood.

"And this is not the only one," the tall Nelding announced, fists tight, white, against his black trousers. "Tentdirad came upon us in the night with their horns and their knives and took open our barns. We lost three clean cattle, six mosheep, and a horse. Even poultry was destroyed, wrung at the neck and trampled into the mud."

Silence stretched between them, unsympathetic. "And why have you brought your dead animal to me, Fathers?" Beck demanded.

Glitter-ridden eyes swept to Jahna in the doorway. "You have your star woman now."

"Yes. This is the Peace cadet I requested." Beck's tone conceded nothing further.

"It was understood that when she came there would be no more tentdirad crying in the night and destroying crops and stock." The tall man's eyes were fierce. He flung a gesture of accusation at the dead heifer. "Now we have this!"

Beck's eyes moved from face to angry face. "It was understood," he said slowly, "that when I had my star cadet, the huttown infants we find abandoned in the vines would have the care any human infant is entitled to. Now they will."

The three huttowners exchanged indignant glances. Then gazes refocused on Beck. "Maybe it was not plainly spoken, Lord, but it was understood by us that when we obtained this star trollop for your use, you would secure us freedom from tentdirad. We have come today to demand it."

Beck spoke deliberately. "Demand then. It will accomplish nothing because I made you no promise. I only committed myself to the statement that mockdirad's hostility stems in part from your practice of abandoning certain infants in the vines to die—and contributing nothing to their care when we bring them here for salvage."

"Now we have contributed," the Father crackled, eyes indicating Jahna.

"One small concession—do you think it immediately cancels centuries of crime against your own children?"

The short Nelding's beard twitched righteously. "In the matter of our offspring, clean *and* monster, we have only done what our conscience dictated."

"Oh?" Beck turned to Jahna. "Peace, fetch the tangling from the small nursery."

Jahna hurried up the stairs. She found the tiny tangling in his swaddlings, eyes open, color—to her surprise—good. Quickly she scooped him up and hurried down the stairs.

Beck took the small body. "So this is what huttown conscience dictates? This infant was left to die of exposure."

Three huttown faces went rigid. "Lord, do you think we have time to waste on this garbage?"

"Now how much time do you waste by letting it die in its own crib? If it must die?"

"And what does it matter where garbage dies?" the short Nelding huffed.

Beck held their eyes. "Exactly. What does it matter?"

The three men stared back at him wordlessly.

"The question then becomes, what does it matter where it lives, if it fails to die?"

"It will never live with us," the tall Nelding asserted aggressively. "No garbage uses its hands in our clean fields. We haven't enough fit food for those who *do* work. Our own children are waking hungry today."

Beck returned the tangling to Jahna. "Trees give milk —all you need is a tapping pipe and bucket. You will find brindle squash growing wild year round. Ask any tentback how to use it. Pull in the mud and you have halma bulbs for your breakfast. I can tell you more."

Huttown faces engorged with outrage. "We will never soil ourselves."

Beck's eyes became remote. "Starve then," he said dispassionately. It was an evocation of their future, grim, final. Turning, he stepped past Jahna into the quad.

The faces of the three huttowners were terrible in their

wrath. Three dark beards waggled. Three pairs of dark eyes glittered. Then the trio turned and withdrew stiffly through the archway.

Jahna heard the wagon creak down the roadway. She stared at the abandoned heifer. Evidently Humble Nodd's compatriots considered it beneath dignity to exit dragging a dead domestic. Then her glance fell on the tangling infant in her arms. Warmth and nourishment had revived him. The head was still a blunt extension of the neck, and the eyes, although they were open, were dull. But at least the thin flesh had color now. Certainly, death no longer appeared imminent.

Before Jahna could return the infant to the small nursery, Valor and Elda appeared from the quad, an ill-assorted pair. They stood over the dead heifer, Valor's face grim. "This does not remain in our yard," she declared, granting the dead animal a distasteful glance before bending to tug a stiff leg.

Half an hour later, while Jahna sat at breakfast, Beck himself appeared, basket in hand. Jahna was startled to see the tangling infant she had returned to the nursery packed snugly into the bottom of the basket. "When you are ready, we are walking tentback way to find this tangling a home," the Father of Pengalen informed her. "Have you fed infants before?"

Jahna's eyes narrowed. "Didn't you check that before you brought me here?"

"I checked a number of other factors—but no, not that."

"I've fed a few babies," Jahna admitted slowly, freshly baffled.

"And have you fed a tangling?"

On Peace? "Is it any different from feeding a normal infant?"

Mockery appeared at the corners of his mouth. "In this case, no."

Jahna frowned, bristling. "Then I'll manage," she said shortly.

Meal completed, she hurried to her room to fetch cape

and boots, at once elated and apprehensive. Venturing into tentback, she would surely acquire valuable data about the Nelding situation. But her guide seemed more interested in provoking than in enlightening her. So we'll contest with shouts again, she resolved. That might constitute the entirety of their relationship for the time she was here.

For the short time she was here? Today, she discovered, she felt less eager to be dismissed back to her own sunny corner of existence. She came down caped and booted to find Beck waiting in the courtyard, a single black dog at command, two baskets in hand. "This one is yours for now."

Jahna hefted the smaller basket easily. "Will we be gone long?"

"Not more than today," he assured her, leading way.

They passed through the archway into a day as gray as any Nelding day. Vines, gray-green, dense, tangled away from the roadside in unpicturesque confusion, half hiding the dead heifer. The air was thick with mist and morning chill. Jahna gazed around her, drawing lightly of the sodden air. "Do you have seasons here?" The informational letter had not contained such superfluous data.

Beck inclined his head. "Yes, sometimes the sky is gray for months on end. Other times it becomes black for comparable intervals."

Somehow the prospect was unencouraging. Jahna elected to abandon the topic. Black dog cantering before them, they picked their way around the flank of Pengalen and squished toward the small grove where Jahna had sheltered the evening before. Tree branches sagged wearily beneath moss and damp leaves. The springy bed of leaves where Jahna had settled to watch the rain was curtained with shadow.

Beck indicated the sweeping branches. "Did you find my tent when you met weather last night?"

Jahna glanced at him warily. "I thought I might have to spend the night under these trees, if that's what you mean."

He stooped to peer into the musty shadows. "I have

74

spent nights here myself. Many nights when I was younger."

Keenly Jahna's thoughts took focus. "It's safe, then? To sleep out on Nelding?"

Beck straightened, his eyes curious on her face. "For me it's safe."

"But not for me?" she demanded, peering out into the deep pocket of shadow beneath the trees. "Are there carnivores out here? Dangerous life forms?"

"There are." Slowly a mocking smile crept across his lips. "Don't you have them on Peace? They're called men."

Jahna's lips tightened. "We have them," she said grimly. "And on Peace we place them in therapeutic villages for intensive treatment until we can call them men again."

Dark brows arched. "All so women can wander in the dark when they should be in their beds?"

"All so women can be free from unnecessary fear," she said sharply.

He lifted his shoulders, a deprecating shrug. "I do not believe many males here would consider that a value of significance."

"I believe you," Jahna responded tartly, turning away.

Morning progressed, sodden, unjoyous. Once, two sullen layers of cloud parted to reveal a small yellow sun. It disappeared again within moments. Occasionally scarlet spears were seen growing from the tangle of leaf and vine, lancing the mist huskily, spilling orange, scarlet, and black kernels from lateral pockets. "This was one of the original crops," Beck explained, shucking kernels off a fat brown cob.

Jahna examined the bright, tough kernels. "Corn?" she guessed in amazement.

"That's what it was called. Now it is called redspear in tentback. In huttown it is properly termed garbage."

Garbage indeed, she thought, fascinated by the colorful kernels. In appearance this corn was very different from Peace corn, which grew tall and slender and bore delicate cobs with tender pink kernels. "Is it still edible?"

"Dirad think so. So do the chitterling."

"Chitterling?"

"They chitter."

Jahna remembered the noisy little creature that had fled from her the evening before. "Food crops seem to alter rather radically here," she speculated. "Do you have any idea why? Unusual ground radiation?"

His eyes met hers directly. "Now, my personal theory is that Nelding is a fussy woman. She takes whim and changes everything she sees. Nothing satisfies her. But what she has created doesn't suit her either, so she changes it again and again—constantly fussing, this woman. After a while then, she decides she liked it better in its original form. But by then she's forgotten what that was. So she has to go on with the tinkering. A finicky lady."

Jahna let annoyance show in her glance, and found, from his answering flicker of expression, that he had been playing for it. With a frown she tossed down the kernels of corn and stalked ahead.

Her annoyance gradually simmered low and she found herself curious again. She pushed through the soggy tangle, her eyes ranging wide over her surroundings. "Are there established communities out here?" she asked finally. "Comparable to the huttown villages?"

"Oh, yes. Some people live in the same grove for all their years. Other tentbackers are nomadic. They come and go, usually in small groups."

"Family groups?"

"Sometimes."

"And the population is composed of disturbed individuals who were once confined to Pengalen, their descendants—and tanglings?" As she spoke she found she had a new question to confront herself with. How was her poise going to weather first contact with tentback? Her previous experience with the frankly abnormal had been almost nonexistent—just as nonexistent as her credentials for managing a nursery of putatively mutant infants.

Beck's long jaw set. "The population is made up of

tentbackers,'' he said with emphasis. "The first came into the tangles and groves well over two hundred years ago. This is the real Nelding, Peace, out here in the groves. This is where our people live the real life of this world, not a schematized and artificialized life brought from Earth in an iron coffin three centuries ago.''

"I see,'' Jahna said slowly, not entirely certain she did. Schematized, rigidly so, huttown might be. But she had seen nothing there that she, citizen of Peace, would classify as artificialized. Everything, everyone, had seemed depressingly of this Nelding earth. "You grew up out here, then?''

He shook his head emphatically. "I grew up in huttown. Why else do you think I scrape off my beard?''

She peered dubiously at his naked chin. Such were common on Peace, but here, where the shaving implements could only be primitive, it seemed foolhardy, even dangerous, to shave each morning. "I can't imagine why you bother, wherever you grew up.''

He shrugged lightly. "My aim is to offend.''

Jahna smiled, remembering the bearded Fathers. "Big black beard being high among the virtues, I suppose.''

Beck nodded. "God himself wore one when he was young. I hear he also wore baggy black trousers and a scowl.''

"And his hair in a knot?''

"Over his left ear. But your own group—you didn't carry virtue with you to the stars. I have read your early history. You brought reason. Even God had to subject Himself to reason to obtain passage to Peace.''

"Then, you do study comparative cultures in your schools,'' Jahna said eagerly, warmed to have Peace called back from the limbo into which it had slipped these last days. Beck Lord, Father of Pengalen, had read of Peace. Therefore Peace existed.

Beck Lord, Father of Pengalen, smiled tightly at her sudden buoyancy. "We study virtue in our schools, Peace, and our schools meet for the most part in the fields. That is to say, the scholars work with their hands while the

Fathers lecture behind. However, a few books and planet reports fell into my hands and I had time to study them, since I was never permitted to enter the fields or to occupy myself with the stock.''

''You weren't? Why?'' Surprise made her questions sharp.

''I suffer storms.''

It was a statement full of austere dignity—and completely devoid of meaning to Jahna. She looked at him blankly.

''A convulsive disorder,'' he elaborated, meeting her gaze evenly.

''Epilepsy?'' she guessed. At his nod, her mind rushed forward. ''But why would that keep you from—''

Then she remembered the tall huttowner's indignant statement that morning. No garbage would use its hands in their clean fields. ''But epilepsy doesn't result from mutation, Beck.''

''It doesn't? Who knows? And who is willing to take the chance? Who would want a field of contaminated grain to transmit disorder to the clean humans who consume it? And to cause them to bear monsters?''

''But that's nonsense!''

He shrugged. ''That nonsense at least allowed me time to read and to do a number of other things no normal huttown boy has time for.''

''Then you weren't exiled?'' she concluded quickly. ''Your parents didn't abandon you?''

''No. My parents could have sent me away at the onset of the disorder. I was four at that time. But they refused, just as they refused to have me formally labeled garbage. You see, illness is permissible, even in huttown. The strictures are that no person who is unaccountably ill is allowed to be near the crops or the stock and that no person who dies of unaccounted causes will be given sanctified burial.'' He shrugged. ''Of course, despite my parents' tolerance, the Fathers regarded me as garbage. It chokes them to address me as Father Lord.''

Jahna frowned, the situational counselor in her rankled.

"But that's an appalling way to manage a pioneer society," she objected. "In the first place, the business of weeding out seedlings and young domestics because they show slight variance. And then not utilizing full manpower, refusing to allow—"

Beck shook his head. "Peace, you can shout all day. Three centuries ago a group of unreasonable people came to settle an unreasonable planet. Since then neither party has yielded even one point to the other. Neither party ever will."

She accepted his words with impatience. But glancing ahead, he waved aside her argument. He nodded toward the horizon. Peering, Jahna realized that the dark blur in the distance had become a long dark stretch of trees. Alert, she followed Beck forward silently. As they drew nearer, the grove took detail. The trees were towering, taller, and more massive than any she had seen, and they were laden with moss and wet leaves. A log wall stretched for some distance along the front rim of the grove. Near the edge of the grove, Jahna's eyes found movement, random, unhurried—humans. She glanced quickly at Beck. His face was set. Her own muscles tightened in response.

With an eager cry, the black dog loped ahead of them, but Beck summoned him back to heel. "They'll spot us in a moment, Peace. Don't leave my side," he instructed Jahna.

She glanced up at him sharply, found his face suddenly less than conducive to peace of mind. "Am I likely to be assaulted at midmorning?"

His reply was short, distracted. "Wander away and learn for yourself."

Jahna tensed. But the time for preparing herself for encounter with this alien milieu had already slipped away unutilized.

Chapter Eight

THEY GOT little nearer the grove before its inhabitants sighted them. There was a hoarse outcry from the edge of the grove, and dark bodies were suddenly swarming from shadow and bounding across the field, closing the space between them. As they vaulted near, Jahna stiffened and recoiled, her throat suddenly closing in panic. For those racing bodies were not clothed, but furred, furred with brown, in some cases heavily furred, and the faces that grinned above the furry pelts were only semihuman. With shock she saw that the features appeared to be formed both upon the dirad and the human models. Flattened nostrils, misplaced eyes, nonexistent lips. . . .

"What are they?" Jahna's voice squeaked out the top of her head.

"In front, mockdirad. And delighted to see you, Peace. Here, don't—" He grasped her arm, drew her around beside him. "Don't get behind me. They'll misinterpret it."

"How could they?" Jahna tried to bring her voice down. Failed. Mockdirad covered the distance from the grove with unnatural speed, seeming to grow across the landscape like creatures accelerating at her from another dimension. Then the exuberant creatures were flying a wide circle around Jahna and Beck, cavorting wildly, using their heavy bodies in ways of which no normal human would be capable. Some had muscular midarms growing from the waist region, and they bounced back upon them, waggling arms and legs in the air, grunting, shrieking, uttering calls and cries—inhuman calls and cries.

Totally inhuman.

Beck held Jahna tight beside him, his fingers coiled deep in the flesh of her forearm. "All right, then—don't give them the chance to interpret your reaction correctly. Show confidence in your male. *Show it, Peace.*" His fingers bit deep for emphasis.

Wildly Jahna seized at self-possession. She pulled her shoulders back square, stuck her chin out at the world, and stared straight ahead, eyes half-focused.

Mockdirad danced and called in a ragged circle, each muscular body seeming to forcibly expulse a powerful excess of energy. The naked genitalia, she saw, were without exception human male. In some cases the hands and feet were likewise human. In others they were dirad, except for the opposed thumb. Some chests were heavily thatched, others were almost bare. Likewise some buttocks, some backs, some faces. Several of the creatures carried male infants or very young male children created in their own image but, Jahna saw in consternation, they did not restrain their antics in consideration of the hapless youngsters. The older children contributed their own voices and gestures to the furor of the celebration.

Then, her first shock receding, Jahna saw that others had come from the grove community too. These were not mockdirad. These might more properly be called mockhuman. They were male and female, young and old, but uniformly muddy, unkempt, and malformed; most of them grotesque, a few strangely, horribly beautiful, caricatures of the human. Foreheads bulged wide over flattened faces. Hair hung in gaudy feather-banners. Arms and legs were carried at strange angles, some mere flippers, others long, too long, and oddly engineered. Bodies bore the stigmata of a hundred varieties of wild mutation. A young woman with amber scales danced around the circle of mockdirad, lips pulled back to reveal yellow fangs. Bringing up the rear was a tall woman trailing three young, all female, all as haughty as she, all as multiply endowed of breast. The youngest, a toddler, carried a proud row of ten nipples down her chest and abdomen.

The tall woman stalked through the ring of antic mock-dirad. Her first gaze was for Jahna. Dark eyes swept her, consuming every detail from hair to boottips, arrogant, angry. Threateningly so. Involuntarily Jahna shrank against Beck. Then the woman saw the basket in Beck's hand. "You have brought me," she stated firmly, reaching for the basket. The tangling's eyes were open now, and his lips moved in vague sucking motions.

Beck shook his head. "This grove has enough, Yuba. The babe goes to Tirammer's grove."

Distant storms scoured the back surface of the haughty eyes. "I will take it," the big woman restated, as firmly as before.

"No. Not for you." Beck's refusal was unequivocal.

For a moment Jahna thought the tall woman intended to slam Beck back against the circling mockdirad and confiscate the basket by force. But storms blew and passed. The woman's gaze shifted and reencompassed Jahna. Anger came back into her eyes. This time it had less the quality of storm than of animal, brute and bloody. Her nostrils flared, bullish. Abruptly she turned and stalked away, her young trailing her, her haughty carriage repeated three times over in theirs.

Jahna stared after her, her legs suddenly quivering. The woman's gaze had been an assault even though her hand had never touched Jahna's face. *If she had met me alone*. . . .

Why?

"Now we will press forward, Peace," Beck said, moving her with him.

Together they pressed through the ring of mockdirad, rupturing it, and submerged themselves in the firmless mob of miscellaneous mutants. These in turn packed tight around them, patting, clucking, uttering murmurous greeting. Beck made response, mouthing names, grasping hands, pressing cheeks. Jahna's hair was stroked, the fabric of her daysuit smoothed and patted, her bare hands and face touched with patent curiosity. She cringed against Beck, struggling to keep courage in her face, if not in her heart. *At least none of these hate me on sight*.

Again, *why?*

Functioning as an object of wonder was not, she learned, her natural metier. She found the pushing bodies, the reaching hands, the often bizarre and always muddy faces totally unnerving. The more so for their aggressive insistence on physical proximity.

Slowly they passed into the shadows of the grove. They were borne like some precious seed past the log compound Jahna had seen from the vines. Beyond that broad wall big trees formed a leafy ceiling over an entire village. At the base of each tree were individual shelters, shadowy leaf-caverns. From these more tentbackers peered, the fearful, the shy, and the most hideously malformed, those who could no more than squirm or crawl to their doors to watch her passage. Dark eyes stared from manes of hair pulled forward over facial features. When Jahna met the eyes, the heads shook, immediately curtaining even the eyes with grimy hair. Involuntarily Jahna glanced down at the tiny tangling. Was this his future?

Was this any future at all?

Then the way opened and they stood before a broad, deep bed of dried moss. "The communal couch," Beck informed her. "We'll have to sit and be sociable."

Hastily they crawled a distance into the moss bed and sat. Immediately there was a tussle to determine who would sit near, who would touch. Bodies closed around them. Jahna's breath clutched painfully in her throat, raw panic on the rise.

"No, no," Beck ordered loudly, sweeping his arm in a broad radius to indicate the area they claimed for themselves. "We want to see mockdirad dance. So leave us room."

His words had effect. Bodies melted back almost superstitiously from his gesture and hovered at the edge of the invisible circle he had sketched. A hundred pair of hungry eyes stared at them over the immaterial barricade he had flung up.

But Jahna gained no calm moment to reclaim her com-posture. With a cry and a leap, a massive mockdirad was before them, baring a vestigal cylinder of teeth. His eyes were human in a flat alien face. His gravelly voice grated from a lipless mouth. "So what have you brought to pay the dance, Becklord?" Arm and midarm reached abruptly. Furry fingers curled over Jahna's hair. With effort she refrained from cringing.

Beck stood, shaking his head firmly. "I haven't brought anything but an audience."

Fingers burrowed into the golden twist of Jahna's hair. Despite paralyzing fear, she managed to glare up at mockdirad with what she hoped was the threat of barely leashed feminine ferocity. "Not even this?" Mockdirad's odor was strong, salty.

Beck slapped the hairy arm away casually. "Especially not that, Hurak. You know what I'll bring when time is ready."

Without warning, mockdirad leaped and spun away, uttering a loud squawk. Another leap and he was back, grinning into Jahna's face with human teeth as well as dirad. "So my time is now, Becklord."

Jahna inched away from him. Mockdirad's behavior, she realized, had the air of display, of masculine aggressiveness played out to demonstrate social rank. But she did not care to encourage it even on that level.

"No, your time is not ready. And you know it. So have you forgotten how to dance?" Beck's voice stung at the pelted male almost casually.

"Ha! What do you give for dancing then?" Other mockdirad had leaped to center stage now and they gyrated behind him, a bouncing, flexing chorus.

"We'll give audience, if you hurry. Otherwise nothing at all."

"Audience and tangling?" Hairy fingers curled over the handle of the basket.

Beck shook his head. "I owe this one to Tirammer. I expect you to convey it there for me."

Abruptly mockdirad squatted down and peered back up at Beck. With the adoption of new posture his voice altered and became earnest. "So owe him here, Becklord," he urged, suddenly man speaking to man. "We're goodback here. You see us."

Beck shook his head, deliberately refusing to acknowledge the man who had stepped from the animal. He resumed his seat on the moss bed and wound his arms around his knees. "Tirammer, Hurak. And now we are waiting for the dance."

Jahna's glance slid sideways, hastily reinventorying the unprepossessing little being in the basket. His appearance was in no way encouraging. He would surely never walk, never use his hands. And if the conformation of his skull were any indication, he might never speak or even truly take thought. Yet he seemed to be coveted here.

For a moment angry disappointment was dark in human eyes. Then, leaping, Hurak became animal again. With a cry he summoned the dance.

And bodies flew. Before she was two minutes into her role as audience, Jahna ached to be released from it. Mockdirad dance was as chaotic, as alarming, in its swift meaty rushes and bounds, as had been the fury storm of mockdirad cry outside Pengalen. Bodies flew the air with massive power, veering just short of impact. Mockdirad tumbled and vaulted, somersaulted and pirouetted, muscular torsos flashing frighteningly near—near one another, near the mute and cringing audience. The effect was savage with power.

Savage, paralyzing—and fiercely victorious. Mockdirad claimed this place with his dance. He claimed this sheltered circle of ground, this grove. He claimed this world and made it his own, mud and vines, sullen skies and dark groves. He claimed this Nelding, but the name he claimed it under was other than Nelding. It was an older name, a name that had never been spoken, a name that belonged to the soil, to the shadows—to mockdirad.

That name was a part of mockdirad. For this world was of him, just as he was of it. He sprang from this soil and this soil sprang from him. They were intricately intergrown, body with body, spirit with spirit. He danced upon

85

this world, this world danced through him—danced with his muscular torso, with his swift limbs. He was its animate spirit, its single sentiment expression.

He was its dazzling expression. As mockdirad danced, Jahna's muscles drew taut, hardening around her like armor to protect her from the possessing spirit of Nelding. Then, when she was queasy with the insistent visual assault of mockdirad's dance, the horns appeared. Harried tanglings brought them at command. Crude and battered, they were tossed to flying mockdirad, but they served their purpose. They filled the grove with the cry of mockdirad.

Drums appeared too, and then sound blotted out thought. Sound became time and eternity, a continuum that stretched through each individual in the grove, possessing him, uniting him with all others in agony and confusion.

Sound blinded the eyes, made the flesh numb. Later, when the insistent din had taken the first edge from Jahna's hearing, her sight cleared and she gazed dumbly around the clearing. Mockdirad had settled into a rhythmic bobbing dance, lost in cry. The rest of the community had crept back from the center of chaos and huddled now on its fringes, eyes large, pained. Jahna took inventory of them, the sad, the hideous, the hopeless. But there were the beautiful, too. There was the grace of total unselfconsciousness, the dignity of surviving human flesh, however distorted its expression of the racial form. In some cases there was actual beauty of face, of body, of bearing.

With a start, Jahna realized her half-focused eyes had touched a face she had seen before—the face of the girl in Nodd's wagon. Quickly she retraced the route her glance had taken. She found those eyes again, staring stark and straight into hers, remarkable in their intensity.

Remarkable in their virulent hatred. Like an electrical shock it jolted across the space between them and struck Jahna, stunning her.

Why? But before that thought could articulate itself in Jahna's numbed mind, the girl had dodged away and was gone. Jahna stared at the spot where she had been. *Why?*

What have I done to her—and to the woman Yuba—that I haven't done to anyone else here?

Did Beck know? Her glance flickered to his profile, set and stern, one solid point of reality in this nightmare grove. He was the one who had brought her here. Somewhere behind his untelling features lay the answers—answers to everything.

But the furor of cry was too great to permit her to frame questions. Slowly her eyes began to move again, touching without assimilating.

Jahna hardly realized when the cry died because it continued in her mind, pounding, insistent. Then Beck touched her forearm. "Now we tell them how much we enjoyed it and we walk away. Peace?"

Jahna shuddered back to time and place, aware that her eyes were too large, that her mouth gaped gracelessly. "Wh-what?"

"We walk away now. Before they go into the second half of the program."

That mobilized her. Quickly she stumbled to her feet. Sleeping legs immediately prickled with agony. She gasped and clutched Beck's arm.

The husky mockdirad Hurak was before them in a leap. But the animal melted quickly from his features, leaving the man to face them. "Now you see we are goodback," he asserted earnestly, clutching Beck's arm.

Beck's brow creased lightly with frown. "I know you're goodback, Hurak. Every one of you is goodback, and the dance was strong. But this little tangle is promised to Tirammer. So now I trust you to convey him there."

To Jahna's relief, mockdirad reacted with dejection rather than anger. Massive shoulders sagged. "Promises," he muttered, taking the basket. His glance swung to Jahna. His eyes remained very human as he took her measure. Objectively he weighed her every feature and facet. Then he met Beck's gaze again. "Your promises are always sure, Becklord." Obscurely it was a demand.

"I've never made you a promise I did not intend to keep."

The fur-thatched head nodded pensively. "Then you will sit for the second dance."

"No, we have to return to Pengalen. This woman is tired. No dance where she comes from."

"None?" Mockdirad was patently astonished. "None at all?"

Jahna shook her head. "No, we—don't."

Hurak's eyes took animal pride. "Then sit. You have waited long enough." He bounced elastically, midarms beginning to flex.

Before he could leap away, Beck restrained him. "No, we can't stay, Hurak. Be pleased that this woman has given you this much time. None of the other groves have been honored."

Despite this mollification, their decision was accepted reluctantly. Their departure was a replay of their arrival, pressing bodies, circling mockdirad, and from the shadows of the leaf-tents, human wreckage watching from curtained eyes. Jahna was alert for other eyes, hating eyes. Those she did not see. Neither the girl nor Yuba was among those who conducted them away.

They approached the perimeter of shadow when Jahna heard a furious shriek from behind. She spun. Mockdirad suddenly flung themselves out of orbit and flew upon a creature in skins who leaped from the branches. Landing, the creature faced the shrieking mockdirad with animal bravado, leaping and cavorting awkwardly at bay, snapping human teeth from beneath a stiff fur helmet. Mockdirad, however, were not intimidated. Massing, they closed quickly around him, ripped away his skins, flung off his helmet, and left him naked and hairless, totally hairless. He lashed out at them, attempting to retrieve his collection of pelts. But mockdirad leaped and spun away in a dozen directions with the skins, taunting.

"So now you see mock-mockdirad," Beck said. "And while everyone is occupied with him, we'll begin to walk a little faster."

A little faster was quickly stretched to a half run. Their escort fell away and they left the noisy fray behind. They emerged from the shadow of the giant trees and trotted through tripping vines. "This way," Beck urged her. "They won't expect to find us lakeside."

Jahna glanced back. "That man—in the trees—"

"He broke tentback law. Only true mockdirad are entitled to fur. You didn't see any other man there with body hair, did you? Or even a beard?"

Skipping awkwardly through the vines, Jahna tried to draw relevant visual images from the uncatalogued confusion of her mind. "I saw tanglings who wore their hair pulled straight down over their faces," she offered.

"Permitted. But beards and body hair are to be scraped off, singed off, plucked out—fur is mockdirad's virility. No one else is allowed to display it."

Jahna labored for breath, the image of the hairless man still distinct in her mind. Defiance, courage—what would they cost him today? "What will mockdirad do to him?"

"Oh, they'll give chase into the vines and he'll live in the mud for a few days on halma bulbs—something you haven't sampled yet. Then he'll return and take a few cuffs and the incident will be forgotten." He nodded to their left. "There is a hummock over here. Let's sit and take our breath. Then we will return by the lake."

The promise of a lakefront detour was not enough to allay Jahna's anxiety. She glanced nervously behind, question in her face.

"They won't come after us now," he assured her.

The hummock was a rocky protrusion upholstered with clumped grasses. Jahna sat and drew a dozen deep breaths, admitting as she did that her exhaustion was more nervous than physical. She glanced around for some sign of water. "Is it far to the lake?"

"A short distance. You're not ready to walk again already?"

She peered up at him. "I am if you are."

He smiled wryly and sat beside her. "I am just as ready as you are. So let us both spend another minute breathing."

When Beck forged ahead again, Jahna sagged behind.

Somewhere overhead it must be noon, somewhere beyond the glum cloud. No one at noon should feel so enervated, so chill. Absentmindedly she touched the seat of her daysuit. Hummock grasses had soaked it. She glanced around dispiritedly. Nelding: cold, wet, primitive.

Nelding: her home for two years? She hugged herself, a futile attempt to infuse comfort. But there was no comfort, not today, not in the muddy vinelands of tentback Nelding.

Gradually, as they walked, she became aware of a sulphurous stench. She raised her head and found they were approaching the top of a gentle slope. Below stretched an expanse of bubbling mud, broad, glossy, sluggishly astir with its own welling turbulence. It lay in a sprawling body, its irregular arms reaching wide into the vines. Streamers of sickly yellow liquid rode its surface. Near its edges darker yellow bubbled up, an obscene effusion from the bowels of Nelding.

Jahna gagged violently, her heart dying. It couldn't be. Not this.

It was. "Here is our lake," Beck informed her.

Disaster-struck, Jahna stared over the mud surface. Her feet refused to carry her farther. Her shoulders began to shake, her eyes to blur. The laughter that emerged was ragged. *Beautiful Lake Nelding!* Helpless, Jahna was torn with hysteria. *By these calm shores, Peace, we dedicate ourselves. By these clear waters we pledge ourselves, our eyes soothed, our feet cooled, our minds and spirits renewed, Peace*—wildly the Lake Peace-side pledge reeled through her mind. Breathless, she struggled to recite it to this foul mud surface, to deny its reality.

But the words emerged in a hysterical garble. Beck took charge of her and she found herself huddled on a dark spread sobbing hysterically. When she was finally too weak to follow that course farther, she wiped her eyes, ashamed, and raised her head.

Beck's eyes held neither condescension nor challenge. He nodded pensively, as if in answer to question. "I have seen pictures of your Lake Peace," he offered. "However, I thought perhaps certain cosmetic changes had been effected.''

"In the pix?" Her voice wobbled. "No. *No*. It's *just* like the pictures. I took my pilgrimage there three months ago. It's—" What could she tell him about Lake Peace with this smelly abortion spread before them? "Lake Peace is spring-fed," she said finally, weakly.

Beck squatted, his own eyes roving the surface of the mud lake. "Well, here we do not seem to be so blessed. This lake is fed by sulphur mud sinks. And you must never walk this area without vigilance, Peace. Anytime you see the slightest stain of yellow in these vinelands, turn and seek another approach. Certain of our mud sinks can swallow you alive—take you down without a trace."

Jahna touched her lips with a dry tongue. "You mean there are other mud areas too? Like this one?"

"There are small sinks throughout the vines. In most cases you can spot them easily because the vines do not grow there. Usually, in fact, you can smell them before you are in danger. When your nose clears, you will understand what I mean by that."

"I already understand," she said, her glance groping over the mud lake. It seemed fitting that it should be odorous as well as visually repellent. "In fact, I'd like to go before my nose does clear."

His brow arched. "You're ready so quickly?"

Determined, she jumped up. "I make a fast recovery." While her hysterical outburst had done nothing for her self-esteem, it had certainly unburdened her psyche.

An hour later Pengalen loomed upon their horizon, welcome haven. They had walked the vinelands silently, Beck pointing out half a dozen small mud sinks along their way. Now he indicated a rolling grassy hummock. "If you will sit, I will forage for halma to accompany our lunch."

"Small game of some kind?" The delay was not welcome with the security of Pengalen near.

"No fear. I will not ask you to skin anyone today, Peace."

Reluctantly Jahna sat. Beck stalked off through the

vines, eyes intent. A few meters away he pointed out a slim spear of green lancing up through the tangles. "This is the finder-leaf. Do you see another near?"

Jahna cast about unenthusiastically. Beck located the second leaf first.

"Good. These, the two of them, give us the line of growth, in case the first finder pulls loose in my hand. As it probably will." He tugged at the base of the first green spear, which promptly did come loose in his hands. He shrugged philosophically, tossing it aside. "Now watch how I get my hands muddy—a Nelding art." Kneeling, he burrowed to his elbows in the mud, grappled, and finally began bringing up a reluctant length of root-rope. He followed it toward the second finder leaf, tugging until he carried a thick strand long enough to loop twice over one shoulder. With his knife he severed the rope. Mud clung to rough fibers.

Flopping the severed loops of rope down on the hummock, Beck wiped his hands on nearby vines. Then he inserted the knife tip and began splitting the fibers of the rope longitudinally. "I was hoping this strand would be shallower. Halma grows sweetest near the surface." As he pulled back the split fibers, pristine white bulbs appeared. He popped them out into the provision basket, careful not to touch them with his mud-stained hands. "However, on a few handfuls of these you can walk all day."

Jahna examined the waxy bulbs in wonder, rolling them on her palm. "They don't require cooking?"

"Not at all. Try one."

She took the smallest bulb on her tongue experimentally. It was cool, faintly sweet, crisp when she bit into it. She chewed, smiled approval, and selected a second.

"So now I've showed you something our ugly Mother does well. Do you forgive her the lake?"

Jahna glanced up. "I'll put it on the agenda," she offered, her spirit reviving.

"And mockdirad?"

Jahna evaded his glance. "Now *that* I don't know," she admitted. Her feelings about those hairy Neldings were ambivalent. Human-non-human union was something that had occurred on no other world, to her knowledge. "How long have humans and dirad been interbreeding out here?"

Beck shook his head. "They do not interbreed."

Jahna peered up at him. She sighed. "You know, I'm almost too tired to ask what those were back in that grove then."

"I've noticed your legs tire long before your tongue, Peace," he commented. His eyes roamed across the vinescape, foraging for answers. "Well, this old Mother Nelding—I see you object when I call her she, but that's what she is—received our race with a smile three hundred years ago. At first she took our seeds happily to her bosom, but the crops that resulted were a little lacking, by her standards. So she began tinkering, trying to set us a better table. She took a plant with the untantalizing name yellow squash number 116 and an equally untantalizing flavor and she created sweet brindle squash. She found our corn dull, so she gave us redspear. She's still experimenting with wheat and rice—and all the other crops we brought with us.

"Naturally when she saw the success of her first experiments, she decided we humans needed a few changes, too. So she began adding and subtracting and making interesting substitutions. Unfortunately the settlers weren't pleased, even with her most inspired alterations. They had come out here to live a very specific sort of life, a very righteous sort of life that was to win them salvation, eternal freedom from human corruption. And now half their offspring were being born barely human.

"A number of settlers broke during the first few decades. What was happening to them was beyond their reason—and their faith. And without their faith they were nothing. Finally the others built Pengalen to contain them—*and* to house the mutant offspring who survived. Most did not, and do not, I should add. So the mad and the mutant coexisted in the compound until they tired of confinement and began to move away into farback. Hut-

93

town saw no reason to detain them. I doubt that huttown even expected them to survive.

"But mockdirad was born in tentback a few years later to mutant mother and father—genesis in the vinelands. Now, two centuries later, huttown is dying and tentback has become cradle of Nelding's future. So I think old Mother Nelding begins to be pleased with the results of her experimentation."

Jahna frowned, trying to digest his account. "Do you mean then that mockdirad is just another type of mutant?" Was that any more incredible than what had happened on Coronel?

His eyes returned from their journey to meet hers. There was lack of frankness in them. "That is what they are."

Obviously he was withholding something. "Well, do they breed true?" she probed. The fact that there was a distinct group of them bearing the same general characteristics suggested so.

"Under certain conditions they do so better than fifty percent of the time."

She waited. When he failed to elaborate, she drew up a mental image of the community in the grove. Mockdirad, tanglings, male and female: she populated her mind with them. And she found an odd discrepancy. "But, Beck, I didn't see any female mockdirad in the grove." None at all, not even one.

"Ah." He studied her thoughtfully. "Would you consider dirad development particularly desirable in females?"

"No," she admitted. "But I saw a lot of other females there with characteristics I wouldn't call particularly desirable either."

"True."

She frowned, trying to fathom his sudden taciturnity. "Then what becomes of females who do show dirad characteristics?" Valor had said that tentback never abandoned young to the vines. Was there an exception?

"Nothing happens, Peace. Females never show those characteristics."

She studied his unrevealing face, curiosity piqued. "But the mockdirad strain predominates better than fifty percent of the time?"

"It does, approximately."

"So it's sex-linked. Limited to males."

"Its expression is limited to males," he specified shortly.

She frowned, puzzled by his reticence as well as by the sparse information he released. "Then certain females must function as carriers of the syndrome, even though they don't show the physical signs themselves?"

His brow arched. "So now you make it sound like an illness, Peace."

"But do they?" she demanded in exasperation.

Frowning, Beck split the last length of halma rope and popped out a dozen tiny-bulbs. "You could say that. But any tangling woman in tentback is likely to produce mockdirad. It appears spontaneously, without pattern, except in those certain cases where its likelihood can be predicted." He tossed aside the spent rope and sheathed his knife. "So are you ready to walk again?"

"Meaning will I now please refrain from asking further questions on the subject?"

He nodded brusquely. "Correct, Peace. Are you ready?"

Briefly she played with notions of obstinacy. But she doubted the tactic would be effective. She stood, brushing at her daysuit. "I did observe that mockdirad weren't numerically a very large proportion of the grove population," she pointed out. Despite their obvious social dominance, they had been significantly outnumbered by tangling males.

Beck sighed and stared out over the vines. "For one thing, Peace, the largest part of the tentback population was born in huttown. And mockdirad are never born anywhere but tentback. Because both parents must be either mockdirad, tangling, or female carrier, as you term it."

She frowned, trying to draw the pieces he reluctantly

95

offered into a coherent pattern. She shook her head. "Beck, it just doesn't seem possible that a planet can mold the human race in the image of an animal. I can understand random mutation, like you have among the tanglings. Obviously there are mutagenic factors in the environment, something we simply haven't encountered on a comparable scale on Peace. And I can understand the type of thing that has happened on Coronel, and even on Smith's World. But to have humans take animal form, to have a substantial number of them take the *same* animal form, mimicking a native form—"

A new thought struck her. "Do the parents of mock-dirad share special characteristics themselves? Aside from being tangling, mockdirad, or carrier?"

His face closed. "They do. They're fertile."

She stared at him. "Fertile?" A fatuous reply.

"Not all tentbackers are fertile, Peace, any more than all the fertile ones can produce liveborn children. That's why I could easily find a dozen groves for little tangling. He doesn't look promising now, but if he lives he may eventually be productive. Someday he may even father a mockdirad."

Jahna's stomach suddenly hung limp in her abdomen. Now she understood why Hurak had tried to claim the unprepossessing infant for his own grove. "They're going to breed him when he matures. Like a domestic."

His gaze was curious. "Would it be better to let him starve? Or die of exposure?"

"I—" Struck, she examined the question. "But what will they do if he isn't productive? If he fails? If he isn't even able to—to go through the motions?"

"By that time, Peace, he will have protectors. There is a certain respect for life out here. It is protected. Not as skillfully or as rationally as on your own world, of course, but what can be done is done. So if tangling is not able to function, he will be fed and tended anyway. After all, there is no scarcity of food—only a scarcity of individuals who can parent new life."

Jahna stared down into the vines, suddenly bleak. "Old

Mother Nelding'' he called this world. But Nelding was no benign mother. She corrupted the germ plasm, twisting and scarring the human heritage almost beyond recognition. And if that weren't enough, she rendered her victims sterile too, a final sadistic flourish.

Old Mother Nelding—what was the malevolent matriarch wreaking upon her own hereditary material while she sat here? What damage was being inflicted on her own future descendants?

And how? By foods grown in soil containing mutagenic agents? By tainted water? By ground radiation? Jahna hugged herself, beginning to better understand Humble Nodd. Her voice was faint. "When are you sending me back to Peace, Father Lord?"

Beck's face registered surprise. "In two years, Peace, as agreed before you ever came."

"I thought you intended to determine if I were acceptable for the work before you decided to retain me."

He nodded. "Yes. Now I have determined. You are acceptable."

Jahna frowned, finding scant comfort in her own embrace. "Well, I can't imagine what you've based your decision on. I've done absolutely nothing to qualify myself to bring six babies through their first two years. Most of my pediatric courses were sked for next year. Even those weren't much oriented to physical care."

"Ah? Then what about bringing twelve babies through one year?"

She looked at him blankly.

"That is what your assignment will be. When the infants in the nursery have stayed one year under your care, they will be replaced. By six more infants."

"They—but what about the first six? Will you return them to their mothers?"

He shook his head. "No, to their fathers. Hurak will receive one, Tirammer one, Carock, Narrd, Drammar, Kethl. Some may be granted back to their birth mothers in turn, but the fathers will retain most."

97

"But who will raise them, then?" Jahna demanded in consternation.

"Mockdirad. They raise their male offspring."

"They—not from birth," she protested.

He nodded. "From birth, Peace. If the infant shows mockdirad signs, he is taken directly to mockdirad compound. You saw it, the log structure at the edge of the grove. For one year he is secluded there. After that he is allowed to emerge, but only in the custody of his father. He may be able to identify his birth-mother by name someday, but he never comes directly under her care—or her claim."

"But that's—that's—" Barbaric hardly seemed strong enough a term. "The mother has no rights at all?"

"None, if the child is mockdirad. If his father is unknown or a tangling, the grove Dirad takes custody and designates one of the younger mockdirad to act as pelt-father."

"But then there *is* no family structure in the grove. No father-mother-child constellation at all. Not living as a unit."

Beck sighed. "Peace, this is Nelding tentback. There are pairings of male and female. Sometimes they are formalized, but there are also random pairings. Tangling babes are raised by their own birth mothers or fathers, unless they are deeded away by voluntary agreement. Any mockdirad, I should add, has access to any female in his grove, even if she is formally pledged to a tangling male. Tentback social codes, you see, are entirely different from those you observe on Peace."

"I—yes. I'm becoming aware of that," she said weakly. "I am." Slowly her head dropped to her knees. Intellectually she had been prepared to find tentback social mores alien. Emotionally, however, she was unready for this casual devastation of the mother-child relationship, even if it operated only in certain cases.

But she had not come here to be devastated. Determined, she raised her head. "Beck, I think you should realize that I have codes, too. There are certain practices I won't permit in any nursery where I work."

He accepted her declaration with gravity. "You may remove the masks and plugs as soon as you assume the nursery, Peace."

She frowned, unprepared for the abrupt concession. "There may be other conflicts that won't be so easily resolved," she pointed out.

"No." He shook his head emphatically. "There will not be. Everything we have will be provided for your use. You will be expected to do nothing beyond rendering the best possible care."

"But who is going to determine how that is defined? You? Mockdirad? Or me?"

He met her insistent eyes levelly. "You are, Peace. That is why you are here."

Her glance dropped. "I see," she said, unconvinced. "When am I expected to take over the nursery?"

"Tomorrow I go into tentback to confer with the grove Dirad. When I return, you will begin."

She studied him uneasily, sensing evasiveness again. "Is there some particular reason I can't begin tomorrow morning?"

Beck hefted the lunch basket. "There is."

"But you don't intend to illuminate me now?"

He swung the basket. "You glow brightly enough by your own light, Peace. Are you coming?"

She picked her way through the vines pensively, occasionally glancing up to study his uninformative back. Certainly, she held a kinder opinion of him than she had that morning. But as they approached the dank fortress, she wondered what she had learned today that Beck Lord had not intended her to learn. Anything?

Anything at all?

Chapter Nine

ZUNIIN HAUNTED grove shadows defiantly. Three days, Dahda had said. But no days had Zuniin yielded to exile. Now, as tanglings and mockdirad returned to the grove, Zuniin matched their mood against hers. Hers was bitter, ripe with resentment. Today StarMother had marched on this grove. Now her subjects were gathering back to crouch in groups and whisper their hundred histories of her visit. The chase had not dissipated their excitement. It still peaked through the grove. Feet still pattered it from tent to tent, fire to fire.

StarMother came.
I touched her.
I stroked her hair.
I pulled her sleeve.
I breathed her breath straight from her nostrils.
I felt heat of her body on my arm.
StarMother came!

Teeth gritted, Zuniin slipped in and out of shadow. StarMother came—but I did not touch her. I did not breathe her breath or feel her heat. I only thought her a message.

And my message was this: You came to end my line, StarMother, but now I am going to end yours. You came to end my face, but I am going to end yours. I am going to end your hair, I am going to end your eyes. I am going to end your blood, I am going to end your flesh.

I am going to end StarMother. Zuniin crouched against a rugged trunk, shoulders hunkered around her racketing thoughts. Rabid chitterlings, they streaked through her mind. Yes. I am going to end her. But how? Not with my hands. Not with my teeth or fingers or even my knife, because I know about the witch-blood. Abruptly Zuniin flipped her hair forward over her face, then poked eye-holes in it to stare out at earth. How? The question was a ferment in her mind, like the ferment of unresolved excitement in the grove.

Gradually Zuniin became aware of stillness around her. Warily she spread her hair and peered up, around.

She peered straight into the face of arrogant young mockdirad. Narrel's sardonic eyes met hers with sadistic pleasure. Instantly Zuniin threw her hair off her face and scrambled up.

Too late. Before she could dodge away, Narrel caught her with hands and midhands. "So you are here now," he clucked, his voice breaking into whistles and crows. "My Mother sent you vineway for three days, she told me."

Zuniin lunged wildly, but it was useless. She grunted, her breath painful, her eyes trapped. And all around her, tangling faces paled, avid with anticipation. She glared, bristling. Tanglings shivered back, but she saw the covert triumph in their eyes. "This is my grove!" she cried fiercely.

Narrel jerked at her arms, and her words ended in a shriek of pain. "Get whips!" he bellowed. "Go get whips—we'll have girl-song." Half a dozen tanglings lunged hastily away, and Narrel pulled Zuniin up on her toes. "You want pelt, so let's hear song, Zu!"

Zuniin glared at mockdirad. *Dirad, if I had magic, I'd tear off your pelt with fire, I'd grind out your dirad-mouth and scatter its teeth, I'd shrivel your dirad-throat until you died choking.* You want my son? *If I had magic—*

But Zuniin had no more magic than she had pelt, and tanglings brought snapping whips for Narrel to flick and lash through air and then across her struggling flesh. And it was her own mouth that screamed and died, not Narrel's. It was she who brought the lingering excitement in the grove to climax, she who satisfied and resolved it with her victim's screech, her flailing limbs, her lashing hair and bleeding belly.

Then she was dumped out on the edge of the grove bloody and violated. She stumbled away, only her racking sobs to warm her as she fell into a cold night-nest of stiffgrass. Even the vehemence of her emotions had deserted her for the night.

It was first dawn when Zuniin struggled back to consciousness. She huddled in the grass, belly and back tender from Narrel's whipping, spirit desolated. There was no one in the grove to whom she was more than renegade Mother, rebel unloved and uncherished, ready victim, unwelcome intimate. There was no one to stand with her against indignity, no one to defend her, no one to comfort her. If she crept grove way and made her way to tent, bodies would roll against hers. But to possess, not to cherish, never to defend.

Gradually hostility displaced self-pity. Anger displaced hurt, and she rose out of her nest and limped lakeside way, stopping twice at mud sinks to smear her wounds with yellow foam. She sat on the shores of the slowly surging mud body and watched streamers of yellow fluid ebb and flow across its surface, sulphurous arms now reaching for her, now retreating, now spreading, now contracting. She delved toes into warm mud and hugged her knees, pressing her sore belly against her thighs. There was no one in the grove.

No one in Hurak's grove. Even less was there anyone in any of the other groves. If she crept the shadows of Keth's grove, of Tirammer's grove, of Carock's grove, she might see her own face riding through the dimness on her own body. She might see her own discredited breast bobbing, scarlet and matted on its underside. She might see her own rough hair, in some groves groomed into compliance, in others allowed to stand out full. She might see her mold-sisters.

But they would never defend her. They would never comfort her. If she spoke to them, if their eyes met hers, some, the younger, would run. Others, the crueler, would

102

call down mockdirad to chase her.

And she had neither birth-mother nor mold-Mother living. Not that either would care about her wounds. No one cared about that. No one at all.

When she was well steeped in her anger, she left lakeside and fished halma from the mud, ripping the tough fibers with her teeth and munching the white bulbs viciously. White eyes, enemy eyes, she devoured them and incorporated them into herself.

Finally it began to be dark again. Her exile was expired. Zuniin picked her way through tangles toward the grove. It was dark by the time she reached first shadowrim. Fires burned low and mushpots steamed. Zuniin stalked sullenly through the grove, glance averted from all those staring eyeless sockets, to the Mother's area.

There was only Yuba-bull hunkered in the dirt ripping at chitterling with her big teeth. The big woman glanced up dumbly and went on with her feast, fingers dripping fat. Slowly Zuniin pressed near the fire and sat, warmth welcome against arms and face. Gradually fire and satiety dispelled active thought and she stretched out with animal torpor. When Yuba had torn the last shred of meat and licked the last drip of fat, she crouched silent too, face empty, eyes puddle-gray.

Then Zuniin glanced up and saw Narrel in the shadow. Quick alarm flashed through her muscles. She sprang to a crouch. "Three days are gone," she hissed belligerently.

Arrogant young mockdirad stepped from his shadow, firelight glistening on his dark pelt. His shoulders were massive and hard, his face taut with power. Slowly he approached, growing in her eyes. "You are not to attend," he hissed back, spreading his legs to tower above her.

She did not like this angle, his genitalia flaunted in her face. She backed away. "I am not to attend what?" she demanded warily.

He stalked near again, his lips twisting. "You are not to attend the ceremonies in Pengalen. You are not to see StarMother take pelt. I told Becklord what you were

103

speaking against StarMother and Becklord said to me that if you come Pengalen way, he will call out the whips and lash your belly raw. Then StarMother will take your blood and turn it into chitterling dung and make you eat. She'll use her witch kit and turn your skin to reedcloth. She'll turn your eyeballs to halma—''

With a gasp, Zuniin scrambled up and dodged away from mockdirad. She crouched on the opposite side of the fire. "She'll never!"

"She'll turn your face to brindle squash and make herself mush. She'll rip the scar off your breast and turn it into worms to chew you. She'll—"

"She'll never!" Would she? What was in the magic kit? What star magic couldn't it do against her if Star-Mother ordered? Already her discredited breast began to crawl with fear. She groped desperately for a weapon to use against mockdirad. "You'll never own a star-molding," she jibed. It was true. Hurak would have one. He was big pelt here. Tirammer would have one. Carock. Narrd. The other powerful pelts. But Narrel would never because he wasn't birth-son of any of them. "You're tangling-son!"

Fur rippled, erecting with quick anger. Narrel's dirad mouth began to flex and chew fiercely.

"Twelve while she is here and then twelve years till there are more," Zuniin taunted. "You won't have one of them either! They'll go to born-sons, all. By the time there is one for you, your pelt will be bare. Your mouth will be cracked. Your eyes will be oozing. You'll never have star-molding, dirad!"

Narrel's midarms formed hard grapples reaching for her. "So I am pelt-son of second dirad here!" he gargled, his vocal apparatus beginning to spew dirad nonsense into his words. With a bellow and a call, he lunged across the dying fire.

But she was away before him. She whipped around the fire and put Yuba between them. "So ask your pelt-father if you get star-molding before his born-sons."

Mockdirad crouched. His voice came in a low rumble,

104

building to a belligerent chant of dirad-nonsense. With a powerful spring, he leaped the fire again and landed with a meaty thud, one big foot grazing Yuba's shoulder.

The big woman was on her feet before he could fully regain his balance. Breasts heaving, puddle-gray eyes deepening dangerously, she launched herself at him, the charge of the she-bull. As her head rammed his furred abdomen, she seized at his genitals and jammed one big fist into his groin.

Zuniin retreated swiftly, eyes blazing. Mockdirad shrieked with pain and flung himself away into the shadows. Yuba lowed, her chest expanding and contracting like bellows. "Leave my fire."

Mockdirad crouched gasping, face transfigured with mortified anger. "I am dirad here."

Before Yuba could meet his challenge, Dahda appeared from her tent. She strode into the circle of fire, breasts asag, old face grim. "What is this noise?"

Narrel lunged from shadow and crouched beside his birth-mother. "This bull charged dirad. And this—this mud crawler has come back to your fire."

"My three days are done," Zuniin flared. "So this is my fire now." Even dirad had a Mother to hide behind. She was the only one alone.

Dahda's creased face considered the two of them implacably. "So what have you done to my son?"

"Nothing!"

"The bull!" Narrel snarled, pounding his feet.

"I am not bull," Yuba asserted, stubborn intelligence storming across her face. "I am a Mother of this grove and this dirad put foot on me."

Dahda peered from Mother to mockdirad and back again. The lines of her face sagged. "This is Mother's fire," she pronounced finally. "So go back to your compound to your own fire, dirad."

Narrel's midarms twisted together violently. "I am dirad here," he insisted, his voice deep.

"And I am Mother," Dahda snapped. "Go."

Mockdirad's horny cylinder flexed viciously, impotently. Slowly the muscular torso straightened. With a frustrated cry, mockdirad lunged away.

And Dahda's attention turned back to Zuniin. "I notice trouble by this fire when you are here," she observed sternly.

"I was sitting here asleep. Your dirad-son came and attacked me."

Dahda turned to Yuba for confirmation. "So?"

Intelligence had retreated again. The big woman's face was sullen and dark. "Dirad put foot on me."

"So who attacked? Dirad or this useless Mother?"

"He put foot on me."

Dahda's heavy body firmed angrily. "So you go to your tent, bull. You have nothing to say here."

For a moment it appeared the big woman would offer violence. Her face suffused. Her neck hardened. "I am no bull."

"You're a dumb beast! Go!" Dahda's eyes flared.

With a belligerent mutter, Yuba turned and stamped away. Dahda turned back to Zuniin. "So are you bringing more trouble tonight?"

If I had a Mother behind me, old skin. . . . "I came here to sleep."

Dahda's eyes did not relinquish the young Mother for long moments. "So sleep," she pronounced finally, turning away.

Zuniin glared after her. *If I had a Mother. . . .*

But she had no Mother and no mother. They had both deserted her, died tentback way, old women. Died the way she would die, and in not so long.

Died the way her line would die if StarMother lived. Three years now she had refused to be Mother or mother. Three years now she had contributed nothing to her line. Now she would contribute. She would contribute Star-Mother's death.

How? She squirmed next to the fire, hugging herself. How? What instrument would she use, if not her hands? She stared into the glowing embers and made fire magic. Squinting, she created scenes of death: StarMother's mouth round and dying, StarMother's body disintegrating. But she could make no instrument.

She became aware of a presence behind. She jerked around, but it was only Yuba returning to the fire, sullen and dumb. Zuniin turned again, flipped her hair over her face, stared through poke-holes.

And the instrument came to mind. It was sitting not two meters away, brute and silent—Yuba. Yuba-bull, stalwart and dumb, inflammable, bloody-eyed.

She would end StarMother with Yuba.

So would she? She shook her head, closing the poke-holes, darkening herself for thought. With an instrument like Yuba, what could she accomplish? Yuba offered strength, certainly. But control, no. Yuba was unpredictable in her storm-fits of anger. Yuba was a tool, but a clumsy one.

However, Yuba was the only tool that came to hand. She was the only one brute-dumb enough to forget StarMother's magic in a storm of rage. Decided, Zuniin swept the hair off her face and scooted back until she sat near the big woman. Fascinated, she watched Yuba's dozen breasts rise and fall with her heavy breath. Grease shone on her broad cheeks.

"StarMother came," Zuniin whispered.

Chapter Ten

THAT FATEFUL morning after her babe was stolen, Piety straggled up from the vines. Her skirts and shirtwaist were wet with mud, caked on one side, slippery on the other. Her face, she knew from examining it with fingertips, was a grimy horror. *Like some tentback monster*, she realized weakly. The fingers she pulled back were blue with cold. As she sat, her entire body resisted her, an unwilling bag of grain she had to forcibly heft upright.

For a while she sat, dumb with exhaustion. Then, cumbersomely, she gained her feet. Erect, she swayed perilously, a human prominence jutting above some vast and threatening plain. Briefly her head was a light, hollow vessel riding dizzily on an overlong neck, blown by otherworldly winds. Then it filled and settled and she was standing in the familiar gray-green viny profusion of the tangles.

Hoisting her skirts, she turned, trying to locate some familiar landmark. But there was nothing to orient herself upon. There was no settlement, home or otherwise, no outbuildings, no roadway, no field. There was only a musty grove on the horizon—and stretching vines.

Lost, she stood for a long while at the center of an empty world. Occasionally, returning from the fields, she had lingered behind her work crew. But that bore no relation to the present situation. Today she was totally alone, open to wind and rain, ready victim for whatever dark forces might move across the face of this Nelding-world when no human eye was watching.

She was paralyzed there forever, every joint frozen.

Then she snatched up her skirts and, in a sudden, activating burst of panic, began to run. Mud splashed over her legs. Vines caught her feet. She made no effort to select direction. She flashed across the vines blindly, panic-driven, until her breath would no longer sustain her flight. Then she crumpled down.

Her second flight was less precipitous. The grove drew her, offering shelter from the threatening openness of the vines. Her third spurt of running brought her there. She plunged under its tenting limbs like an animal harried to its den. Tossing herself down, she gasped and sobbed drunkenly for breath. She was safe, enclosed in dimness.

But then, lungs replenished, adrenalin still surging in her bloodstream, she found her mind torturingly clear. The entire procession of recent events marched across her memory in sharp tones, the starhand riding past, her own defection, the birth of her babe, its loss.

It was a short procession. Another followed it, a train of future happenings. She saw herself stumbling out into the vineland again, wandering alone until she found some landmark, some cluster of cabins, perhaps, or the roadway, then delivering herself to the first work party she met. But when its Father reared up and bellowed his indignant questions, what did the muddy wraith reply, her eyes swollen from grief, her skirts and shirtwaist solid with mud, her hair unknotted around her ears?

Piety shrank against the leaves, trying to find words for that wraith to defend herself by. And what did she say later when she was returned to Father Hoock and he demanded their firstborn? What did she say to Sister Nair's knowing eyes? To Sister Cree's? The filth she had scrubbed from her mouth the day before last was still visible to anyone who looked with knowing eyes. Piety hugged herself, moaning under the ordeal of those eyes. As she had the night before, she began to search for alternatives.

There seemed to be none. She could die here. Or she could return to her Father Hoock and die under his eyes. Of slightly different causes, true, but she would soon be dead nevertheless, whichever course she chose.

However, there was a stubborn kernel at the center of her that would accept neither death. Yesterday dawn she had become mother of a child. A monster-child, true, but a child who needed her nevertheless. And just as she had not heard him cry out in dirad's grasp, neither had she found his mangled body in the vines today. She had even heard Father Lord claim dirad beasts were vegetarian. Despite their appearance and bearing, he had said, they represented no menace to human life. Sometimes they even carried monster-babes from the vines to him at Pengalen.

Now she made herself sit and think about that. Perhaps dirad had done nothing more with her babe than carry him a distance and drop him. Perhaps he lay somewhere in the vines now, cold and blue and helpless, too small to call her. Or perhaps dirad had carried him to Pengalen and he had been taken to the nursery there. Perhaps the starhand was already dripping milk into his mouth and holding him warm against her.

Piety had to know. If he were in the vines, she had to find him. If he were at Pengalen, she had to see him. If he were dead—

She would not admit that possibility. Because his death would remove the last barricade between herself and her own death. Quickly she rose and emerged from the grove. With trees at her back, the vinescape was less threatening. Glancing overhead to orient herself, she plotted the probable direction of Pengalen. That would be the primary focus of her search, she decided, because it offered the greatest hope.

Her body was still heavy, her head still light, but her spirit was stubbornly resilient as she set in the direction of Pengalen to find her babe.

As she walked, Piety found her strength multiplied. Her limbs became sure, her head steady. Once, at midday, the clouds thinned and she had glimpse of the sun, pale golden overhead. Gradually her clothes dried and caked mud crumbled off into the vines.

But then it was afternoon and her legs were reluctant again. She rested at frequent intervals, torturing thoughts invading her mind. Growing around her, mingling with the native Nelding vegetation, were the forbidden melons, fat and tempting. *If I took strength from these,* some small voice kept whispering, *I would walk that much faster, I would find my babe that much sooner.*

The inarguable validity of those thoughts tormented her. Somewhere, here or at Pengalen, her babe needed her. But her legs were reluctant, her pace slow. She had eaten nothing since giving birth, almost two days now. Even if she found her babe not ten paces ahead, there was no milk in her breasts. Nor would there be if she did not eat. Once, her hand extended and rested on the cool rind of a black melon. She jerked it back fiercely, lunged to her feet, and hurriedly put distance between herself and temptation.

Later in the afternoon she spied a settlement on the horizon. She clutched her skirts, peering intently, trying to bring detail to focus. But the afternoon air was thick. She could discern no more than the presence of cabins.

She glanced uneasily at darkening skies, trying to re-orient herself. The main road, she knew, curved wide to service a crescent of settlements extending from Forgiven, the nethermost, to Seldenbog, the last before Pengalen. If she described a straight line across the vineland while the roadway described a curve, she would reach Pengalen that much sooner. But she did not dare go nearer the hut community to learn its name. Instead, she set course vineward from it, alert for feeder roads, wagons, or field crews.

She crossed no cultivated field. She met no hand or any Father. When dusk came, she went to ground in the arms of a small grove. At a distance she watched night-darkness mingle with the special ominous black of storm. But she was curled snug in a nest of leaves, her hair spread loosely over her shoulders, her skirts hugged tight around her legs. When storm swept her way, she was dry and warm. She closed her eyes and rain-on-leaf sang a night song to her, lulling her to sleep.

Hers was an alert sleep. Sometime later, in the black of

night, her senses were suddenly engaged. She sat, eyes staring. In the distance she heard a discordant cry, riotous, running. Holding her breath, she crept to the edge of the grove and peered in the direction of the settlement she had passed in late afternoon. But she could see nothing. The cries became more distant as she hovered there, alert.

At last they were gone. Slowly Piety crawled back to her nest, chilled now. The world had been empty today, barren of any sentient creature other than herself. Evidently the night was less thinly populated. It was a long while before Piety closed her eyes, longer still before she drowsed again.

She walked through the next day, searching and hungering, hungering not just for sustenance but for sight of that small body, useless arms reaching to her, needing her. She kept the one hunger constantly before her, a shield against too keen an awareness of the other.

But when she had slept and risen still again, weakness overcame her and the vision of her babe did not suffice to keep her from temptation. Piety's hands grappled down into the vines and, shaking, seized a yellow and black melon. Savagely her teeth tore back the tough skin. Then, the melon consumed, she staggered across the vines to a stand of garbage corn. She tore off cob after cob and choked the hard grain down half-chewed. And her only regret was lack of water. On her knees, licking rain-wet leaves, she satisfied even her thirst.

But contrition claimed her within the hour. She staggered across the field, stomach in nauseous revolt. *I regret,* she cried silently. *I regret, I regret. Never again will I let filth touch my mouth. Never will I even see the corrupt melon at my feet hereafter. Never again. . . .*

But she knew it was a lie. She had let hunger overwhelm her not one hour ago. When her stomach cried again, her eyes would seek the vines once more, her teeth would tear, her nails bite, and she would bury her snout in filth like a common hog.

She would. Because she realized now that she could never return home from this search. No one would be

112

deluded that she had gone so many days without food. Sister Nair, Sister Cree, the others, would denounce her on sight. Father Hoock would disown her without appeal. And her own Father would never reclaim her now. She would be an outcast, an object of shame wherever she went, until she died—which would not be long.

So, for her now, there was only her babe. Resuming her search, Piety plunged through the tangles with frantic energy, driven, hopeless, victim of fresh and painful urgency.

Abruptly, an hour later, she dropped in sudden exhaustion. Her eyes closed and sleep overtook her in one leap, a consuming beast.

Sleep became its own special torture when her babe came to her in dream. She had examined him only once in life, with cringing haste, but now she saw him from every angle, in every aspect. Now she saw him newborn, child, youth, and man. His flaws took freshly horrible reality with each stage of maturation. It was the blossoming of a loathsome flower that fed on the flesh of her own innocent babe. Piety thrashed in the vines, hands tearing leaves, hair sopping mud. Her babe—she had to find him, to help him, to hold him—to kill him? She did not know.

She woke on her knees, crawling blindly through the vines. Her hair was thick with mud, her clothes slimy. She peered at the landscape from veils of ropy hair. The world was empty. Haunted nevertheless, she scrambled to her feet and stumbled forward.

Or perhaps she stumbled backward. It did not matter. Because once she was on her feet, her babe returned. He floated before her in an image of terrible clarity, guiding her, compelling her across the vineland. Several times she fell, but he waited for her, waxing and waning, now bright and terrible before her, then fading so that the vinelands glimmered dark through his thin flesh. When dusk fell, his image took a soft halo and drew her on.

At last human strength deserted her. Her babe faded and she was alone in the vineland. She dropped and lay like a dead animal.

It was much later when the moon slipped from cloud and transposed her monster son into the heavens, silvering his pinched features into divinity. With a moan, Piety struggled up again. And not so very far she saw the hulking dark walls of Pengalen. Her son had led her to the fortress! Somewhere, behind those moldering logs, he waited. What he wanted she was not certain. Sustenance, or a merciful end to his monster-sufferings?

She did not know. Her soul was chaos. But her mind remained clear enough to realize that she could not simply stumble into the log fortress and demand her babe. Father Lord would never release him so casually, particularly not to a muddy wraith-mother who might as readily give death as nourishment.

Reeling, stumbling, she found the small grove near the walls of Pengalen. Tomorrow she would hide in the vines near the archway and observe comings and goings. When she knew something of routine at Pengalen, she would be ready to dodge into the fortress and secretly claim her son and give him whatever it was he most wanted.

Chapter Eleven

UNDER VALOR'S tutelage, Jahna quick-fried squash and slid it to an earthen platter, found the small bowl of halma left from yesterday's trek into tentback, and poured tree milk for them both. Beck had returned to tentback early that morning. Through the first hours of day, Jahna had enjoyed the quiet of her room. But by midafternoon leisure had begun to pall. "Will Beck be back tonight?" she wondered hopefully as they sat to supper.

Valor glanced up from her platter. "He did not say."

Jahna lapsed into brief quiet, unsatisfied. "Valor, I've wondered," she ventured, "are you and Beck contracted in any way?"

"Contracted?" Valor rolled the word off her tongue warily.

"That's what we call it on Peace," Jahna explained quickly. "When two individuals want their relationship formally recognized, they arrange for representatives to negotiate a contract. They have clauses drawn up to cover every aspect of the relationship from the number of children to—"

The suggestion underlying her explanation was plainly unwelcome. Valor stood, her face suddenly dark. "There is nothing between us. We are two people living our separate lives. It only happens that we live them here, in the same place, dedicated to the same work."

Jahna's cheeks reddened. "Valor—"

"Beck Lord may make contracts and he may make liaisons. I will never speak of either matter." The Nelding woman left the dining area abruptly, her slapping skirts speaking offense.

Jahna slumped in distress. She had assumed Valor's rejection of huttown life implied rejection of its more rigid conventions. Evidently she had assumed wrongly. She jumped up. "Valor, I didn't intend to offend you. I—"

Valor faced Jahna from the stove. "Then is it enough to say that I am here because I cannot live in huttown and will not live in tentback? Beck Lord will have to speak for himself."

Jahna recoiled from the Nelding woman's obvious sensitivity. "I really didn't intend to pry," she offered untruthfully.

Gradually Valor's color subsided and they both returned to their meal. "You know, Beck studied planet reports and many old books before he decided he would have a Peace cadet here," Valor commented finally. "But since I do not read, I know very little about your world."

"Oh, I brought pix," Jahna offered, eager to cement the reconciliation. "Lots of pix."

An hour later Jahna closed her album, a sickening emptiness claiming her heart. Peace was still there somewhere across the stars. Skies were still bright, hills still golden, Lake Peace still blue. But for two years she was condemned to this moldering fortress on this wet backworld.

Valor gently touched the leather cover of the album, "Now that I have seen your world, I am not sure my eyes could ever accept it. In those colors, it has an appearance of unreality."

Jahna smiled faintly. "Well, it doesn't stick to the boots quite like Nelding does."

"And everyone on Peace is schooled to read and write," Valor went on earnestly. "Your Fathers were not even a religious group like our own. Beck has told me that much."

"They weren't religious in any conventional sense," Jahna agreed. "There certainly was never any supreme being anyone was required to accept or honor. Some of our people recognize a deity and others don't. All of us are encouraged to consider it the responsibility of each indi-

116

vidual to arrive at his own world view.''

Valor frowned. "But the world is as it is, Jahna. You cannot decide for yourself how it will look. Can you?''

"You can decide to examine it through your own eyes, though,'' Jahna pointed out. "You can decide to develop your own philosophy instead of letting someone impose an arbitrary system of belief and preconceptions on you. You must have done that yourself, when you decided you couldn't live in huttown.''

Valor's fingers rubbed at the face of the leather album. "Perhaps, although it did not seem so noble at the time.'' Her eyes, dark with memory, met Jahna's. "It seemed, in fact, that I simply threw aside everyone and everything— everything I had ever been taught—and stepped out into nothingness.''

"But haven't you put together something else out here? Something to replace what you threw aside?''

Valor considered gravely. "Now, that I do not know. Sometimes—in a way, you see, what I created here was myself. Certainly I am not now the person who left huttown, and I will never be that person again. That much is good, I think. But now I find that I stand out here all alone. I have no God left to protect me. I have no family to claim me. My mother is dead and my father is a true huttown Father. So I have only the person I elected to become. And sometimes I wonder: What is that?''

"It sounds like a good beginning to me,'' Jahna asserted positively. "Maybe it's even everything. It's my own feeling that you have to possess yourself before anything else you do or own can have worth.''

Valor's eyes shied away. "Perhaps,'' she agreed. "And now it comes to me that I do have duties. I must go back to the nursery so Elda can return tentback way to visit her sisters.''

Jahna bit her lip, suddenly eager to prevent the older woman's withdrawal. "Valor, I—maybe this doesn't seem relevant to the discussion, but I want to know what Beck is doing here. I—it's important to me to understand what I'm being asked to help him in.''

117

"Ah." Valor stood, her dished features pained. "I have specific instructions, Jahna, that I am not to discuss the babes with you again until Beck returns from tentback. Then he will discuss them with you himself."

"But you do know what he's trying to do? Why he wants me to care for them during their first year?" Jahna persisted.

Valor plucked at her skirts. "Jahna, won't you have faith—for just a day or two?"

Jahna met Valor's eyes with full seriousness. "I need facts before I can move on to faith, Valor."

Valor studied her silently, solemnly. "I have faith in you," she said finally, "that you will do the work Beck has brought you here to do and that you will do it well. Not only because your government pledged your services but because you will see the necessity when it is explained "

Jahna's lips hardened. "My own conscience will have to come before my government's pledge."

"Then find it in your conscience to believe that what you will be doing will be beneficial and lasting. That much even Beck would permit me to say."

"Beneficial to the babies themselves?"

Valor's eyes flickered away. "Yes, one day, in terms of the lives they will lead because of you."

Jahna's brows creased thoughtfully. "Then what kind of lives would they lead without my—well, my services?" Whatever those were actually to be.

"Ha-ha!" Valor took herself quickly to the door. "I told you about Beck's instructions. And now I must go check those selfsame babes."

And she was gone. Jahna stood alone in the dim room, leather album clutched in hand. Troubled, she sat and opened the album again. Peace seemed very far tonight, a world captured flat and arranged in a leather-clad album to tantalize her. Impossible to believe that a few weeks ago she had walked under that bright sky, moving confidently toward her carefully chosen goals. Now she was alone on a strange world, a baffling and unpleasant world. A world, furthermore, where her training and experience seemed to have very little applicability. She was alone except for the reticent woman who had just withdrawn and Beck Lord, Father of Pengalen.

Father of mystery. What could she possibly be expected to do for twelve infants that could justify bringing her all the way from Peace? What could she possibly give babies who faced life on this muddy purgatory that their own mothers could not? Here, how could she even judge what was helpful and what was harmful? There were universal standards, certainly. There were equally universal gray areas, ambiguous areas, areas where succor and hurt blended and fused into one, inseparable.

As she herself was blending into one with despair. Engineering herself up from her chair, she found her way down the hall to her own room. She stood for a long while at her window, staring into darkness. Once, for a few minutes, the moon appeared. Soon clouds obscured it again, leaving her alone with her doubts. Finally she sought bed and oblivion.

When she awoke next dawn, Jahna lay in the depths of her mattress assessing the pull of weariness on shoulders and chest. Then she became aware of a sound from below, a scratching. She struggled out of bed and stumbled to her window.

She stared down, unbelieving. In the mud of the courtyard a small body in huttown garb lay sprawled. Near it sat dirad, rocking on his haunches and scratching at the log wall with his midarms. Jahna looked at the motionless child, unable to believe. He could not be dead, not so early in the day.

But did children, even on Nelding, lie face down in the mud to nap? Quickly she pulled on worksuit and boots and hurried to the stairs.

When she reached the courtyard, dirad bristled and scooped the child's loose body into his midarms. Fur erect, he danced away uttering a low cry of alarm. Tetz whimpered from a nearby doorway. Glancing around, Jahna saw the little dog and two large companions cringing in musty shadow.

"Dirad—give me!" she commanded, her voice shaking. This dirad was larger than the first. His shoulders and torso were thick with muscle. His legs were bristling columns of flesh. But he did not enjoy the same antic confidence the first dirad had enjoyed. He hastened to the protective shadow of the archway, where he squatted, uttering a series of deep barks, the limp child clutched to his chest.

Jahna approached the big animal cautiously, offering both hands, trying to speak with quiet confidence. The animal crept deeper into the archway, a spate of threatening garble tumbling from his vocal organs.

"Dirad, come! Give to us!"

Jahna turned, relieved to see Valor hurry into the courtyard, dark hair disarrayed, a rumpled gray gown hanging to her bare ankles. "I woke and saw him sitting out here," Jahna explained. "I don't think the child is alive."

"Almost certainly he is not," Valor agreed. She stepped past Jahna and approached the archway briskly, one hand held forth. "Dirad, come. Give me so you can have cakes."

Threatening garble came deeper, more menacing, from the archway.

Valor paused, studied the rumbling animal. "Normally this old fellow would come directly to me with his find. I think you frighten him, Jahna."

Jahna's gaze flashed from Valor to the animal. "Should I go get his cakes?"

"Go," Valor agreed. "They are in the kitchen, stale, but dirad will not mind. Bring them only to the doorway, however. Do not step out until I have this child."

Jahna ran the stairs. On a shelf in the kitchen she found a platter of tough yellow cakes sprouting moldy beards. She hurried downstairs in time to see dirad meekly bestowing his find upon Valor. When the tall woman held the lax body securely, dirad bowed away, clucking and hawking almost apologetically.

"Now you will have food," Valor assured him. She sidled toward Jahna. Gently she lowered the limp body to the ground and took the platter of cakes.

Jahna knelt quickly. The child's face and garments were caked with mud, his hair stiff with it. As she pressed his wrists and throat, she found cold flesh stretched tightly over protruding bones.

Valor joined her, grimly taking the bony wrist from her. "He is dead. He would never have been left in the vines otherwise."

Jahna gazed helplessly at the emaciated body. The child appeared to be four or five years of age. "He looks like he died of malnutrition."

Valor stood. "No. In that case his family would have sanctified his death with burial. It is when the cause of death is not understood that they are left in the vines to rot."

"They—oh! Beck told me that no one who died of unknown causes could be given sanctified burial," Jahna remembered. "But I thought—"

What *had* she thought? That the body would be buried anyway, but without ceremony? That the righteous Fathers of huttown would grant their dead that small indulgence?

"Clean ground can never receive unclean bodies. So now, since Beck has not yet taught dirad to distinguish between a live tangling and a dead huttown child, we will have to sanctify this death ourselves." Valor's deep eyes viewed the prospect grimly. "Bring a spool of ragging from the nursery to wrap him. I will fetch digging implements for us both."

An hour later they had placed the child to rest outside the walls of Pengalen. "It is our blessing dirad can at least distinguish an adult body from a juvenile," Valor commented as she scooped the last shovelful of mud into the oozing grave. She gazed down at the wound in the earth. "When my young sister was given to the vines like this child—it was many years now—I took my shovel by night, I searched until I found her body, and then I buried her in clean ground, wrapped in the blanket from my own bed. So each time I bury one of these children, I pray for them both: May they find kindness in Old Mother's embrace. Certainly they found it nowhere else.''

Jahna stared down at the bleak gravesite. "What did they do to you? When they found out?" Her voice was an appalled whisper.

"The Fathers?" Valor's mouth twisted. "I do not believe they know yet that one unclean body is fouling their sanctified burial tract. The next day I left huttown forever. So you see, my Father lost two daughters within one day. And I am sure he has never once considered it might in any way be his own doing." She glanced up. "Now I think we should return, Jahna. Old Mother appears to be preparing a tantrum."

Jahna studied the darkening sky apprehensively, following Valor back to the archway.

In her room she scrubbed and changed. By then Mother Nelding had unleashed her temper across the dark skies. The heavens cracked and rumbled angrily, the dark cloud layer turning liquid and falling in a heavy sheet across the land. Jahna stood at her window and watched the courtyard liquefy. Tetz and his two companions peered anxiously from their doorway shelter.

I helped Valor dig a grave, Jahna told herself leadenly, struggling to capture the full reality of the morning. I helped her bury a little boy under that mud. Somewhere in huttown his parents are looking into the rain now. And feeling—what?

She could not imagine. She paced across her room. "EarthExodus" in her mind had always been a proud and evocative term. She had seen the human race reaching out from its native rock to people the universe, to anoint the galaxies with its sentient will. Now she began to see another side to EarthExodus. She began to see ships of hopeful men and women flashing toward remote tragedy, toward unknown hurt and devastation, insidious destruction that would touch not just their own bodies, but the bodies, minds, and souls of their descendants as well. Who of Nelding's original pioneers could have visualized his seed dying in mud, rotting in vines? And the survivors becoming father and mother of creatures other than fully human? Jahna had studied the saga of Coronel, where the human race had evolved into something strange and touching, a gaudy new race. Now she viewed the backside of that saga, this world, where the human race suffered and disintegrated into chaos.

How long could huttown produce enough normal children to replace the parent generation? How long could they survive in their stubborn refusal to utilize altered crops and domestics? And just how vigorous was the rebirth in tentback? With so many of its inhabitants sterile, could tentback reproduce itself in sufficient numbers to survive the next centuries? Or was the life of the groves a final defiant flourish on the journey to extinction? Jahna stared into the drenching rain, wondering.

Chapter Twelve

JAHNA LAY on her bed after lunch staring at the ceiling, listening to the rain, when she heard a strangled yelp and a canine bellow from below. She hurried to her window. A tangling cantered through the archway on spider-long legs, rough hair thick down the back of a massive head that sat directly on broad shoulders. His arms were in proportion to his legs, long and thin, hanging past his knee. His feet stirred mud turbulently across the courtyard. Pausing, he peered up and around. "Va-*lor!*" he cried, cupping his mouth. "Va*lor!*"

Jahna heard Valor's door, heard her feet on the stairs. Then the tangling disappeared into the doorway below.

Jahna ran to the top of the stair. Below, the two Neldings conferred, the tangling gesticulating urgently, Valor peering out past him in distress. Finally they reached some accord and the tangling disappeared into the rain. To Jahna only his feet were visible, plowing mud.

Valor turned and glanced up, her face tense. "We have work to do, Jahna. There is to be a congregation in our courtyard tonight."

Jahna's eyes flashed to that liquid zone. "In this mud?"

"That is what I am told. We will have to harvest moss quickly and spread it. Otherwise our guests may sink from sight."

"But—why would anyone come in this weather?"

Valor shook her head. "It is already decided. Tonight is the night. And these violent tantrums seldom last long. We may see the moon later. So come. I'll fetch gathering poles for us both."

Mystified, Jahna followed her to a small supply room. There Valor found two long poles with crossbars tied to them at regular intervals. She also found a long fabric bag. "You'll see that our overgrown halls do us some benefit," she explained, leading way back upstairs and down the first corridor.

Together they confronted the moss-choked hallway. Following Valor's example, Jahna extended her gathering pole before her into the billow of moss and slowly twirled the pole to wind moss onto the crossbars. Then, when the poles were wrapped, they tore the moss off and stuffed it into the long bag. "This is how we gather moss for mattresses, too," Valor explained. As they cleared their way down the choked hall, the air shifted before them in torpid layers, particulate and gray by lantern light. Thick pads of flocculent moss spread across the revealed walls in involuted patterns. When the bag was filled, they dragged it downstairs and emptied it across the mud, patting it down with their feet into a thick, soft pad.

It was dark when they picked their way down the decrepit third-floor stairs with the last bag of moss. Light from their lantern bled away into dark crevices and cavities; rotten planks complained underfoot. Jahna stepped onto solid floor with relief. Outside, the rain had ceased.

"You wash and change while I spread this last bag," Valor instructed. "Our guests will be here within the hour."

Jahna's shoulders ached from her unaccustomed labors. "Will we be expected to feed them, too?" she asked, prepared for the worst.

"Oh, no. Food is no part of this celebration."

Relieved, Jahna returned the gathering poles to their place and hurried to her room. When she released her hair, particulate moss clouded the air. She slapped at her suit, producing a second cloud. Hands and face were gritty-gray. Quickly, coughing, she dodged across the hall to redeem herself.

Before she could change into a fresh daysuit, Tetz

croaked wildly below, his two black companions adding bass accompaniment. Jahna ran to her window. A stocky figure appeared through the archway, loping raggedly on mismatched legs, torch in hand. He shouted hoarsely, flurrying his flame at the frantic dogs, driving them back in yelping panic. His bare legs were splashed with mud.

Valor appeared from her doorway, hair still gray with dust. "Guard!" she commanded the dogs. *"Guard!"*

At the second command, the dogs retreated to a doorway and the stocky figure cantered toward Valor, bellowing raggedly, incomprehensibly.

Quickly Jahna pulled on her fresh daysuit. By the time she reached the head of the stair, the stocky figure was gone again, bellowing back out the archway, and Valor was pattering up the stairs. "They're coming. We must pad the babies quickly."

They ran across the moss-strewn courtyard and met Elda at the top of the nursery stair. By the time the last baby was padded and lidded, they heard the cry of mockdirad on the moist night air: a garble, a shout, a growing storm of discord, the call of horns. Jahna ran to a window. The courtyard was empty with the special hollowness that foreshadows chaos. Sound howled around the log walls, attracted. Jahna clutched her ears desperately, In the grove mockdirad cry—*song!*—had been painful enough. Contained within these high walls, it would mount to sanity-shredding agony.

Desperately she ran across the nursery and fished in the container of gum plugs. She kneaded four small plugs into two larger ones and slid them into her ears. The fury beyond the walls retreated, its impact dulled.

But then mockdirad began to funnel through the archway, and the gum-muted swell of sound surged loudly again. Glossy-pelted bodies burst into the courtyard, torches brandished in hands and midhands. Caught, Jahna provided mute audience for their entry. Bodies flew, flames flurried. With swaggering dance mockdirad claimed the courtyard. Seen from above, their dance was compelling in its vigor, in its violence, in its defiance of

126

gravity and restraint. Unlike the dance in the grove, however, it seemed to possess form. There was ritual substance to the claim mockdirad placed on the fortress of Pengalen tonight.

Then mockdirad formed a ragged crescent across the yard, bodies crouched on flexed legs, torches suddenly thrust high. From their communal throat rose a hoarse cry of fealty.

Two personages, fur-draped, powerful, strode through the archway. Inside they paused, surveying their roaring audience with barbaric grandeur. Torchlight made two gaudy idols of them; splendid in their dark furs. One was the mockdirad Hurak, his eyes flashing. The other, lean, autocratic, was Beck Lord.

Despite gum plugs, Jahna was drawn into a vortex of sound as mockdirad abandoned their posture of fealty and flew again into noisy dance. As they racketed about the yard, Beck and Hurak made their way through the field of flying bodies. Behind them, the archway filled with twisted tentback bodies. The mutant following crept and hobbled into the courtyard and lined the walls, cringing from the flailing torches of the antic mockdirad.

Jahna became aware of Valor beside her, face strained. Simultaneously she became aware of fear rising in her throat, acrid, paralyzing. As if summoned, Beck raised his eyes to their window. With a bound, Hurak emerged from the welter of flying bodies and landed beside him, deep chest heaving. His glance followed Beck's. Meeting Jahna's eyes, mockdirad flung back his head and bared his cylinder of dirad teeth. They flexed yellow and horny, a declaration of power. His massive body poised to leap for the doorway which led to the nursery stair.

Beck restrained him. Mockdirad spun and presented argument, gesturing upward urgently. Beck's eyes rose to meet Jahna's again. He spoke to Hurak, gesturing forcefully toward the assembled dirad and tanglings, and then dodged into the doorway himself, alone.

Jahna could not hear his feet on the stair, but in a moment he was with them, a commanding presence in

127

furs, legs leather-laced. Valor weighed his fur cloak impassively with her eyes. Beck's glance swept quickly between them, settling upon Jahna. "Peace, we need you now."

Jahna stiffened, recoiling. Her plea was muffled by gum plugs, drowned by mockdirad cry. "I have to help in the nursery!"

"No, I will send tanglings here." His eyes flickered to her ears. "So remove those insults and come. Mockdirad is ready to give shout."

Jahna shrank against Valor, her heart curdling. "And then what? Will you award me to the one with the loudest cry?"

His brow creased with impatience. "Mockdirad has come to give shout, not to contest with shout. There is a difference." His hands reached earward to implement his order.

"I can do it myself!" Fiercely she dug the gum plugs from her ears. Before she could wad them together in frustrated fury, she was taken by sound.

Total sound. It rocked her back against the wall, stunned. Her mouth went dry, her legs weak. She raised her voice to protest the agony of cry, but her words dribbled away into storm, inane, inaudible.

Beck seized her arm and pulled her to the door, down the hall. At the bottom of the stair she clung to the doorframe with ripping nails. He grappled with her briefly, unsuccessfully. Then his hand drew back and descended in a broad arc, palm connecting with her jaw. She saw the blow coming. It hung in the air forever and she was helpless to shield herself. Only when pain stung her could she react. Then, with a wild twist, she flung herself upon him, raking him with uncoordinated nails.

He seized her wrists. His dark eyes blazed. "Peace, *mockdirad are watching*."

She sagged in his grasp. Slowly she peered back over her shoulder. Dark bodies arced past, staring at her with avid eyes, fur erect on massive shoulders. A single mockdirad landed beside them with muscular impact, man-face twisted, arrogant with animal power. Furry hands cupped Jahna's cheek, fondled her neck. Jahna drew back with a hysterical squawk. Imperiously Beck gestured the hands away, twisted Jahna around until she stood beside him. "Take control of yourself, Peace. Put on your proud face. Stand above these animals."

She seized desperately at self-control, grasped it by the tail. With a will she composed her face, made of it a white, staring mask. Then Beck led her through the cloud of antic bodies until they stood near the center of the courtyard. The freshly harvested moss was disconcertingly springy underfoot.

Hurak appeared from the field of mockdirad and landed beside Jahna with a meaty thump. "So!" he bellowed. With a piercing male scream, he spun and wielded his torch in a wide circle, pounding his feet to the ground ferociously.

As if ordered, mockdirad came to rest. The dance halted. The outcry ceased, its echoes bouncing turgidly off the rotten walls and dying. The courtyard became still.

Hurak bellowed and a bent tangling stumbled through mockdirad with dark pelts flung over his arms. Hurak whipped the pelts from him and flung them down in a heap before Jahna.

"Sit," Beck instructed her.

Tense, Jahna knelt and sat on the glossy heap. The skins crackled stiffly under her weight. She raised her head, glancing around uneasily, painfully aware of the pressure of dark eyes, of the growing silence.

Hurak's massive chest swelled. His voice was a play of thunder across the crowded yard. *"So, Becklord, is this indeed the StarMother you have promised our groves and our camps?"*

Beck's voice was incisive. *"This is."*

"And have you examined this StarMother and spoken with this StarMother and have you determined that she is indeed what she must be to accomplish her mission here?"

Jahna stared up at Beck, alarmed to find herself suddenly catapulted into some ceremonial investiture. *"I have,"* he declared. *"She is."*

"And do you certify, on authority of the mighty pelts you wear tonight, that this StarMother is sister of the moon, daughter of the sun, and that she rides across the stars in the belly of a metal insect that births kings, queens, and wizards throughout the known universe?"

"I certify."

Jahna shifted uneasily on her furs. Although Hurak's phraseology had the ring of ritual, she was reluctant to allow herself to be so grossly overrated.

"And do you certify that this StarMother will now mold our daughters in her own bright image, so that they too will ride the wind and look down upon our world with the eyes of the moon? So that they too will bear gold upon their heads and blue in their eyes, so that their bodies will be perfect and straight and strong and their minds swift and able?"

Jahna's gaze shot to Beck's face. Mold their daughters in her own image? Her mouth opened in alarm.

"I certify," Beck declared. *"This is your StarMother."*

Whatever protest Jahna might have voiced was lost as gathered mockdirad gave birth to a furious bellow of celebration. Beck knelt and sat beside Jahna on the furs as dark bodies began to leap, to bob, to fly in celebration. Jahna's body was racked with painful tension. *What had Beck Lord brought her here for?* What did these antic semihumans expect of her?

Abruptly the celebration was aborted. A shrill scream pierced the rising furor and Hurak brandished his torch in a flaming circle, pounding his broad feet insistently, uttering again and again his high cry.

Chaos died. Mockdirad not only ceased their dance but, cowed by Hurak's shattering cries, ducked into crouching posture, arms and midarms wrapped tightly around their chests, heads bowed.

When all were quiet, mockdirad and tangling alike, Hurak uttered one rending bellow and raised his torch to the sky. Jahna's glance rose anxiously. And over her head the moon appeared. Small and white it drifted from a cloud, a pale body, empress of night reigning from the dark throne room of the heavens. Floating and distant it crowned her, its emergence publicly proclaiming Jahna its royal sister, co-empress of the realm.

Raising his torch twice again, Hurak flung himself flat before Jahna. Across the courtyard other mockdirad slowly stood, saluted the crowning power, and flattened themselves in submission before Jahna.

Jahna shuddered, unable to swallow. It was a moment frozen in time, a moment, she knew, that had come before in human history, a moment that would come again. It was a moment of spiritual coronation and she was its temporal goddess. She sat in the flicker of torchlight, enthroned, made divine by the silent will of gathered mockdirad and tangling—and by the distant silver smile of the floating moon.

She raised her head and gazed up. As she watched, the moon disappeared back into the cloudy maw of the sky, a night-queen withdrawing to her private bower.

Beck jumped to his feet. His voice was harsh. "So, dirad—why have you left StarMother bare for her own coronation?"

Across the courtyard alarmed faces rose into view. "Ah!" Hurak's head snapped up. His expression entertained superstitious fears as old as time. Quickly he flew to his feet bawling incoherently. A lantern-jawed tangling, his gray hide like armor, thick and plated, crept through the fear-struck mockdirad. Ducking his head abjectly, he offered an arm laden with dark pelts.

Hurak flicked free a cape of furs. With arms and midarms he held it high, dedicating it. *"So, StarMother! Take this pelt!"* Majestically he bent and bestowed it across Jahna's shoulders. With obsequious reverence he bowed away from her and crouched, head hunched on his chest, furry nape exposed. "So now, StarMother, you wear our strength and our wisdom. Now, StarMother, you carry our pride and our hope on your shoulders."

Jahna squirmed uncomfortably. Hurak's pride and hope was not only stiff but distinctly odorous. She glanced up at Beck, uncertain whether she was to make verbal response.

"So now we will see your dance, mockdirad," Beck announced haughtily. "Are there other furs for us to rest upon?"

Furs appeared from bags and were quickly heaped before the middle wall of the quad. Beck led Jahna to position, gesturing her to sit. Lowering, she arranged herself stiffly, feet tucked under, spine rigid. Her face, she knew, must be white and staring. The furs crackled.

Beck himself sat. "So now we are ready."

Hurak leaped straight into the air, uttering a harsh, gravelly bellow. And the dance began.

Mockdirad made of themselves muscular missiles that filled the air. Massy bodies arced and somersaulted, leaped and swung. Some flung themselves back and dashed across the yard on their midarms, legs and true arms waggling in the air. Others flipped themselves in blind patterns, colliding with their fellows with meaty grunts. Their hoarse cries shook the air.

For the first eternity, Jahna was completely anesthetized by chaos. But the dance stretched on and gradually she became aware of cramping muscles, of hot scratchy discomfort. The cape of pelts lay heavy on her shoulders. She half turned. "I thought only mockdirad were allowed to wear fur."

Beck leaned toward her, his voice low. "You are not only crowned royal, you are adopted into the order of mockdirad, Peace. So be glad. You are sitting on the ancestors themselves."

Jahna's thighs stiffened involuntarily. "I—what?"

"When mockdirad dies, his kin strip off his pelt and preserve it for ceremonial use. It's a great honor, Peace, to sit on these furs with Hurak's grandfather draped over your shoulders."

Jahna's head spun. She stared at him full-face. His expression told her that he spoke literal truth. She gaped, nausea forming a sour tidal wave in her throat. She choked it back, struggling to rise, to escape.

"No." He restrained her. "Look honored. No one insults the ceremonial furs."

Sick, she settled back and sucked breath against the aggressive rise of nausea. Malevolently the pelts pricked her legs, each stiff hair demanding recognition of its individuality, of its transcendance of time and death. Hurak's grandfather settled possessively around her, hugging her, holding her. Her entire body grew clammy. Pain slashed across her abdomen. She swallowed convulsively, struggling to choke off a second inundating wave of nausea.

When the horns appeared, they were almost welcome. Because, as mockdirad settled into song, Jahna was finally carried away from the bed of furs, carried away from Pengalen, carried away to a place where sound was the only dimension, where color and form and motion were perceived by the inner ear, where nothing mattered but the cry, the call, the undulating din that formed an ever-cresting wave which flowed around them eternally.

Flowed around them forever and then a while longer, linking them to every age of man, past and future. Jahna grew heavy with eternity. Beck was stone beside her. Hurak's grandfather was cement on her shoulders pressing her down into the soft earth of Nelding, claiming her.

She was one of the order. That and more.

Finally the horns were lowered. Mockdirad bent their heads, gulping massively for breath. Sweat glistened on fur, tipping it, beading it, slicking it flat. For the first time Jahna saw the furred order in exhaustion.

A second command from Hurak and mockdirad crouched and slowly backed away until a broad aisle was formed before the fur couch. Then the tanglings began their procession past the throne. Hesitantly, fearfully, sometimes boldly they came, the horrible, the beautiful, the grotesque, the pitiful. Some hobbled, others strode. Each fell to his knees when he reached the bed of furs and kissed air first before Beck, then before Jahna. Then, regaining his feet, he backed away, his dark eyes searching Jahna's face for revelation.

Those who had crowded into the courtyard for the ceremonies passed in review. Next came the hundreds who waited beyond the walls. They pressed through the archway, eyes glistening by torchlight, to make their obeisance. Jahna huddled miserably in her cape, helpless to deny their homage, loath to accept it.

One of the order. But more, obviously. Much more, at least for tonight.

As the tanglings of tentback passed, Jahna began to observe an unsettling fact. Some of them—that scaled woman with fangs, that magnificent dark woman on disproportionately short legs, the big Yuba—a handful of them were coming again and again. But each time they passed, they were different in some detail of dress, of grooming, of expression. Once, she raised her head and found herself staring into the eyes of the rough-haired girl who had boarded Nodd's wagon. But in her eyes tonight there was neither recognition nor hatred. There was only avid curiosity. And the rough hair was tamed into a thick mat on the girl's neck. Jahna stared up at her, disconcerted.

The woman Yuba came twice, once very young, once older, flabby, and then, when the procession was near an end, she came again. This time she swaggered, towering over the others, her dozen breasts jutting aggressively, eyes aloof, refusing to recognize Jahna and Beck. Only when she was abreast of the couch did she lower her glance. As her eyes met Jahna's, dark storm billowed across her haughty features. Bitterness, jealousy, finally twisting hatred, and the storm became animal, bloody and bawling. Sweeping Jahna with the turbulence of her wrath, this third Yuba did not kneel.

Instead, with a cry, she lunged. Muscles rippled with animal power. She caught at Jahna's hair and yanked her head violently sideways, at the same time throwing herself across her body and bruising at it fiercely with her free fist. "Steal-baber!" she grunted viciously, a half-snarl.

134

After a moment's startled helplessness, Jahna struggled to pull clenched fingers from her hair. She sobbed with effort, the fur cape sliding off her shoulders. The big fingers were like steel claws. Desperately Jahna tried to kick the woman, to elbow her, even to bring her teeth into use. Her eyes blurred with futile tears.

Then Beck and Hurak fought the woman off Jahna. With a bellow, Yuba relinquished her hold on Jahna's hair and spun to lunge at Beck. Jahna rolled back against the log wall, head down, gasping for breath.

It was minutes before Beck, Hurak, and three younger mockdirad controlled the bellowing Yuba. Even in their grasp she rocked with fury. "Steal-baber!" she shrieked, her breasts shuddering. "Steal-baber! I bite out your eyes, stealer!"

The males hurried her across the yard and through the archway.

Jahna sat, holding her head. The courtyard presented a prospect of frozen faces, tangling and mockdirad. From beyond the archway, Yuba's voice rang in fury. Jahna stared around, stunned. *There was no one to stop her now*.

No one to stop her if she stood and ran across the yard and up the stairs to her own room. Quickly, before Beck could return, she was up. Mockdirad and tangling, as stunned as she, shrank back to allow her passage.

In her room, she leaned against the door, fighting to regain breath. Then she zipped out her mirror. Although her hair was wildly disarrayed, her face was unmarked. Hands shaking, she let down her hair and began brushing it back into order. *Steal-baber—StarMother*. So she had two new names to work with, to define for herself her mission here. *She had two useless names to work with*. She had stolen no babies. And if they had been stolen by someone else in her name—if they were in fact the six babies upstairs—what was she expected to do with them? Mold them? In her own image?

How? And what was her image? Sister of moon, daughter of sun, passenger of a bewitched bug that carried kings and wizards the length of the universe. Throwing

135

down her brush, she cradled her head in her hands, pressing her temples spasmodically, trying to squeeze comprehension into her mind.

Then she heard Beck on the stairs. His step was unmistakable, sharp-edged, urgent. Her door opened. "Are you hurt?" His tone held little concern, much impatience.

"Not seriously," she snapped, her voice matching his.

"Good. So shake out your hair again. We must get down."

Her eyes flared. "Oh, must we? Is there someone else down there waiting to get her nails into me?"

Beck's dark brows arched. In his furs he was an impatient princeling, intolerant of delay. "There is the remainder of the ceremony to be played out, and now we have extra advantage. At least we will have if you do not fail me." Before she could draw back, he reached out and raked her hair forward across her face. "So stalk down there like a woman outraged, Peace. There is a show to be played."

She retreated, her eyes blazing. "What—"

"Peace, we have the other party on the defensive. So let us seize our advangage before it evaporates." He grasped her arm, hard fingers biting. "Keep anger in your eyes, Peace. I will manage the rest." With a twist, he dragged her into the hall.

Indignantly she fought him down the stairs, half stumbling. When they reached the doorway into the courtyard, Beck abruptly twisted her arm back, thrusting her sharply off balance.

Pain scalded her shoulder. She gasped, her eyes filling. Before she could retrieve her balance, they were hurrying across the yard, Beck striding, she half stumbling beside him. Furiously she blinked back tears of pain, too startled to struggle effectively.

"So now you see what your woman has done!" Beck barked, dragging her before the fur couch.

"Ah." Hurak's knees flexed. His dark eyes became contrite, as if he were personally responsible for Jahna's

136

bedraggled condition. "But you know Yuba-bull, Beck-lord. There is nothing behind her rages but muscle and bone."

"I know every one of you," Beck snapped. "And now, I wonder, do any of you accept this StarMother? Or is the same treachery in every heart? Is each one of you willing to risk the magic to express your hatred? Do all of you secretly concur in my decision to send this Mother back to her own world, where she can pass unmolested?"

Under different circumstances, the alarmed moan of the assemblage might have been gratifying. But with Beck's fingers digging her arm, with Hurak's grimy forefinger reaching to sample the tumble of her hair, Jahna was unable to summon appreciation. She cringed from Hurak's touch. Her expression, she realized from his reaction, must be formidable beneath the serpent's nest Beck had made of her hair.

Hurak withdrew the rejected hand quickly. "Becklord, you know that Yuba does not act for any of the rest. You saw how we kicked her into the weeds to eat mud and crawl home with our curses in her ears."

"I saw that," Beck agreed implacably. "But did I see blood on her face? Or whip marks on her belly?"

"So." Hurak flexed mighty muscles, fur bristling. "You will see it," he vowed. "You will see blood on her every breast, on her buttocks. You will see it mingling with the mud of her legs. You will see her cheeks torn out, you will see—"

"I did not ask you to destroy her. I only inquired after your true feelings. If you had bloodied her without my asking, I would have no doubt. But you did not. And now the moment is past."

"Moments can be regained," Hurak pointed out, his big body poised to leap.

Beck shook his head. "No. The matter is left to Star-Mother's magic." Maneuvering Jahna, he sat her on the fur couch. "So do you all know what this StarMother told me before she consented to come down and take your

137

insults again?'' He raised his voice to whiplash the entire assemblage. ''She told me that tonight in this yard were gathered nothing but weaklings.''

This time the moan was of disbelief.

''When I reached her, she was already packing her goods to return to her own world. She would not stay here with savages and pulings, she told me. There was contempt in her every word. So that is what your treacherous thoughts have accomplished here tonight while you made your puny dance and uttered your hypocrite's shout.''

Hurak's shoulders bristled indignantly. His cylinder of teeth began to flex, shredding some phanthom enemy. ''You saw our dance, Becklord. You heard our song.'' In his outrage, his voice broke into cackles and whistles.

Deliberately Beck lowered himself to the furs beside Jahna, ''I saw your dance. And now I know why it was so feeble. Now I know why this StarMother laughed behind her face while you danced. Your dance was nothing! *You* are nothing!''

With a wounded bellow, Hurak leaped straight into the air. Descending, he lunged past Jahna, the flame of his torch singeing her cheek. With a frightened gasp, she tried to duck away.

Beck seized her forearm and forced her bolt upright. ''Face him down, Peace, Show him how much you care for animals!''

The big mockdirad made a series of passes, his flame fluttering past Jahna's cheek each time. She struggled briefly against Beck's grasp. Finding that futile, she fought to match Hurak's flame with the fire of her eyes. Hurak's cylinder of teeth writhed in answer, and he spun away with a harsh cry, only to appear again.

Flame grazed Jahna's cheek, but she glared it down, unblinking. This time mockdirad spun away uneasily. He took stance and lashed the air furiously with his torch. With a bellow, he threw himself back upon his midarms and raised and lowered himself rapidly, rhythmically, on flexing elbows. Then he flipped backward, landing on his hands, at the same moment catching his casually tossed torch with a sidehand. He began to march a tight circle on his hands.

There was an intervention. From the backdrop of mock-dirad a single furred body appeared. With a cry of declaration, he landed before Jahna, man-face twisting aggressively. Gasping, shrinking, she recognized the arrogant young mockdirad who had cupped her face in his hand earlier. Now he reached his furred fingers into her hair and pulled her head up firmly, flattening his nose to hers.

Hurak bellowed, acrobatics cut short. Swinging his torch, he swathed its flame across the young mockdirad's rump. Young mockdirad leaped back, releasing Jahna to flurry his own torch against Hurak's. His dirad teeth flexed and chewed viciously. From his throat, a trail of garble grew, menacing.

Hurak backed away, beginning to grunt and haw fiercely. Then suddenly he leaped again, landing on young mockdirad's shoulders. Younger mockdirad grunted, carried to the ground under Hurak's weight.

Quickly Jahna scrambled back against the wall. Rolling across the courtyard, the two mockdirad pounded each other mercilessly. Clots of dark fur flew. Blood spattered. The cries of the combatants were gut-deep, vicious. Jahna hugged Hurak's grandfather, knuckles white. "Can't you stop them?"

Beck knelt, his profile tense. "I can't touch them. If Narrel tops Hurak—"

Jahna's eyes widened. If the dominant male were displaced now, in the middle of the ceremonies, chaos would surely ensue. And what would be the consequences in terms of her own circumstance?

Fortunately she was not to learn tonight. Hurak, despite his years, was the stronger male. After a long, grunting tussle, he wrestled younger mockdirad to the ground and shoved his face into the moss. Vengefully he rocked on his back, both the younger mockdirad's arms twisted painfully behind his back.

Beck stood beside her. "So now you have shown us you can whip the pup," he stated caustically. "But Star-Mother still has seen no dance fit for dirad. And she has heard no song but that puny tune you sang earlier, dirad. So throw the pup into the vines and let us have shout—if you are capable!"

Hurak's dark eyes flared with emotion. With a bellow, he leaped up and gestured to his hairy lieutenants. They wrestled young mockdirad toward the archway. Leaping, Hurak brandished his torch fiercely at Jahna and Beck, drumming his feet insistently.

But as he whipped his fellows into dance, Jahna realized, his fury became more demonstrated than felt. And Jahna's desperate scorn soon took the quality of assumed role, too. Deliberately, as furred bodies flew, Jahna relaxed her taut muscles. Order was restored to the assemblage, at least for tonight. Hurak's authority had been vindicated. Beside her Beck sat again, cross-legged, unreadable.

At first the theme of the renewed dance was anger, but fury was quickly displaced by sheer animal exuberance. Mockdirad leaped and bounded, heavy bodies boasting their power.

Finally horns reappeared and dance became song. Sound filled the courtyard, possessing them all. Now Jahna found that in her ears mockdirad cry had begun to take pattern. Call answered cry, completing it, elevating it. Voices contributed to horn, horn to voice, swelling out the noise-song until it took perceptible form, tangible substance, until it was a thing that moved among them, prophetic.

Aeons passed in the cry, until dawn came sodden to the Nelding sky, diluting shadows, diminishing torchlight. The cry died, but with serpentine sinuosity. Jahna stirred, both legs numb, the interior of her head a vast empty chamber. She stared at crouching mockdirad blankly, unable to comprehend their silence or their exhaustion. By gray dawnlight they were a clutch of spent animals.

Beck stood as Hurak strode forward. Big mockdirad had saved a final driblet of animal vitality for challenge. "So now you see our dance and hear our song, StarMother."

"StarMother has heard and StarMother has seen. There is no scorn in her now," Beck responded. "She will wear pelt in full respect."

"And she will remain to leave her mold-daughters in our groves?"

"She will leave them proudly. Stand, StarMother."

Numbly Jahna gained her feet, legs prickling in agony. With heavy pride Hurak approached. His odor was overpowering. Bowing, he kissed air on either side of Jahna's shoulders. "So wear my ancestor in pride, StarMother."

This, obviously, was not the moment to voice reservations. "I will wear him," Jahna mumbled.

That sparse effort seemed all that was required. Mockdirad backed away. "And now that this StarMother sees our strength, there will be rededication. All will come, even those who came before."

At Beck's touch, Jahna sat again. First mockdirad filed past the fur couch, kneeling and kissing air before her. Then the tanglings came again, their faces drained and pale in the harsh dawn. Various, many, they passed.

When all had come and gone, Hurak approached again. Bowing, he wrapped midarms around his chest and backed ceremoniously from their presence. Halfway across the yard he whirled and with a raucous bellow propelled himself into the archway.

The courtyard emptied in a riot of cry.

Finally all were gone. The trampled moss was bare. Jahna turned to Beck. He shook his head. They continued to sit, staring into the shadowmouth of the archway in ceremonial silence for minutes after the last celebrant had gone. Then Beck stood.

Jahna followed suit, stretching reluctant limbs. Grimly she declared herself. "Now there are a number of things you are going to explain to me, Beck," she said, her tone offering no room for evasion.

The Father of Pengalen nodded heavily, permitting his exhaustion to surface to visibility. "Yes, there are, Peace. A number of things."

Chapter Thirteen

HURAK'S GRANDFATHER, mercifully, accepted exile in Jahna's room. Her hair brushed and twisted up off her neck again, she met Beck in Valor's apartment. A quarter hour later Valor cleared bowls and mugs from the counter and Jahna pushed back her chair firmly. "The first thing I want to know," she stated, "is what I'm expected to do for, or to, the babies in the big nursery."

"Now, that is very simple," Beck responded, standing. "You are to mold them."

Jahna studied his profile, waiting. Her voice sharpened. "Couching my function in proper imagery then, I'm expected to teach them to float with the moon and fly the known universe—with the help of a starship and a qualified captain, I hope?"

He smiled faintly. "As you say, that couches your function in imagery. More realistically, what is expected is that you will bequeath to them, by being the only person they have sensory contact with during their first year, your own features and physique, your health, and many—with luck, most—of your mental and emotional capabilities and capacities."

Jahna stared at him, her capacity to believe suddenly acutely stressed. "I'm—*what*?"

Beck met her startled gaze squarely. "You are to mold them, Peace. It is a tentback procedure perfected these last two centuries. When a tentback child is born bearing certain characteristics—or, more accurately, lacking certain characteristics—he or she is designated a molding. If the child is male, he is immediately taken to mockdirad compound, where his dirad-father or his pelt-father—the first being the natural father, the second an adoptive father—give him pelt. That means they undertake to mold him after themselves. So for the entire of his first full year, he sees no one but mockdirad. He is handled by no one but mockdirad. And by the end of that year, he has taken pattern. He has become mockdirad.

"If the molding is female, however, she receives a less well patterned rearing. If no one claims her from her birth-mother and if her birth-mother is a tangling, she will soon develop the tangling characteristics of her mother and of any other individuals to whom she is much exposed during her first year. If, however, she is granted to one of the grove mold-Mothers, or sent by the grove dirad to a Mother of some other grove for her first year, she will be shielded to a large degree from exposure to any individual except the mold-Mother until she has successfully taken the Mother's characteristics. Until she is *molded*, Peace. Then she will be returned to her birth-mother to grow into a mold-Mother herself someday, if she survives childhood. And most moldings are vigorous. A high proportion of them actually do survive childhood, even in tentback."

Jahna was aware of a disbelieving laxity in her facial muscles. "You don't mean that. . . ." She faltered. Obviously he did mean what he had said. "But, Beck, that goes contrary to everything we know about human heredity," she protested. "A child's physical appearance can't be altered simply by—by arranging proximity to individuals bearing desirable characteristics. And a child who is born normal, even to an aberrant mother, never—"

"But moldings are not born normal," Beck interposed. "In appearance, yes. There are no physical abberations. That is, in fact, how it is determined at birth that a tentback babe will be moldable. He has no recognizable mutant features. But his developmental processes are in no way normal, not in the conventional human sense."

Jahna gaped at him, scouring her mind for coherent argument.

"You admit, don't you, that a normal child's emotional

and intellectual development can be influenced by the people and stimuli he is exposed to during the first year?'' Beck prodded.

"Well, of course. Everyone knows—"

"So, in moldings, Peace, the process is carried a step farther. Their physiological constitution can be programmed through exposure, too. When you go to the nursery and remove plugs and masks from our six girl babes, they will immediately begin taking clues from you. They will take clues from the texture of your hair, from the color of your eyes—and from the acuity of your vision and the state of your health. If you expose yourself to them adequately, within a few weeks you will begin to see yourself reborn. By the time they leave us a year from now, they will be six small Peaces, golden hair, blue eyes, restless tongues. Every one of them will return to her grove and grow into tentback you.

"So if your blood descendants should ship here two centuries from now they would find women in our groves far more like you than your descendants themselves, even though by then the resemblance will be less positive than in this first generation. You see, each molding does develop certain individual characteristics. Likewise, certain individual differences in temperament develop, sometimes due to the mold-Mother's emotional circumstance when she took the molding, sometimes simply due to some quality in the molding herself. Or himself, in the case of mockdirad.''

Slowly Jahna shook her head, unable to accept. "Beck, no. I—no,'' she pleaded helplessly.

He regarded her steadily. "But yes, Peace, that is what Old Mother has given us. This is her gift. Call it what you want: mutability, adaptability, perfectibility. On other worlds, there have been changes, too. You know that.''

"Of course. But this—"

She pressed her temples. Was this really so much more incredible than what had happened on Coronel? Was postnatal physiological mutability so much more difficult to accept than the development of a feathered species incorporating five separate sexes? Jahna shook her head help-lessly. Did she really, after all, accept the hard reality of Coronel? On other than an intellectual plane?

"All right then, if you cannot accept mutability in fact, why not examine it in theory? Why not discuss it with me as something that might happen someday, somewhere? Your training, I believe, prepares you for that type of extrapolation?"

Jahna frowned. "*No*, Beck. I've never gone into the more technical aspects of human genetics, but I've ab-sorbed the basic concepts. I *know* what is possible and what is not possible. I know—"

"And *I* know what has happened in tentback."

Jahna slumped, deflated. Obviously he did know. And the evidence? Hadn't it already confronted her? "Last night at the ceremonies," she said slowly, "the woman who attacked me came past our couch three separate times."

"She did. The first of her came from Tirammer's grove. She is mold-Mother of a single babe, birth-mother of none. There is some doubt that she can bear. The second is member of a roving band that sometimes camps lake-side. She is birth-mother of half a dozen. But she has been careless. The moldings among her offspring have taken tangling appearance, even the males. There are no mock-dirad in her band to give them pelt."

"And the third, the one who attacked me? She's the one we met in Hurak's grove? The one who wanted to take the tangling?"

"Yes, Yuba-bull. So in these three you see the effect of innate temperamental difference, environmental dispar-ity, and careless molding, all compounded by generations. All three Yubas stem from a common mold-ancestor. But one is a heedless nomad, the second a conscientious grove Mother, the third a dumb brute. And there are other Yubas in farback. Only a tenth part of tentback trekked Pengalen way last night."

"These Yubas, do all of them carry the same name?"

146

"Formally, yes. Usually there is a modifier. Yuba-bull, Yuba-quick, Yuba-netser."

"But if they all stem from a common ancestor," Jahna wondered, perplexed, "who did *she* stem from? Who molded her?"

"Ah. Now, Yuba-first was only a tangling, but one who was considered desirable by mockdirad: strong, fertile, striking in appearance—healthy. So when other tanglings birthed molding babes, mockdirad claimed them and brought them to Yuba. That was the beginning of her line many generations ago."

"And how many lines of—of females are there in tentback?"

Beck shrugged carelessly. "Dozens. Some of the stronger lines have mold-daughters in every grove. Others are dying. Too many discrepancies have appeared in the line. Their moldings are no longer desirable. Their only hope is to birth a molding and hide it from mockdirad until it is too late for it to be molded to a fresher line."

"So it's always mockdirad who decides how the child is molded?" Jahna pressed, dissatisfied.

"Unless the birth-mother hides the child, yes. Or unless she is a nomad."

"Even in cases where mockdirad can't prove paternity?"

"Even in those cases. The grove dirad enjoys presumptive paternity over all moldings."

"But why?" Jahna protested. "Why would any woman permit an unrelated male to exercise that kind of power over her own child?" Certainly no Peace mother would allow her child to be arbitrarily separated from her for its first year.

Beck shrugged. "You have seen these unrelated males, Peace. They do not permit their authority to be questioned. Certainly not by mere women."

"But if the women united—"

"But they have not. Think about it. Mockdirad present a united force. They have their own stronghold in each

147

grove, their own walled compound where no one may pass unless he bears pelt. Inside that compound they may dispute among themselves. There may be occasional challenge to the grove dirad, like we saw last night. But every mockdirad in every grove shares pelt. He carries a visible symbol of authority on his back, and every mockdirad in tentback will uphold the ultimate authority of pelt.''

"And the women, on the other hand, are fragmented," Jahna mused, apprehending his argument. "They stem from different lines. They probably compete for moldings, directly or indirectly. And what influence they do exercise they exert on a one-to-one basis, each mold-Mother alone with the child she's molding—the child she must release after just one year."

"Oh, the Mothers have their special tent area and their special fire circle in most groves," Beck conceded. "And there are lines of authority among the Mothers of each grove. But there are none radiating out to unite the Mothers of one grove with the Mothers of another. Line rivalry prevents that. A Mother who exercises authority in her grove often finds the dominant Mother in the next grove of a line she feels disputatious toward. And there is an established taboo against speaking to a mold-sister who belongs to another grove. So that effectively quells any attempt by the Mothers to unite tentback-wide.''

"Then they need what mockdirad has," Jahna speculated. "They need some unifying symbol of their power, some clear-cut—"

Abruptly her words died. She stared into Beck's eyes, suddenly chilled by the affirmation she found there.

He nodded, rising. "Yes, Peace. They need you."

"They—"

Her mouth dried as she grasped his meaning. "Beck, you're planning to copy me and distribute me through the groves," she said incredulously.

Beck paced across the room. "I am," he agreed. "Twelve years after you leave, each of your twelve moldings will be ready to become mold-Mothers in her own turn. But each of her will be much more than Mother. She will be StarMother, sister of the moon—''

"—daughter of the sun!''

"—a personage who has brought magic powers from the stars. Her golden hair and her white hands will be her crown and her scepter. Her faultless body and her keen mind will be passed from generation to generation, and she will quickly learn to use them to best advantage here. She will establish her own compounds and guard her moldings as no other line in the groves is able to guard theirs. There will be no carelessness, no casual neglect, no blur the passage of desirable characteristics. In fact, after the first generations, only superior carriers will be permitted to mold. The others will have other functions to fulfill in the groves. So not only will the line not degenerate, it will actually enhance itself over succeeding generations.''

"But—" Despite his visionary intensity she struggled with doubt. "But then—why is mockdirad permitting this, Beck?" It was obvious that after the first generation, the pelted males would find themselves confronted with formidable rivals for authority.

Beck smiled tightly. "Mockdirad is doing more than permitting. He is sponsoring. Because mockdirad has a taste for display. He sees you as an acquisition, an enhancement of his status. He has never read books, you see. He doesn't know that in some places, on your Peace for example, women do not bow to the muscle-authority of the male. He doesn't know that it is possible for situations to evolve in which intelligence can equal and eventually dominate physical power.

"But now that you are here, now that you are ready to mold, we will begin to evolve toward those situations in tentback.''

Their eyes met across the room. Between them spread a vision, his alone until now. But as moments passed, it began to be hers, too. She began to see a grove society in which the assertive vigor of mockdirad was tempered by a more rational force. She began to see a life that drew on reason and compassion, a life that provided enhancement of opportunity for every individual, tangling and molding alike.

She began to see what the human race could become in the groves of Nelding.

But then, unable to inhibit the flow of images, she began to see what the human race could become on other worlds, too. What had Beck called it? Mutability, adaptability—*perfectibility*. "Beck, you can't keep this here. Nelding is just one world. And I'm—I'm *not* the logical person to mold these babies. Something like this, shared through the settled planets, could completely transform human history. There are men and women on every world with gifts and qualities we all desperately need. In just one generation, we could produce dozens of people with the same gifts that are now confined to a few. We could—"

Beck wagged his head emphatically, one hand raised. "Peace, we could do a number of beneficial things for all those other worlds. But for the next hundred years, for the next two hundred years, we need those same things done right here. Nelding tentback is in no position to export its advantages, particularly when there is nothing of equal value your planets might offer in return."

"But consider what this could mean in terms of human history," Jahna insisted. "Despite everything that's been accomplished in genetics, we can do absolutely nothing to ensure that the gifted pass their special qualities to their offspring. We can do nothing to grant that kind of practical immortality to the people we need most. We can—"

Beck shoved his hands deep into his pockets. "All right, Peace. In two hundred years, return to Nelding, or send a delegate, and ask the Mothers of your line if they are willing to contribute their moldings to the cause. Perhaps they will be eager to sacrifice their own immortality for the immortality of people they have never seen, people whose gifts they may be prepared to appreciate—and may not.

"I don't know what their response will be. I expect it depends on how clearly you're able to transmit your values to the babies upstairs. But you are welcome to try.''

Balked, Jahna rose from her chair and paced across the room. ''Beck—''

''No.''

''All right,'' she conceded, exasperated. ''But really, Beck, I don't understand why you chose me to mold the babies. I mean, the imagery you've swaddled me in is— well, complimentary, certainly. But I've done nothing to prove myself worth duplicating. I haven't demonstrated any special gifts or qualities. Maybe someday I will. But to date—well, I'm a student cadet. A good student cadet. But my field isn't even one that attracts really brilliant people. There are dozens of cadets with profiles that are more notable than mine. And if you had the choice among all those—''

''I had the choice,'' he stated. ''But examine our situation, Peace. Musical genius is already provided for, for generations to come. Don't deny mockdirad that.'' He smiled wryly. ''We have no need in the universe for outstanding mathematicians, artists, or language specialists. We have no physical sciences to speak of. Frankly, I think that gift will appear from our own ranks when we are ready for it. So my primary requirement was for an individual who would be able to think and act in terms of the broad human picture. At first, in fact, I considered securing an anthropologist, one who was strong, healthy, preferably young—female—and willing to spend a couple of years here, most of it occupied in molding, but some of it devoted to field research.''

''You might have interested some very gifted women in that arrangement,'' Jahna pointed out quickly.

''Perhaps. But all off-world communications go through the fax set in Forgiven, you see, and the only person permitted to use the set is Humble Nodd.''

''Ah—and huttown has no idea what is transpiring out here?''

He snorted. ''Huttown knows we have produced some very hairy savages and that we call them mockdirad. Huttown certainly doesn't know they're being deliberately

151

bred from normal-appearing infants—or that I propose to produce a female equivalent from more normal-appearing infants.''

"So you were left with the problem of importing a suitable individual without ever making your exact purposes for doing so clear,'' Jahna mused. "To anyone in huttown *or* to the importee.''

"Yes, and I was determined to obtain a person who would be as inclined to act as to study. You can see I didn't care to breed a race of shrinking theoreticians. Fortunately I had heard of the Peace Cadet Corps. They appeared very eager to obtain off-world experience for one of their cadets. They were even willing to fax me records and profiles to select from. So here you are, Peace.''

Jahna hugged herself. So here she was. *Sister of the moon, daughter of the sun.* "And the Mothers who are already here?'' she wondered aloud. How many were willing to surrender their own brand of immortality for a vision, someone else's vision?

"They feel threatened, of course. I have promised that there will be moldings for every line, but they know that may be only a promise. And they know their own moldings will never have the status yours will have. I haven't suggested, for obvious reasons, that your coming will soon enhance the status of all tentback women.''

"You don't want mockdirad to realize that prematurely,'' Jahna agreed, sliding back in her seat. "But in that case, how many more Mothers are waiting in tentback to claw out my throat, Beck? Will I have any freedom of movement at all? Will my moldings? Or will there be the constant threat of ambush?''

Beck leaned his long frame against a log wall. "Ah, now, remember your magic, StarMother.''

Her eyes narrowed. "Magic?''

"You brought a whole kit of it from the stars, Peace. If anyone tentback way draws your blood, it will sear into his flesh and slowly destroy him. If anyone pulls out a strand of your hair, it will form an invisible band around his own throat, gradually tightening until he can no longer draw

152

breath or swallow food or water. If anyone marks your face or your body—"

"You told them that?"

"I made no public statement. I simply advised key mockdirad throughout the groves. You carry your magic in a small white case, but even if the case is stolen and thrown to the bottom of the lake, your powers persist. There is a magical linkage, you see—"

"But Yuba's attack has already demonstrated that everything you told them was false," Jahna protested.

"Did she draw blood?"

"No, but—"

"Did she pull out hair?"

"I don't know, but it certainly feels like it."

"So then she's already suffering the consequences. Unless you are summoned to lift the spell, she will suffocate."

"But Beck, there was no spell. The only possible way. " Slowly her voice died and she was forced to admit unattractive possibilities to mind. "I suppose there's a strong background of superstition in the groves."

He nodded. "It has no coherent organization, no firmly established system of practices, but it is here. Ready to be used. By us."

Jahna slumped. "So you're counting on the power of suggestion to close the band around Yuba's throat."

"I have no doubt that it is at work already. In every face she will see affirmation of the fact that she is doomed. There is no way she can escape the atmosphere of expectation except to run out into the vines. And there she will be alone with the most dangerous enemy of all: her own mind."

Troubled, Jahna wrestled with her own sense of accountability. She had no desire for vengeance, particularly not for a slow and torturing vengeance inflicted upon a woman who was more dumb brute than malefactor. "If no one sends for me—"

He studied her levelly. "If no one sends for you then your magic must take its course."

153

"But that's—Beck, I thought you were attempting to lift tentback above the level of primitivism. I thought that was your entire purpose in bringing me here, to put grove society on a more humane level, on a more rational level."

"But do you think it is possible to accomplish those ends with rational means, Peace? Last night, your coronation, were no celebration of rationality. If I had simply informed Hurak and the others in stark terms who you were and why you were coming Nelding way, I would have received no support and certainly no babes. The ritual, the imagery, the pagaentry: all those were necessary to establish your power."

My power, she mused. Somewhere in tentback the big woman was feeling her power now—feeling it at her neck. "Intellectually I agree with you, Beck," she said slowly. "But—"

"I am not speaking intellectually, Peace," he emphasized. "There is no tradition of intellectualism in these groves. There is a tradition of power, of superstition—and of manipulation, sometimes overt, other times covert. We are necessarily playing our game by the rules that prevail on this board."

"But if we ourselves revert—"

One fist balled, a gesture of impatience. *"So we revert.* We take advantage of superstition. We wield every iota of power we can corner. We manipulate. We do all the things you admire least, Peace. But we do them with full awareness. That is the key. And we do them with higher intent than has ever been conceived in tentback before.

"We have a mission."

She gazed for a long time into his intent eyes. Beck Lord had a mission. True. Beck Lord was prepared to sacrifice means to end. He was prepared to sacrifice the big Yuba too, if necessary.

Jahna Swiss was not. Yet it clearly would accomplish nothing to argue the point further. Her glance flicked away from his. Her fingers played across the rough countertop. She had further questions, she realized, for the Father of Pengalen, questions that would buy time for thought. "So

154

what are you getting out of this, Beck?''

He patrolled across the floor, his profile set. ''I will be granted three male babes when you have molded the first set of females and three more when you have molded the second set. Thereafter I will receive an additional three each five years. That was my price.''

Involuntarily Jahna caught a sharp breath. *Of course.* He was grasping at immortality too, grasping at it as no other unpelted Nelding male had hope of doing. Her hands tightened into fists. ''Each five years in perpetuity?''

He nodded crisply. ''That is the agreement.''

So her own moldings would not carry the burden of bringing order out of chaos alone. There would be a parallel line to complement the sisters of the moon—and to manipulate and maneuver them. Jahna's eyes held Beck's—as the eyes of her line would hold the eyes of his line down through the years. *We may be together for centuries,* she realized. *The two of us, side by side, two minds pitted against mud, vine, mockdirad, and each other.*

My ally, my opponent. What won't we see together? What contests of will won't we wage against each other? And what compromises won't we reach, the two of us against the world?

Slowly her breath seeped away. She lowered her eyes. She could hear his breath and feel his will in the room, ready to contest her own. She stared at the countertop, aware of unresolved issues between them. ''There are still things you haven't explained, Beck,'' she said finally.

''So?''

She shrugged lightly. ''You haven't told me how the first mockdirad were bred.''

Beck pulled his chair back from the counter and lowered himself into it, tilting it precariously on its two back legs. ''Now, that is not so mysterious. When the first tanglings left Pengalen and settled the groves, they had neighbors: dirad. Life was casual then. Dirad offered no threat to the tanglings, and so, during those first years, they were permitted to co-occupy the groves. They were even permitted to handle the tangling young, right down to the babes. Dirad aren't always gentle, but then babes aren't particularly fragile either.

"So it happened that the first moldings took pelt. A few years later an epidemic of lung-wad swept the groves. The tanglings who had taken pelt survived, every one of them, even though most of the other tangling babes and many of the adults died. The pelted ones had taken immunity from dirad, you see, along with pelt.

"But no one understood it in those terms. Their survival was magic. They were protected by the spirit of the groves, the same spirit who animated dirad and made halma sweet and caused the lake and the mud sinks to bubble.

"After that babes were deliberately exposed to dirad. It was noted which ones took pelt and which did not. Those who did were considered carriers of power. So from there it is a very short step to the present situation."

"But now mockdirad are molded directly from one other? Not from dirad?"

"True. When the human population increased, dirad moved away into farback. They do not much like to be crowded."

Jahna nodded thoughtfully. "And the disease, lung-wad, is it still a problem?"

"In isolated instances. But our people keep themselves dry and fed now. There have been no more epidemics." His eyes narrowed. Arms clasped across his chest he studied her. "So do you think you can survive a few centuries on our world, Peace?"

Jahna felt her brows draw tight. "I can survive," she said doggedly.

"Good!" His chair thumped to the floor. "In that case, I suggest we both get some sleep. Tomorrow we will begin the molding."

When he had gone, Jahna rested her forehead in her hands. Tomorrow she would begin creating half a dozen new sisters to the moon, half a dozen new daughters to the sun, half a dozen new bearers of star magic.

Tomorrow she would begin reviewing all the broad implications of her mission to Nelding. Today she would sleep. She groped the dim hall to her own room, fell across her bed, rumpled daysuit and all, and numbly pulled up her coverlets.

Tomorrow. Despite exhaustion she stared at the ceiling, unable to sleep. Would an emissary arrive from tentback tomorrow to fetch Jahna to break the spell that was closing Yuba-bull's throat? Or would the big woman hide herself in the vines to die, the first casualty of StarMother's coming? Finally Jahna slept, restlessly, her own throat constricted by a phanthom band.

It was dusk when Jahna woke. She sat in bed, her heart clutching in her chest. In the distance she heard the cry of mockdirad, ragged, harsh. Quickly she jumped up, ran to the hall. One plea flashed phosphorescent through her mind: *not again!*

Beck was already clattering down the stairs to the courtyard. Jahna followed. Valor appeared from the nursery wing, her face pale and strained. Beck whipped around, his lean face taut. "Peace, get back to your room. And mark this cry for future reference as you go."

"They're not coming here!" Jahna cried desperately.

"They are not. That is no social cry. Valor, accompany her up. Both of you stay out of sight until they are past." Quickly he darted across the courtyard to the archway.

"Valor—"

"No, listen to their voices," Valor commanded urgently, drawing her to the stairs.

As they stumbled up the stairs and down the dark hall, Jahna concentrated on the ragged cry. She shook her head, unable to differentiate it from the cry that had filled the courtyard the night before.

"You can hear their anger. They are running huttown way," Valor informed her.

Jahna halted, torn. "A raid? They're going to attack the settlers' barns again?"

"They are."

Jahna hesitated. Valor's face was shadowed, unread-

157

able. She felt no desire to expose herself and invite mock-dirad's attention. But if the pelted males were running huttown way, anger in their cry, someone should attempt to stop them. "Beck isn't—isn't Beck going to turn them back?"

"Beck is no wizard, Jahna," Valor declared strongly.

"But he has influence. He could—"

Valor shook her head, exerting pressure on Jahna's arm. "No. Come quickly so we can pad our ears. Mock-dirad travels fast."

Indeed, the storm of sound was billowing near, and now Jahna began to sense its particular qualities: offence, belligerence, raw anger. "The babies!" she remembered in tardy alarm.

"Elda and her sisters will pad them if possible. Come, Jahna!"

In her room, Jahna scrambled to the bed. Sinking, she pulled her knees tight to her chin and braced herself for the ordeal of sound. The storm call of mockdirad was very near now. It gained in volume, in body. Then, parting, it seemed to flow to either side of the compound, a turbulent stream of sound rushing swiftly around an obstacle.

Around and on. Mockdirad was gone, his voice dying in the distance, vengeance on the run. Victim of anticlimax, Jahna looked up. Valor moved to the window and peered out, eyes shadowed, mouth grave. "It was not so bad, was it?"

"I—no," Jahna agreed lamely. Not so bad here. But it would be bad in huttown when the clean cattle were released from their barns and slaughtered. Bad when the clean poultry was strangled and thrown flopping into the mud. Bad when the labor of dozens of gaunt huttown families was destroyed in an hour's animal fury.

Bad when the destruction might have been averted. Jahna jumped up when she heard Beck on the stair. She met him at the door. "You didn't even try to stop them?" Her voice was brittle.

Beck's dark brows flared in astonishment. "Stop mock-dirad in that mood? Do I look like a barricade or a man?"

158

"You look like a man who promised huttown he would stop mockdirad's raids if they did something for him first," she pointed out hotly. "Perhaps you didn't commit yourself in so many words, but you conveyed that impression. You used their vulnerability to get me here."

Beck's lean body relaxed. "So do you think anyone holds you responsible, Peace?"

"You've *made* me responsible. Oh, in a peripheral way, but I—" Her eyes flashed across the room to Valor's frozen features. Disturbed, she found new thoughts bobbing to the surface of her mind, unwelcome thoughts. "Now I even wonder whether mockdirad originally began raiding huttown on their own initiative or whether it was suggested to them—by someone with an interest in the situation."

Beck's jaw hardened. "Peace, divorce yourself from the ethics of my dealings with huttown. Concern yourself instead with the effectiveness of my dealings in tentback. That is the crucial factor in this situation."

"You obviously don't need much help there," Jahna snapped. "I suppose last night—the coronation I believe you termed it—was actually a stimulus for this raid. Mockdirad certainly went home primed for action. And now huttown is going to feel the full impact of my arrival."

Beck inclined his head. "That seems an accurate analysis. But there was certainly no intention on my part that mockdirad run huttown way with torches and horns. I have no interest in destroying the Fathers by violence. They are destroying themselves quickly enough to satisfy me."

"But you had no interest in going after mockdirad and stopping them, either. Did you?"

Deliberately Beck paced to the window. His eyes sought the dark. "Peace, I will not leave Pengalen until I hear mockdirad return tentback way, even if that is several days. Because I will not risk encountering mockdirad while they are in blood-cry. Our safety here, and a lot more than just that, is dependent on the strength of my personal authority. I have very carefully created for my-self a precedent of success. One failure at this point, just one, and I am plucked."

Jahna frowned, unwilling to accept the validity of his argument. "Plucked?"

"Shaved, skinned—on your world, unmanned. Not an eventuality I can risk, even though it would be more figurative than literal. I cannot risk asserting myself on any issue that I cannot hope to see resolved in my favor. There are not many of those, I admit, but tonight is one."

Disconsolate, Jahna sagged. His argument had the undeniable force of reason. Pengalen was a frail outpost caught between two harsh cultural milieus, tentback and huttown. Soon Beck would move out into tentback with her moldings and his. Their safety, their entire future, depended on the force of his authority. To risk com-promising that tonight, when mockdirad were already lost in the frenzy of cry, when the likelihood of success was plainly minimal, even nonexistent—no. "You're right, of course," she admitted dully.

"I am," he agreed. He peered into the dark again. Then his gaze shifted to Valor. "So have you begun the evening meal?"

"There is squash sliced," Valor responded quickly, skirts bunched between white-knuckled fingers.

"So fry it for us. We have missed too many meals lately." He turned back to Jahna. "One thing, Peace. You have boots and you have a light cube. Do not attempt to leave Pengalen with them tonight."

Her jaw sagged. "You scarcely have to worry about that."

"Good. I didn't seriously think I did."

But afterward, as they ate, Jahna reviewed his warning. Last night she had been crowned and granted pelt. She was celestial sister, commander of magic and myth. So how much power did she actually wield here? Could she have turned mockdirad back to tentback herself?

Guardedly she glanced up at Beck, at Valor. Gathered physically, the three of them were separate in their thoughts. Beck's eyes flickered up to meet hers. In their depths, Jahna caught brief question. She glanced away. Beck Lord had brought her here. Beck Lord had arranged her coronation. Beck Lord had determined the course events were to take around her. How vulnerable was he to rebellion? And how alert was he to its possibility?

Silently she wondered. The more she knew of Beck, the more she doubted he had left any contingency unprovided for.

Finally Beck pushed back his chair, his features taut. "If I am needed, you will find me in the archway. Later, when the order returns to tentback, I will follow. Try not to admit anyone to the compound until I return."

Valor acceded to his instructions gravely.

When supper platters were cleared, Jahna returned to her room. She sat on her bed, thoughts somber. Huttown had done nothing to warm her affections, but she did not like to imagine how those gaunt and bitter people felt tonight as mockdirad came crying down the mud track to ravish barns and granaries.

After a while she lay back. It was then that her eyes, moving to the window, found something new in the night sky. Quickly she jumped up. At a distance, the sullen darkness was embered with orange and red, somber, fierce. Appalled, Jahna stared into the angry glow that was the horizon.

So mockdirad had done more than open barns and slaughter livestock tonight. Jahna's body was rigid, her breath shallow. The surfaces of her eyes captured the distant conflagration. Its heat reflected on her face, searing her. Mockdirad was burning huttown. Perhaps the order had torched only one settlement. Perhaps they were reducing the entire system of villages to ashes. And it was her coming that had lit their torches.

She stood alone at the window for an hour, for longer. Finally the dark night sky smothered back the fiery glow. Orange conflagration became scarlet smoulder. Numbly Jahna rubbed her forearms. First Yuba had fallen victim to StarMother's coming. Now huttown had fallen. How many other victims were to follow?

Reluctantly Jahna paced back to her bed. There was no way she could retreat to the bright-sky rationality and humanity of Peace now, no way she could slide inobtrusively back into her past. That required a starship. She was stranded here and, thanks to Beck, she was committed here. To withdraw her cooperation now would surely engender further chaos, further bloodshed.

She stood to her knees in the mud of Nelding. Wiry vines tied her. Moss was already a hoary growth congesting heart and lungs, smothering spirit. Some of her own innocence had been torched huttown way tonight. So what had she left to bring to bear on the Nelding situation?

Education? Ideals? Principles? How could any of them guide her through the moral morass of this dark world? Bleakly she pulled up her coverlets and stared at the dark ceiling. Later, much later, she slept. It was not a slumber that brought oblivion. Her dilemma continued to confront her in the format of dream. When she woke at dawn, she was more oppressed by her situation than she had been the night before.

Chapter Fourteen

PIETY'S NIGHT under the trees stretched long and chill with her babe glowing moonbright from the sky, dappling the perimeter of the small grove, haunting her. But she slept near dawn and when she was wakened a short time later by dirad crackling through the vines toward the fortress her strength was restored. The inner fire of purpose burned bright again.

And what dirad carried in his dark-furred arms—no, it was not Piety's monster-son. It was another child, an older child, a child terribly lax and gray. But to know that the animals did bear precious burdens Pengalen way, that it was not all some cruel legend, to know that her babe was even now inside the fortress, warm and safe. . . .

Piety emerged from shelter and tripped through the vines to the front wall of the fortress. There she burrowed deep into the thick foliage that covered the ground. The cold was nothing to her today, nor the mud that soaked her garments and turned her hair to snakes. Because she knew she had only to wait here for the right moment. Then she would enter the fortress and search until she found her babe. And when she felt the smoothness of his flesh against hers again she would know what he wanted from her.

She waited, watching the entryway keenly. But when the starhand and the tall woman emerged from the archway shortly carrying—*what they carried*—and when Piety crept through the rattling vines, sprang up, and dared the mouth of the arch, a black brute materialized abruptly at the interior of the arch. Tense, growling, he barred her way, while behind him a small furry grotesquerie croaked and barked indignantly.

Piety flattened herself against the arch wall, strength and bravado suddenly fled, her breath turning light and shallow. If she were to enter, she had only now, while the two women were absent from the fortress. But before she could steel herself to brave the guardian of the arch, a fleshy apparition emerged from a doorway in the courtyard, summoned by the smaller dog's outcry. Gross, horrifying, wattles of excess flesh flouncing on its jowly face, it advanced across the courtyard. Its hair stood in sparse clumps on its scalp. Its voice was menacing. ''Who there?'' It sought the archway with eyes glittery-wild. ''Who out there?''

Electrified, Piety lunged sideways from the archway and hid herself in the vines again. The apparition waddled through the archway and glowered out across the vinescape, head panning with behemoth slowness. Piety pressed her face into the vines, every muscle quivering with fear.

Time passed, time unspeakably cruel. Finally Piety dared look up. Mercifully the apparition had retreated into the fortress, taking the dogs with it. Piety's tense muscles relaxed abruptly, liquefying, spilling her helpless, face down, in the vines.

But that did not mean she was defeated. Soon she organized herself to her feet and retreated to a better vantage point. Her babe had called her here. He waited for her inside the fortress. Sometime, somehow, she must reach him. Vowing fervently that she would she settled into hiding again.

She held purpose before herself like a brightly lit candle through the day. Soon the two women returned to the fortress, but they must leave again sometime, everyone must leave. Somehow her babe would shoo them all away, just as he had led her here. If not today, then tonight when he looked down from the sky and saw how she ached to be reunited with him. And the dogs—Piety shivered—he would send the dogs away too.

But the day stretched sodden and uneventful, until the drenching storm swept across the vinescape, sending Piety in swift retreat to the small grove. Rain found entrance through the thickly thatching limbs of the trees, soaking her. And then when the storm was spent, when she crept from the trees and stood to her ankles in mud, her gaze detected lights on the horizon.

It was torches, many torches, coming in procession toward the fortress. Coming, their direction told her, from the very heart of monsterland. With a frightened gasp she fled to cover of the trees and watched. Like a snake the strand of torches wound from the gathering darkness. Soon the cries of the monsters were raucous on the wet air. Trembling, Piety retreated into the dark heart of the grove.

The grove was scarcely large enough to hide even one wraithlike fugitive. Even so, for a while, Piety thought it would do. For the monsters converged not upon the trees, but upon the fortress, funneling through the entry arch with raw cries of celebration. But that structure soon reached capacity and scores of monsters milled around the entrance and straggled out into the roadway and into the vines, still calling and crying restlessly.

Those cries seemed to leap and bound ever nearer Piety's sparse shelter. Her pulse pounded in fright and she pressed herself against the trunk of a tree, trying to draw the darkness of shadow around her like a concealing cloak. But she knew, hearing the cries come nearer, that it was only a matter of time before she heard the first monster footfall under the trees.

And she was right. For soon there came a whoop so very near that the breath left her lungs. Her eyes, detecting the shadow of the beast that had penetrated her shelter, slowly rolled up, and her slight body slid slowly, helplessly, to the base of the tree in a faint.

And so it was that next morning Piety's eyes opened slowly on the purgatory of captivity. She lay confined between mud-caked monsters, her arms pinioned with rope, her body stiff and chill on its sparse bed of grass and reeds. The reek of sulphur thickened the air. With painful effort she arched her neck to peer around the demon-den. Dimly she remembered her arrival. After whatever celebration was consummated in the fortress, the monsters had carried her here like a bound domestic, flinging her from one set of shoulders to another, laughing drunkenly.

They had gone to earth in this stand of reeds near dawn. Now her captors sprawled ingloriously in sleep, mouths gaping, faces lax, eye sockets deserted. Piety's head dropped and her eyes closed, squeezing out hot tears. She was helpless, bound, hemmed by sleeping bodies, her fingers dead, her arms useless. Her mind trembled with terrified images of what the monsters intended for her when they woke. She raised her head again. There were better than a dozen adults in the band, the big woman breasted like a domestic, five younger women, grotesque in their muddy carapaces, and the men. There were two youths too, a single girl, and two toddling babes. But Piety suffered no delusion that this was in any way an association of proper families. This was a band of degenerates.

Her head sank again. These were garbage—but how was she better? She had loosed corruption on the flesh of her very own unborn babe. And, wandering alone, she had stuffed herself with filth and licked water from the leaves of the garbage vine. If Sister Nair saw her now, covered in mud, her hair loose on her shoulders, her feet bare—Sister would recognize garbage!

Piety flailed herself with contempt. She was worse than these monsters! They had been corrupted against their will before birth, but she was an active corruptor—of herself and of her babe. Whatever they did to her when they woke, she deserved!

Later, in the dark, yellow stench harsh to her nostrils, she started awake at a touch. Torches were lit. The many-breasted woman bent over her, dipper in hand, hair loose, flesh flabby. She lifted Piety's head and laid the dipper in her mouth. "So eat, huttown," she muttered, her words throaty and indistinct.

Liquid touched Piety's lips. She trembled with conflicting emotions. Her devil-weakness won and she sucked the

166

edge of the dipper, drawing thick sweet ooze through her lips into her grateful mouth.

When the big woman left her, other members of the band came to examine her. The mood of celebration was past now. Tonight the members of the band stooped over her solemnly, one laying back her shirtwaist to examine her breasts, another divesting her of her skirts, a third pulling her hair away and examining her head and back intently. She peered up at them from terrified eyes, tense, ready for ill-usage.

But when her examiners had completed their inspection, they moved away serious and still. The big woman returned and threw Piety's clothes back over her. Then all the members of the band gathered several meters away, squatting in the trampled reeds, conferring gravely. Piety craned her neck to watch them, her heart hammering. That they were plotting her disposition was clear from the speculative glances that darted her way.

However, before the conference reached its conclusion, there was a cry on the night air, distant, compelling. Monster-heads snapped alert. Eyes glistened by torch-light, seeking the unseeable. With a scramble the youths and men swarmed out of the reed-den. The cry came nearer, billowing out into a multiplicity of voices, harsh and angry. The big woman trampled to the edge of the reed bed, muttering command back to her juniors.

The night-cry swelled out into a sweeping storm of anger, running on a hundred pair of feet through the vines. Somewhere beyond the reeds, the men of the band disappeared, bearing torches with them.

Soon the cry sickened and died in the distance. The big woman returned, her heavy features self-occupied. She stood between the cluster of younger women and Piety. Finally she approached Piety. Turning her, she worked her hands free of their bindings. Piety gasped as blood flowed back into her fingers. She managed to sit, trying to pull her clothes with her. But her hands were numb. The garments fell away, leaving her exposed.

The big woman was no more desirous of Piety's nakedness than Piety herself. Pulling Piety to her feet, the big woman yanked her shirtwaist over her and anchored her skirts at her waist again. "You will not leave us," she commanded, when Piety was dressed. "You do, mock-dirad eat you tonight."

Piety was aware of weak tears sliding down her cheeks. Even her lips were numb. "No," she replied, her voice trembling, "I—"

The big woman tried to read her intentions, staring at her long and deeply. Finally she gestured downward. "So sleep," she instructed. Before she left, she turned back again. "You don't leave us," she reiterated.

"I won't," Piety quavered, huddling back into her reed bed.

The big woman returned to her companions. Together they crouched in a circle, their grim faces rendering the night a vigil. Piety watched their silent huddle miserably. Her hands were free, her feet unhindered. But she was in monsterland now. Even if she slipped away, even if she stumbled back across the vinescape, there was no geographic referrent to guide her back to Pengalen. And all the males of the band had disappeared into darkness, following a cry in the night. Who knew what she might meet beyond the reeds tonight?

Piety closed her eyes, hoping fervently for her monster-son to appear, to guide and inspire her. But he did not show himself. And she knew she would never survive the tangles of tentback without his guidance this night.

Chapter Fifteen

ZUNIIN BREACHED shadowrim at first dawnlight, hard legs still pumping, lungs sucking, teeth bared to the morning chill. Face and body were streaked yellow and black: Sulphur and ashes she wore, her waistlet tossed into the flames of a bawling huttown barn. Now she laxed her pace through the grove, relishing the earthen familiarity of treehome, the mossed timbers of mockdirad compound, deserted now, the dozen dead fires in their pits, the tangling bodies sprawled dreamless in their tents.

Sleeping! Last night the timbers of huttown had felt flame. Damp, dark, they had smoked alight, then flared to lick the skies, their occupants spilling out into the mud, helpless in black-trousered fury, weaponless against the pelted powers of tentback. And while huttown burned, tanglings and Mothers had slept in tentback!

Zuniin snorted. Reaching the Mother's fire, she threw herself down panting. Greasy stakes poked earth in a circle. A caked mush pot was tossed to one side. Voraciously Zuniin snatched it and scraped it with her nails, gouging out the leavings of last night's meal, devouring them. She picked the pot clean, then seized a roasting stake and sucked chitterling grease. But that was more flavor than substance, and hunger was suddenly total.

There was nothing here to satisfy her. Urgently she took foot to the larder tent. On her knees she pawed at containers and cool-pots. Her hands quivered as she pushed aside reedcloth and found coiled ropes of halma. Urgently she tore one rope from its pot, dragged it away, and sank down, slashing though fibers with her teeth.

169

As halma energy infused her, she was gripped by exhilaration. *She* had run the flanks of the order, throat erupting vengeance, her limbs matching theirs. *She* had torched the Fathers out into the night. *She* had burned huttown. So who was only Mother now? And who was mockdirad unrecognized? Who was brother of the order, as swift, as strong, as savage? Zuniin's eyes glittered, relishing memory of the night.

Then she heard the furor in the vineland. Pattering swiftly back through the grove, she saw heads raise from sleep, faces startled pasty. Exhilarated, she reached shadowrim to see the first rank of mockdirad bawl across the vines, torches windtorn, dark fur matted with perspiration, stained with ashes and mud. Zuniin caught a savage breath. *We burned huttown.*

Bellowing, calling, mockdirad surged across shadowrim. Horny teeth gnashed. Midarms flexed. Their odor was strong on the damp air, an acrid assault. With a ragged cry, mockdirad spread through the grove, bullying its inhabitants from bed with their torches.

But the dance was brief. Mockdirad was quickly spent. Soon, sooty, the pelts lunged back to their compound. Behind those walls their cry babbled and died into day's sleep. Only the shrill complaint of one mockdirad babe coursed through the morning air, peevish.

And Zuniin was left crouched alone around her anger. For her victory had died with the dance. *She* had run with the order. *She* had fired huttown and smeared its ashes across her breasts and buttocks. But at dawn she had not dared dance with the order. She had not dared inject her unpelted body into the pattern of lunging celebrants. She had cowered instead, afraid of challenge, derision, rejection. And when the order sprang to the compound, Zuniin was abandoned to the company of tanglings and Mothers.

That was the company of impotents and fools! For a long while she huddled in shadow, her sudden fall bitter in her craw. Finally she stood and flipped her hair over her face. Doggedly she groped back to Mother's fire, to her own dark tent. There she threw herself down on her moss bed with a black curse. *If she had pelt*. . . .

She rolled on her back and glared up into the woody roof of her tent. So what was pelt? Hair, nothing more. Hair of a certain texture, hair growing in certain places.

Hair growing on certain individuals.

Her breath noised in her ears. What was pelt? Pelt was everything!

And more.

Finally, as life settled around grove fires, Zuniin's eyes closed and she plummeted into sleep.

She did not grovel long in the pit of dreams. Soon old Dahda was rapping at her shoulder, voice crackling. Twisting, Zuniin was awake and away in one motion, across the small tent, back pressed to its woody trunk.

Dahda's eyes were dark with anger. "So here you are, mud crawler."

Zuniin flashed teeth defiantly. "So I ran huttown way and helped the burning. That's where I've been." And where were you, old skin?

"So did you think Yuba-bull would never live to tell us?" Dahda crackled, her hand wrenching into Zuniin's hair. She yanked her face near.

Zuniin snarled and whipped her head away, rough hair tearing. "Live to tell what, skin?" she spat, veils of flesh falling back from sharp teeth.

"You know what she told when we ran back here and found star magic choking off her throat? She told who made her throw herself on StarMother. She told who made her pull hair and dig for blood. And the person was you, Zu."

Zuniin's eyes flared indignantly. "I never!"

"So is Yuba-bull clever enough to lie? Or is she a dumb-brute who can be used by any useless Mother who is afraid to take her own curse?"

Zuniin glared at her. "So do you think I got inside Yuba's muscles and moved her? I never made her do anything!"

"I think you got inside her head," Dahda accused, voice silibant, eyes narrowed. "I think you pushed what little intelligence bull owns into one corner of her brain and filled the rest of her with your own intentions. So when she stepped before StarMother she was not Yuba-bull. She was Zuniin. When her hands grappled into StarMother's hair, they were not Yuba's hands. They were Zuniin's.

"So now you are coming lakeside to see what you have done to our grove sister."

Never! Zuniin's head whipped around seeking escape. Never would she go see Yuba die!

But there was no escape past Dahda. Dahda crouched, barring her way. "Leave my tent!" Zuniin grated fiercely. "I came here for sleep!"

"And I came here for girl! So do you want me to call Narrel with his whips?"

"No!" It was not Zuniin's word. It was panic-torn from some other throat, some weak throat.

"Then come!"

Zuniin trembled with powerless fury, her teeth set hard. "I did nothing to Yuba."

"Come!"

Helpless, Zuniin fanned her rough hair forward, hiding her eyes. "Take me, old skin."

Grunting, Dahda seized her arm. With a peremptory blow, she propelled Zuniin from shelter. Zuniin scrambled to her feet, snatching her hair tight across her face, panting with impotent fury. "You never burned huttown, old skin!" she shrieked indignantly.

"And I never crawled inside another Mother's brain and closed star magic on her throat!" Dahda's hand closed on Zuniin's arm again, implacable.

Struggling, Zuniin was dragged through the morning grove. She sensed rather than saw the tangling audience to her disgrace. She sobbed furiously, tears coursing into her hair. "I never, I never," she protested.

Then they reached vineland. Ungently Dahda divested Zuniin's face of its hairy shield. "You slept through Becklord's arrival, mud crawler. If you had heard what he said behind mockdirad walls this morning, you would swallow your tongue about burning huttown.''

Zuniin flared, snatching her arm free. "I burned it!"

Swiftly Dahda landed a kick that toppled Zuniin into the mud. "So do you think huttown is going to do nothing about that? Do you think huttown is a squash waiting to be thrown into the pot?"

"Huttown is dying," Zuniin countered, pulling herself up. She smeared her muddy hands across her torso aggressively. "Becklord said that himself. Huttown is putting half its live babes to the vines so they are tentback now. Huttown is killing itself every new day, draining its blood into us.''

"Huttown is not dead yet. And huttown may not be dead for five hundred years now. You fine pelts burned out so many barns and granaries they may begin eating Nelding to keep from starving this winter. And once huttown stops starving itself on clean food, we will face a well-fed enemy instead of a weakling one."

"So we will roast them and feed them to our babes!" Zuniin spat. "We should have roasted them last night. We should have run after them and burned their clothes off their backs and their beards off their faces. We should have torched their clean babes and their—"

Dahda's second blow was not so casual as her first. It caught Zuniin's jaw with a crack and sent her headfirst into a small mud sink. Zuniin shrilled, hot sulphur mud closing around her face. Thrashing, scrambling, she came out of the yellow mud, her face coated, her nostrils clogged. She sputtered for breath, shaking her head violently. Blinded, she stumbled away, fleeing the old Mother.

But Dahda was not to be fled from. Before Zuniin could clear her eyes, the old Mother grappled her arm again, shaking her. "So where do we get fresh babes if you burn the Fathers, crawler? Are you going to birth enough to balance?" She pounded Zuniin's belly with the back of her hand.

"And if the Fathers don't starve this winter, how long do you think they will continue to feed the ranks of a death-enemy? How long before they decide to destroy their garbage babes along with their domestic monsters instead of setting them out for tentback? And how do you think these groves can grow without Fathers' seed?" She spun Zuniin off balance, fanning her face with her open palm. "So?" she demanded. *"So?"*

Zuniin choked and spat mud. When she opened her eyes, grit invaded them, scratching, stinging. *"So!"* she shrieked, a capitulation.

"So now you know the beginning of what you wise pelts did last night," Dahda muttered, dragging her away again.

By the time they reached lakeside, Zuniin's face had caked and cracked. Her eyes watered, her hair stank. She stumbled weakly, resentfully. Had she destroyed the groves all by herself? Had *she* killed the lines and depleted the tents? She had only run with the order.

And we should have burned them all! Deep, savage, she knew that. *We should have torched every beard and every skirt! Next we should torch StarMother herself.* Where but with StarMother did all these troubles begin?

Where indeed?

They topped the lakeside rise. Before them that dark body spread, yellow-streaked, surface sluggishly surging. The stench of sulphur enveloped them. Grimly Dahda led Zuniin down the slope to the lake itself. There grew a lone stand of dispirited reeds, a trampled path leading to its center. Zuniin balked, but Dahda steered her roughly into the reeds and shoved her forward.

Yuba-bull lay on her side, her dozen breasts laboring, her big face sheened with perspiration. She sucked breath harshly, totally occupied with the process of drawing air past the invisible constriction of her windpipe. Her staring eyes were dull with anguish.

"So now you see how you have lessened our Mother force by two," Dahda stated, her voice raw. "Because now you are banished from our grove too, Zuniin. We don't need a worthless Mother who births no one and kills her own kind. So if you are seen in our grove again, you will be whipped out into the vines and trampled. And any person who gives you tent or mush will be treated like-wise." The old woman's eyes glowed fiercely. "I will not meet you again, Mother. Unless you sprout pelt and return to us transformed."

Zuniin stared up at the matriarch, thunderstruck. Banished? "No," she gasped.

"Yes," Dahda hissed back. "The word is around to Mothers, mockdirad, and tanglings. So do not bother to return. You are no Mother of our grove now."

Exiled? Forever? Zuniin sank to her haunches, trying to grasp what Dahda said. Never pierce shadowrim of tree home again? That meant never pierce shadowrim of any tentback grove again. If Dahda exiled her from home-grove, mockdirad would exile her from all. She would be a nomad, cast adrift in the vines. There would never be Mother's chatter or tangling bodies to sleep against on cold nights. She would be alone, prey to cold, hunger, and roving outcasts. She would be anyone's victim.

"I come from line," she protested, her voice rising. "My sisters live in every grove of tentback. My face—"

"So your face is erased from this grove now. And it will never return," Dahda pronounced heavily.

Zuniin jumped up, suddenly pleading. "My line—"

"You have never chosen to contribute to your line, blood or mold. So run into farback and establish your own grove, crawler. Be everything, mockdirad, mother, and Mother. You were the one who burned huttown. Now breed a new tentback all by yourself. Lift the magic from Yuba's throat and you will already have your livestock. She is banished now, too."

Yuba-bull moaned, hands clutching her throat, her puddle-gray eyes protesting.

Zuniin seized at the matriarch in desperation. "Old Mother—"

"Old skin, I heard it," Dahda snorted, freeing herself. "Stay here and tend your stock, crawler. If you follow me, Narrel will be glad to temper his whips on you." Face grim, the old Mother turned and rattled through the reeds.

Zuniin slumped back to her haunches. The sound of

Yuba's laboring breath was chorus to her own despair. Banished. And from whom did that stem but StarMother?

No one. There was no other cause for what had happened to her. There was no other cause for what was happening to Yuba.

Yuba, big clumsy tool. Zuniin's glance rested on the big woman. "So StarMother topped you," she observed bitterly.

"Steal— babe—"

Slowly Zuniin's stunned mind began to work again. "StarMother topped you because she had Becklord and mockdirad there to lend muscle. But if you had been alone with her, Yuba-bull, if you had taken her in the vines, if you had held a knife in your hand or a rope—"

The big woman's eyes clouded with pain. "No— blood," she gasped in protest.

Zuniin's fists tightened. "So! No blood, no hair, no water, no dung!" she spat. "So how do we kill this StarMother without touching her?" But she was not speaking to Yuba-bull now. She was speaking to herself, struggling with what she knew of the star magic. A drop of blood could kill. A single hair. A flake of skin. How was she to be sure, if they tightened a noose on StarMother's neck, that StarMother would not manage to spit upon them with her dying breath?

Desperately her mind groped through the list of possible dooms. Restless, she jumped up. How could she think in this clump of reeds, with the bull gasping at her feet? "So I'll run back this way at dark," she flung down, callously launching herself from the reed nest before Yuba could voice protest.

Beyond the reeds, she pattered through the vines, racing nowhere, hair wind-torn, legs pumping. How to kill StarMother without risking star magic? There was no way. She flung herself down on a hummock of stiffgrass. No way at all. Urgently she flopped to her back and made pictures in the gray cloud-belly. She made weapons. She made scenes.

All of them were useless! She flung herself up and ran

again, flying through the vinelands until her legs ached and her breath was agony.

All she had was Yuba. She would have to crawl into bull's brain and push bull herself aside, manipulate bull's arms and legs. She would have to turn bull into her own creature—again. It was the only way.

But it would never work if bull expired first.

Near dark Zuniin returned to the reeds with halma and squash. Yuba tossed restlessly on her bed, her face shadowed, her breath harsh. Quickly Zuniin tore into the rope of halma. She popped white bulbs into her mouth, chewed them fine, and then bent near the big woman. Placing her lips to Yuba's, she discharged the mushed bulbs. "Swallow."

The big woman choked and coughed, but by dark she had taken nourishment. Zuniin could detect fresh strength firming her face, making her breath steadier, deeper. Zuniin sank back and bolted her own meal, preparing for a second voyage into bull's brain. But when she had finished, she found bull asleep. She stared for a long while at the sleeping woman, thinking. Then she too slept.

Chapter Sixteen

IT WAS dusk when they looked up from their platters at the unexpected sound of chanting. Jahna's eyes flickered to Beck, to Valor. Both Neldings were startled into stark immobility. Then Beck's features twisted. His chair jarred back. Without word, he clattered to the door.

"What is it?" Jahna demanded, finding her voice. The sound welled heavy on the damp air, measured, solemn, belligerent, a somber liturgy of menace. When Valor did not reply, Jahna hurried to a window. Below, Beck's dogs bounded after him into the archway. Quickly Jahna darted across the room and into the hall.

Downstairs she ran across the courtyard, Valor's anxious call unheeded. Beck was poised rigid at the outer mouth of the archway, dogs reluctantly at heel. "What is it?" she gasped when he glanced around. Beyond the archway the road was a deserted track darkening into dusk.

"The Fathers."

Jahna stiffened. "They're attacking tentback?"

"Ha!" Beck's derision was sharp. "You'll never see any huttown Father step into any grove beyond Pengalen. He knows who rules shadowrim."

Jahna's fists clenched nervously. So the Fathers were marching Pengalen way. Marching to demand what righteous revenge for last night's atrocity? And marching to demand it from whom?

Valor entered the archway, shooing dogs back into the courtyard. "Should we not pad the babes against this?"

"Go," Beck agreed. "And do not come down again, Peace, until the Fathers have withdrawn."

Jahna peered anxiously into the empty roadway before following Valor to the nursery. The six babes were already boxed for the night. Their reaction to the abrupt introduction of windings and padding was combative. But even over their angry protest Jahna could hear the chanting advance of the Fathers. Righteous anger freighted their heavy cadence, bitter, dark, insistent.

The last babe padded, Jahna took a window in time to see two black-clad Fathers advance through the archway, dark beards stern, hollow eyes fierce. Beyond the arch she could see the orange flicker of torches on the road. As the two Fathers strode across the courtyard, the chant beyond the walls fell to a belligerent grumble.

"So what is this?" Beck demanded, barring entrance to any wing of the quad, his dogs crouched behind him, muscular enforcement.

The two Fathers, one lean, one stalwart, halted and crossed arms across their chests, tight-knotted heads erect. "This is the delegation which will now escort the star cadet back to Forgiven to await her ship."

"Oh? It was my understanding Humble Nodd would come for Cadet Swiss in two years' time. Has that period somehow passed already?"

"The period of our tolerance has passed, Lord," the lean Father crackled, his craggy features acrid. "Last night your garbage pelts torched our homes and our barns. All our pure domestics and our clean crops were wasted. Six of our women and children died in flame and others will not tend field for many weeks. The ranks of the Fathers themselves are less by two tonight."

"I fail to see how the fact that four settlements were burned affects our agreement concerning Cadet Swiss," Beck responded sharply. "Does someone testify that she ran with mockdirad?"

The lean father was board-rigid. "Someone testifies that tentdirad ran in her name, Lord. Those who suffered the flame were not deaf, you know. Therefore the First

179

Fathers have determined that this cadet represents an inflammatory element and that she shall be deported immediately. To that end, Father Nodd has already faxed the starwaves for an appropriate ship. In five days it will arrive and she will be returned in the direction of her own world.

"And never will another star trollop be summoned here, Lord," he continued, his voice condemnatory. "Nor will you again be addressed with the title Father. Through your treachery you have shown yourself to be man of the tents. Therefore you will now be treated as man of the tents." His words echoed off log walls with bitter finality. "Now we will take custody of Cadet Swiss."

Beck did not step aside. Nor did his dogs yield. "Cadet Swiss has contracted to stay two years on Nelding, Barr. I do not release her from that agreement."

The second Father spoke, his voice choking up from a deep barrel of outrage. "Then she will be released from her contract at arms, Lord. The ship we have faxed carries weaponed commandos who will take this woman by force if necesssary." His lips pulled wide in a fierce grin. "We need not remind you that no starship is vulnerable to the torches of tentdirad. That is more than tentdirad can say of their vulnerability to the devil's weapons carried aboard the ship we have summoned."

Jahna could see tension tighten Beck's shoulders. Deliberately he crossed his own arms against his chest. "There are other types of weapons, Fathers," he said slowly, "and other vulnerabilities."

The two Fathers exchanged a glance.

"There are weapons and vulnerabilities of many orders, in fact. There is vulnerability, for instance, to universal shame."

Lean Father's voice crackled harsh. "Speak to tentdirad then. They are the ones who have killed and destroyed."

"Ah," Beck agreed somberly. "But they are not the ones who have degenerated."

180

Both Fathers stiffened visibly. "Tentdirad are the garbage here!" stalwart Father spat.

"But they are your garbage, Weyl. They are what you have birthed from your own so-called clean women. They are visible proof that you carry contamination in your genes. Are you eager for the universe to know that?" His gaze probed from Father to Father. "You have gone to lengths to lose your garbage in the vines. When star merchants stop huttown way, you tell them nothing about the monsters you have produced. So no one beyond this world knows yet what the life of the felicitous virtues has produced on Nelding.

"And no one need know. Unless you motivate me to tell them."

Father Weyl had flushed scarlet. "And how do you propose to tell them? There is one fax unit on this world. Do you think we intend to allow you to use it?"

Beck shook his head. "There is a portable fax unit too, Fathers. It has range right across the starfield to Peace. And farther." With a gesture he indicated the nursery window. "There she stands."

Startled, Jahna shrank from the two malevolent gazes that slashed her way.

"If Cadet Swiss is taken by force and loaded unwilling back to her own world, do you think anything will prevent her from telling the universe what she found here? Before she has even lofted above cloud-belly, Nelding and its Fathers will be in the process of becoming synonymous with degeneracy and shame. So the choice is yours, Fathers. But it is not the choice you thought when you breached Pengalen shadowrim. Is it?"

The two rigid Fathers exchanged a long bitter glance. Weyl's voice rumbled up ominously. "And how can we be assured that if we respect this trollop's wishes, she will not malign us nevertheless in two years' time?"

Beck shrugged. "It's surely possible to reach agreement with Cadet Swiss."

Again fierce gazes rose to Jahna's window. "And what

181

is your choice, Cadet?'' Father Barr demanded abruptly, his voice a weapon.

Jahna scraped down into her chest to find her own voice. "I—I can't possibly make a decision of that order on such short notice."

"But you agree that if you are granted free choice, you will not malign the Fathers of Pengalen across the stars?"

Jahna bristled. But this obviously was not the time to argue the Fathers' twisted system of values. "I agree," she committed herself warily.

"And that is a solemn commitment? You are willing to swear it before God the Mighty Power as well as before the Fathers?"

"A Peace citizen doesn't have to swear her intentions before any special audience to validate them," Jahna responded sharply.

Bitter faces creased with distaste. Stiffly Father Barr said, "Then we ourselves make our own commitment. In five days time a starship shuttle will appear on this site. At that time you may state your decision to the commander of that shuttle. In exchange for that freedom of choice, then, do you agree to our terms firmly and finally?"

"Haven't I already said so?"

Father Weyl's face suffused violet. "Very well. Then we will help you make your final choice. Already the pyres have been set against the walls of this structure. When I raise my hand, the signal will pass and those pyres will be lit. These walls will be slow to burn but burn they will, to the ground. That we know from watching our own huts and barns burn only one night ago.

"So if you elect to spend two years in the groves with animals and garbage, it is your choice, trollop!" Stiffly the Nelding raised one arm, hand fisted.

Jahna's alarmed glance shot to the archway. A turmoil of torches flurried to heed Weyl's signal. "Citizen Weyl!" she exclaimed. "This is certainly no—"

"You have committed yourself!" Weyl rumbled, his purple cheeks split by a vengeful grimace. Turning, he stalked to the archway, followed by his lean partner.

Jahna glanced down at Beck. His fists were tight at his sides. Urgently she ran from the nursery and down the stairs. In the courtyard, Beck had not moved. Although his back was rigid, his face was not as grim as she had anticipated. "Can't you stop them?" she cried, aware of the ludicrous repetition of last night's accusation.

His eyes swiveled to hers. "So do I look like a man or a barricade?" he demanded, his lips curling into a taut smile.

"You look like a man who's standing here allowing a crowd of degenerates to burn his home!"

"Ha!" he agreed in appreciation. "But my chance of stopping them seems rather faint, Peace."

"You could—" Urgently she sought for measures. "We could set the dogs on them."

"No, I will save my dogs for another day." His eyes roved out the archway. The road was dark, deserted, but there were hoarse voices at every wall of Pengalen. "Don't you think you could be doing something yourself?"

"I—of course! But what?" The Fathers would not listen to her.

"Packing your personal goods might be an intelligent first step." His face became totally serious. "I am sorry to move you to the groves, Peace, but it doesn't appear there is much choice."

Jahna gaped at him, unable to accept his easy accommodation to the destruction of Pengalen. "Beck—"

But what could they do, she, Beck, and Valor alone? The Fathers would listen to none of them. Fight the fires, then? But even if they commanded an adequate water supply and some means of pressuring it into a stream against the walls, three people could only extinguish so many pyres. "We might be able to save one wing, Beck."

He shook his head decisively, turning to the nursery door. "No. Go pack your goods, Peace, and bring them to the yard. I will help Valor with the babes." Turning, he disappeared into the doorway.

Jahna stared after him, protest still bubbling in her mind. To simply pack and scurry away, to allow the

Fathers to destroy the only establishment on Nelding that was neither a part of huttown nor of tentback—but what choice had they?

None. Unresigned, Jahna took the stairs and threw her personals into cases. By the time she returned to the nursery, dark rolls of smoke were visible, underlit by scarlet and orange flame. Beck and Valor had stuffed unused boxes with nursery supplies and appurtenances. The babies had been unpadded and were shrilling in their relidded boxes.

"Start carrying them down to the courtyard, Peace," Beck instructed, proffering a length of fabric. "But first wet this and tie it over your face."

"But where are we going to take them? We can't carry them to tentback in the dark."

"My tent beyond the walls will accommodate us for the night. We won't even need torches to light our way."

Numbly Jahna ferried boxed infants down the stairs. With a sense of unreality she arranged them in the middle of the courtyard. On Peace, the timbers of Pengalen would have flared up with a bright *pouf*. Here, soggy, they produced musty rolls of dark smoke, heavy and odorous. It hung heavy in the courtyard, thick with particles of ash and moss. Her eyes stung in protest.

By the time they were ready to evacuate their gathered possessions, Jahna could see flame through the rotted front walls of the fortress. It reached in sullenly to kindle the thick sheaves of moss which packed the deserted cells. The damp moss took fire reluctantly, belching musty smoke.

Masked, they deposited the boxed infants in the empty roadway. When their possessions were clear of the fortress, Jahna and Valor followed Beck through the vines to the small grove Jahna had discovered on her second day at Pengalen. Behind them the burning fortress groaned in ancient agony, a hundred timbrous voices expressing in final summation the anguish Pengalen had known in its span.

When the last infant was sheltered, Jahna dropped beneath the limbs of the tent, coughing. "Beck, if the wind turns this way—"

The soot-faced individual who deposited her cases at her feet shook his head. "There is no wind tonight. If there were, perhaps we wouldn't have this cloud of smoke sitting on us."

Jahna shuddered in a coughing spasm, appreciating the accuracy of his observation. Wind might have carried the smoke toward them or from them, but in any case it would have swept the air. Instead, heat carried a certain portion of the smoke up. The rest simply rolled away from Pengalen at ground level, sluggish, stagnating. "Then maybe we should try to reach tentback tonight. If mockdirad see the fire and come this way—"

"Let us hope not," Beck said wearily, dropping to the bed of leaves. "We have difficulty enough populating Old Mother without open warfare between the Fathers and the pelts." He swiped at his forehead, bringing away a blackened hand. "With luck the groves are already asleep and tomorrow there will be only ashes here to inflame the pelts. You can be sure I'll throw water on Hurak and his brothers before they ever see those ashes."

Helplessly Jahna agreed. Valor joined them, her deep eyes reflecting the conflagration with slack despair. Jahna zipped her cape out of her bag and shrugged it around her. A week ago it had seemed impossible that she was to spend two years at Pengalen. Now that sentence was wiped off the books. It was tentback that faced her instead, dark groves, mud sinks, sulphur lake, mockdirad.

She shivered, remembering reluctantly that this new sentence was not irrevocable. The Fathers had already summoned a starship. In five days, if she elected, she could return Pengalen way, board a shuttle, and loft cleanly back to Peace, leaving behind the myriad physical and moral problems Nelding posed.

If she elected. . . . Suddenly the burden of choice was hers. And that was not a welcome circumstance. She glanced up. Valor and Beck were studying her, ash-black faces grave. Beck's brows arched. "Well, Peace?"

She shook her head. "I don't know."

Unexpectedly his hand closed on hers. "You won't break contract, Peace. You've seen enough of Nelding life already to know that we need you more than you'll ever be needed again on any world."

But Jahna could not answer the pressure of his fingers. Tonight, exhausted, conflict-torn, she was unconvinced of her own ultimate integrity.

The babies were soon quiet in their boxes. Valor decanted water. Thirstily Jahna eased her smoke-raw throat and splashed her face. It was not long before both Neldings were stretched asleep on the thick layer of leaves that padded the floor of the small grove.

Jahna lay beside them wrapped in her cape, eyes wide. Her hand rested on her light cube for reassurance. But the thoughts its smooth cubic surfaces stimulated were discomforting. The light cube was an alien artifact on this world. Exposed to conditions it had not been designed to withstand, it would soon prove victim to accelerated deterioration and a markedly shortened life. And she was its human counterpart, already eroding under stresses she had never been conditioned to withstand.

Racked by doubt, shaken by recurrent coughing spasms, she watched the madhouse of Pengalen die in ashes. The sky was graying with dawn before she slept.

Soon Valor and Beck were stirring, tending fretful infants. Jahna rolled away moaning in protest, eyes and respiratory passages raw, flesh hot and prickly. Throwing off her cape, she was immediately assailed by morning chill. Miserably she reswaddled herself, struggling to regain oblivion.

Failing. An hour later she trekked tentback way with Beck. Valor and the six infants remained in the grove. Blue-white mists rose across the vinelands, dawn spirits merging into the damp of day. Jahna moved painfully, the smell of smoke stale in her nostrils. Beck led the way silently, preoccupied, his face drawn beneath random slashes of ash.

Soon they paused to dig halma, but this morning Jahna

found the white bulbs tasteless. She swallowed painfully and slumped on the hillock, waiting dully for energy to reactivate her. For a brief distance afterward, her legs assumed their burden graciously. Then they became lumbrous and unwilling again. Jahna stumbled, aware of Beck turning to study her. "Do you want to wait here, Peace?"

"Wait for what?" she demanded shakily, dropping to the vines to rest.

"I can send mockdirad for you with a litter. In fact, it might make a much more impressive entry."

Jahna groaned, digging her splayed fingers into her hair. "Beck, don't you think we could forgo an entrance today? Besides, I left Hurak's grandfather with Valor," she added, a hopeful afterthought.

Beck squatted, his face thoughtful. "Point," he agreed. His fingers picked at vine, shredding and scattering. "But I consider an entry of some kind necessary to underscore certain elements of the situation."

"Maybe we could just forget about drawing lines today," Jahna suggested plaintively. "Maybe we could just stagger into the grove and pass out. Incognito."

Beck smiled faintly. "We'll pass out later, Peace. When we've made it clear, in a public manner, just where responsibility lies for the present situation."

Jahna's forehead clenched. The matter of blame lay deep in one of those gray areas beyond reach of her fogged mind. Doggedly she wobbled to her feet. "Then I'll make it on my own powerpak," she declared. But as she stood, the world drained dizzily away, green dimming to gray, gray to black. Laxing knees slowly lowered her back toward the tangles.

Beck caught her elbow. He supported her as life slowly pulsed back to her head. "I'm all right," she protested, regaining control of her legs. "It's just a—a—" She sought helplessly for some brisk term to define the etiology of her weakness.

"Smoke inhalation," he supplied. "Valor and I breathe the stuff in quantity every winter. Our lungs consider it a normal component of the atmosphere. Yours are not so sophisticated—yet." He released her. "But the entry, Peace: You can pierce shadowrim this morning as Star-Mother outraged or as StarMother devastated. In either case, my role is to see that blame for your condition is properly assigned. But you must preselect your own role and then resolve to play it consistently."

"Meaning that if I march into the grove in full outrage, I'd better not faint at Hurak's feet." Deliberately Jahna sat again in the wet vines. "Somehow devastation seems out of character, Beck." Did the sister of the moon weaken in the face of woodsmoke?

He inclined his head thoughtfully. "But can you play outrage? In your present—devastated—condition?"

Her head dropped. "Couldn't I be so outraged I—I refuse even to see them?"

Slowly Beck folded to the vines opposite her, his eyes narrowing. "Ah. So outraged you don't even want to raise your eyes to mockdirad today because all you see in his face is shame."

Jahna studied his intent eyes. "Yes. It's mockdirad I'm actually angry with," she ventured, finally beginning to apprehend the trend of his thoughts. "Because huttown wouldn't have burned Pengalen—"

"Correct, if mockdirad had not burned huttown. Star-Mother's is the peace ethic and mockdirad violated it flagrantly. Now they are going to bear the full consequences, if only in terms of disgrace."

"But then I should have given some sign yesterday. I should have gone into tentback. I should have—"

"You sent your first minister," he assured her. "And the words you put into his mouth—well, you have a fine command of imagery, StarMother. Every pelt in the grove was slapped flat." He smiled. "Your analysis of the Nelding situation was, in fact, almost identical to my own."

"I'm very selective in the personnel department."

"Um. But today," he mused, thoughts turned inward again.

"Today, in addition to being exhausted, bedraggled,

sniffly, and gritty, I'm outraged," she asserted decisively. "I'm so outraged I'm going to seclude myself as soon as I reach the grove. I refuse to watch dance or hear song. I don't even want to hear mockdirad's voice before tomorrow sunset. In fact, I think his first act of atonement should consist of submitting himself to a period of silence. And even after he completes that, even after he shows me he understands why I despise his actions, he should realize there is a very good chance I may return to my own world when the shuttle appears. Because I'm not sure Nelding is ready for me, Beck."

His glance flickered up warily. "You'll never find a world readier, Peace. Old Mother has offered Nelding an unparalleled gift. But if we have to follow the evolutionary track up through all the stages of civilization *at a normal pace*, how long do you think it will be before we're able to share our gift with any other world? We may not even survive that far, you know. Because once huttown is absorbed into tentback, there will be no outside focus for mockdirad's aggressive instincts. Our pelts will have no one to move against but one other. And the Mothers, without you, won't be strong enough an influence to counteract the pelts. Without guidance, I can even see the Mothers actively supporting intergrove rivalry."

Jahna evaded his gaze, quickly hustling her doubts to shelter. "That may be." It was her turn to shred and scatter leaves. "But I think you should be warned that if I do stay, I may begin composing my own speeches. And delivering them."

"I'm prepared."

"Even if my views turn out to differ from yours significantly?"

"But I don't think they will. I studied your records very carefully before I made my selection. Why should I import a goddess who was likely to prove imprudent as well as insubordinate?"

She kinked a tendril of vine around her finger. "Perhaps because the formal records only captured certain dimensions of my character. Perhaps because there are other

189

aspects I'm not even acquainted with yet, because there has never been a crisis to key them to life. We have differed, sharply, on several issues already.''

"Now, that is because you have had only a few days to appraise the Nelding situation. There are still a number of factors that are only words to you now. A few days in tentback and they will take flesh. You will be able to weigh the local condition with fully informed intelligence. A while beyond that, Peace, and you will find yourself a second expression of my own fully enlightened outlook.''

"Even to the arrogance?''

His eyes narrowed. "So does that bother you?''

She laughed, considering. "No, I don't mind arrogance. If it's justified.''

"And it isn't?''

Confronted, Jahna took her feet again. "First Minister, if you can talk me into the grove and under shelter until I'm fit to be StarMother again, I'll grant you first planetary right to arrogance—and to a selection of other notable qualities. Including the tongue to make matters clear if I decide to loft back to Peace for a century or two until your hairy friends are fully ready for the benefits a well-trained StarMother can bestow.''

Shutters closed between them. He nodded. "Then let us walk, StarMother.'' His words originated from a distance.

They walked in silence until the shadow of Hurak's grove loomed on the horizon, vague, dark, summoning. Jahna paused in her stride, her throat closing ominously.

This stand of trees, she realized unwillingly, had always waited somewhere on her personal horizon, a fact of her future, incontrovertible, inescapable. Only today was that fact revealed to her. Only today was she drawn forward into the circle of attraction of her own unsuspected future.

But she could see no more than her entry. When would she emerge from Hurak's grove? Under what circumstance? She frowned, trying to bring the future into sharper focus.

It refused to clarify. She could distinguish only mud and vines and in the distance tenting trees that already began to

190

disgorge dark bodies. Turning, protest futile on her lips, she watched Beck Lord, former Father of Pengalen, assume figurative robes of authority. Swallowing back panic, she raised her own head, crowning it. For today, for five more todays, she was StarMother, sister of the moon, daughter of the sun.

Someday she would ride her enchanted bug back across the universe. But not this morning.

Chapter Seventeen

PIETY CAUGHT only disconnected snatches of monster-talk as the members of the lakeside band huddled together across the reed-stand, but she apprehended enough to make her heart clutch and her head empty dizzily. Last night the Fathers had torched the fortress!

And her babe? Agonized, Piety squirmed across the trampled reeds to the skirts of the group. At her approach, talk ceased. Grimy faces closed suspiciously. The oldest male rigidified, glowering at her. "You *no!*" Quickly the big woman jumped up and tugged Piety back to her bed. "You stay," she instructed, her muddy face grim. "Vine-secret."

"But the fortress," Piety pleaded desperately. "I heard you say—did the Fathers burn the babes too?"

"You don't hear vine-secret, huttown." Shaking her head menacingly, the big woman pulled her waistlet from Piety's grasp and backed away to rejoin the circle. Quickly the monsters hunched together again, shadowed faces intent.

Piety peered at them helplessly. *Her babe*—was he buried somewhere in smoking ruins, a charred skeleton? Piety hugged herself against that terrible possibility. Last night while the monsters slept, despite her vigilance her babe had appeared to her neither on the night air nor in the chamber of her dreams. Because he had died in flame hours before? And if he had, what was left for her?

Nothing. Nothing at all. She faced that with bitter certainty. She had no home to return to now, no family, no Father Hoock. Nor was there a life for her among the monsters. Without her babe, she was a corpse walking.

But, she realized miserably, she wasn't even walking now. She had huddled here captive for two days, a corpse sitting, waiting . . . eating! Yes, she had eaten again, twice. To what purpose if her babe was dead?

To no purpose. If her babe lived, God the Power might recognize that her continued corruption was to some end. But not if her babe were dead.

She had to know. Quickly she peered across the reed-bed, her slight features tense. She could not sit one more night waiting for a vision that might never come. She must take herself to Pengalen to learn what had become of her babe. She must do it tonight.

That meant now, before the monsters bedded down around her, making escape impossible. Resolute, she began to move sideways through the crumpled reeds. Sitting, she inched and sidled. Then she stretched on her stomach and continued to move herself, prone. When she reached the boundary of the communal bed, her body bent down erect reeds and slid across them silently. Darting a glance back, she saw she had not been missed.

Painstakingly she reached the outer perimeter of the reedbed and stood. Sky above and tangles below were lost in darkness. Hesitantly she began to move through the vines, picking her way around smaller clumps of reed, the stench of sulphur heavy in her lungs. Like a small wraith she threaded the night.

Like a small wraith she paled and shrank at the angry outcry behind. The stand of reeds she had escaped sud-denly belched dark bodies wielding torches. Piety moaned, throwing herself flat in the vines. If there was God, she prayed fervently, if that God could find within Himself just one grain of mercy for His errant child tonight, if He could briefly make that child invisible to monster-eyes—

Mercy was absent from the vinelands. Piety's captors plunged near. A rattling tread halted near her head. Hope-lessly she raised her eyes.

She was yanked to her feet and dragged through the

vines. The monster who had found her was brute and ugly. He pulled her into the reeds and threw her down. Bellowing, he called back his fellows.

The big woman knelt over Piety, her eyes angry. "I told you, stay! Here!" She pounded the reed bed. "So now you do it, huttown."

Piety's lips trembled weakly. "Please. I have to know—"

They would not honor her voice. They ringed her, a dozen pair of grim eyes, and her words babbled away into nonsense. The oldest male knelt beside her, shoving his terrible face near. "You stay or mockdirad eat you." His lower jaw comprised half his heavy face. His eyes were lost in deep pits ringed around with stiff bristles. "Eat you!" he snarled, baring his canines.

"So sleep, huttown," the big woman warned her harshly.

Slowly they backed away. They reformed their huddle in a half-circle. As their heads bent over their secrets, their eyes remained vigilant on their captive.

Piety shivered in her cold bed, a trapped animal. Hugging herself, weeping, she finally fell asleep under their gaze. Even her dreams were barren, wasteland of emptiness, herself alone at its center.

She woke sobbing. All around her monsters sprawled in sleep. With a bitter cry, Piety rolled into a sodden ball of misery. But even as she sobbed, her resolve was slowly reforming. She would escape. Not tonight. Perhaps not tomorrow. But sometime soon she would rattle through the reeds again and, reaching the lakeside tangles, would run through the sulphur-tainted night, the moon to guide her. For the necessity had become a part of her, and it must be fulfilled. It *would* be fulfilled, however long she had to wait and watch for opportunity.

Sometime. . . .

Chapter Eighteen

JAHNA SAT cross-legged on the elevated couch of furs, shoulders and back rigid, eyes fixed straight ahead. The people of the grove stirred uneasily before her, silent on broad beds of moss. Beside Jahna, Beck was immobile. Jahna had not glanced at him during the hour of penance, nor did she do so when the sunset call finally rang in relays from shadowrim.

"Sundown!"

"Sun*down!*"

"SUNDOWN!"

Sunset, time for the ceremony to begin. Deliberately Jahna lowered her gaze and surveyed the gathering. Tangling faces were pale, layers of mud and grit scrubbed away, filthy hair rinsed, hands streaked half-clean. As her gaze passed from row to row, heads shook. Fearful faces were hurriedly curtained with hair.

Her gaze swept forward to where mockdirad knelt. The pelts were ostentatiously humble today, heads bowed, each muscular chest shaved in visible penance. Hurak took his feet, his head still lowered. "You are in the eyes of my mind, StarMother. Shame prevents me from raising other eyes until I have been invited to do so."

"So keep them averted, dirad," Beck responded peremptorily. "StarMother is not eager to fall into pools of treachery." Jahna's First Minister stood, arrogant in his pelts. Slowly he swept the gathering with his gaze. "So give us details of progress, dirad."

Hurak's head bobbed eagerly. "You have inspected the site yourself, First Minister. Teams of tanglings are already clearing weed and vine. Logs are being assembled and materials are being carried from every grove of tent-back. Messengers run farback way—''

''And do all dirad here acknowledge why it is necessary for a special compound to be erected to house Star-Mother?'' Beck interrupted, his voice abrasive.

Hurak's horny cylinder of teeth contracted until it was no more than a bulging knot in his neck. ''These mighty pelts acknowledge that the cause is our aggression against the Fathers of huttown three nights ago, when the pelted horde ran the night with flaming torches, their cry loud on the wind, their powerful legs carrying them over every obstacle.'' Captured by his own rhetoric, Hurak flung back his head, his voice soaring. ''Then the Fathers of huttown spilled from their doors, their faces blanched with fear, their—''

''And do the pelts of tentback acknowledge now, collectively, that that aggression was in and of itself a wrongful act?'' Beck demanded, shattering Hurak's impromptu hymn.

Hurak's eyes flared briefly, unreadably. He dropped his head. ''It was wrong,'' he muttered.

''Louder!''

The big pelt did not raise his head. He spat the words at his feet. ''It was wrong.''

''And why was it wrong, dirad?''

Hurak was silent, the set of his shoulders suddenly sullen. ''There is only so much of human blood on this world. Therefore it is wasteful for any of that blood to be fed to mud and vine. All of it, even the Fathers', is necessary for the balance and growth of this world.''

''So the pelts formally acknowledge that the Fathers are of human blood, as the pelts themselves are?''

Hurak's dirad cylinder writhed spasmodically. Behind him Tirammer, furred giant of the nearest neighboring grove, heaved his body stiffly erect, fur bristling on his shoulders. ''We acknowledge it,'' Hurak declared hastily, his own fur doggedly flat.

''And you acknowledge that the pelt-power dirad wield

in these groves does not give dirad the privilege to commit certain acts that would be considered reprehensible if committed by the Fathers or by the tanglings of these groves against the pelts?''

Hurak's head rose again, his eyes dark with wrenched pride. ''We acknowledge it.''

Jahna studied him briefly before her gaze shifted to the mockdirad gathered behind him. Four mockdirad she knew by name now, Hurak, Tirammer, arrogant Narrel, Nard. She raised her hand to signal her minister to silence. ''Then you are liars,'' she said with piercing clarity.

Bodies froze beneath the trees. Slowly startled eyes appeared from tangles of hair. Mockdirad lunged to their feet, shoulders bristling, bare chests swelling. Hurak rumbled ominously, his dirad cylinder twisting like an angry serpent.

''Sit!'' Jahna's gaze returned to Hurak and Tirammer, who alone kept their feet. ''I have lived in this grove for two days now. Even while you observed the silence I imposed, I was listening to you. I was testing your thoughts in the air. And what I detected was not regret or shame. Was it, mockdirad?''

The two big mockdirad exchanged a frozen glance. Hurak's eyes shifted. ''It was nothing else,'' he stated piously.

Jahna's eyes held his for long moments, her lips pressed tight. ''It was delight,'' she corrected. ''It was pleasure— that you had slaughtered your enemy before I thought to impose my standards upon your behavior. Minister?''

Beck crossed his arms over his chest. ''That is what you tasted.''

Hurak's glance scuttered away. He remained silent, stranded in the withering gaze from the royal couch. Low on his back, fur erected. In wave motion, the erectile area moved up his back to his shoulders, then flattened again. A low mutter of dirad nonsense emanated from his mouth.

''So did you think I came here merely to be your ornament, dirad?'' Jahna demanded. ''Did you think a

StarMother, sister of the moon, welcome passenger aboard any enchanted insect that plies this universe, would settle here in mud and shadow and graciously accept whatever vile thought and action she found operant?''

Hurak continued to utter dirad garble, his eyes intent upon the ground.

"Did you think I would ask nothing from dirad in exchange for my presence?''

For answer Hurak began to bob rhythmically on flexing knees. Behind him Tirammer crouched suddenly, folding arms and midarms over his chest, bowing his head sharply to expose the nape of his neck.

Jahna allowed silence to embrace the uneasy assemblage. "So answer me, dirad,'' she demanded finally.

Hurak bobbed, arms and midarms whipping air wildly. *"Dirad holds power,"* he snarled, his communication breaking down into furious nonsense. With a lunge, he threw himself across the assemblage and seized a torch from a crouching tangling.

Quickly Jahna stood. Her couch was raised on a structure of logs, so that she looked down on mockdirad. "So do you think I will establish my line on a world ruled by animals, dirad?''

The whiplash of her scorn halted mockdirad's charge. He froze before the couch, torch raised.

"Do you think I will create moldings to live as consorts of brutes?''

Slowly the man emerged from Hurak's paralyzed features. He lowered the torch, his massive shoulders rippling, his dirad cylinder curling in upon itself.

"So?'' Jahna pressed, aware of Beck poised ready beside her. "So, dirad?''

"I am no animal,'' Hurak declared in a broken tone. "I am mockdirad, carrier of the life-power of these trees.''

"I recognize your power. I question the human principles animating it. First the pelts wasted blood. Now they come here and attempt a false appeasement. Did you think I wouldn't read your true feelings, dirad?''

198

Her point told. Hurak dropped to his knees. "Mock-dirad are not brutes," he stated again, his tone a plea. "Our blood is human."

"Like Father's blood?"

"Like that."

"So then you do acknowledge that pelt-power does not bestow the privilege of committing murder?"

Hurak's head dropped. "We acknowledge it."

"Collectively? Each of you acknowledges it? Tirammer?"

Tirammer began to bob nervously, crouched, arms and midarms still folded over his chest. "It is acknowledged."

"Nard?"

Nard was a stolid pelt with balding head. "So Nard acknowledges," he rumbled, his eyes evasive.

Jahna studied them with asperity. In a crackling of furs, she sat. "Minister, we will have one more day of silence. I am not satisfied."

Her audience groaned. Tangling eyes were awed, mockdirad full of pain. "That is the word," Beck declared. "So leave us now. We will gather tomorrow at the same time. We will see then what StarMother has read from your secret thoughts."

Beck and Jahna sat in cross-legged silence while tanglings and mockdirad muttered from the grove. When moss beds were deserted, Jahna climbed from the platform. Beck sprang down beside her, eyes alert. "So, StarMother?"

Jahna pulled Hurak's grandfather tight around her shoulders. "I haven't reached any decision, Beck."

"But tasting thoughts from the air, I conclude that you do not feel optimistic about our pelted friends and their humane tendencies."

Jahna did not respond. They walked the grove in silence. The smells of evening mingled in the air, wood-smoke, damp reedcloth, roast chitterling, nush. As they passed smoking cookfires, tangling faces were hurriedly screened with hair. Awed eyes peered up and out. Jahna was uncomfortably aware of hypocrisy. Was it any more honest for her to pretend to be a skyborne deity than for mockdirad to feign a humility he did not feel?

Yet if she remained here, she would be thrust daily into the role of goddess. She would necessarily function simultaneously as stern mother to these errant children and as a symbol of feminine desirability. There would be no moment, no hour, no day when she did not carry the burden of her hypocrisy.

She sighed. "No one has sighted Yuba yet?"

"So what would you do if she were found and brought here?"

Jahna frowned down at her boots. "I would lift the curse, of course. Wouldn't you consider that appropriate after our sermon about humanity? Or aren't we required to practice what we preach, Minister?"

Beck's brows arched quizzically. "It's mockdirad who's required to practice, Peace. We pursue a more pragmatic course."

"Mightn't it be pragmatic to set the pelts a good example?"

"Um. But first you must consider what constitutes a good example. I recommend physical survival as the first principle."

"And power the second?"

He lifted his shoulders in a negligent shrug. "I am corrected. Call power the first principle and survival its natural concomitant."

"But power is what mockdirad exercises," she pointed out. "I thought our goal was to impose another scale of values, not to outdo mockdirad at his own game."

Beck paced beside her thoughtfully. "True. But we're playing our game on mockdirad's ground. So we have to top mockdirad before we begin to change rules. And in any case, if we lose sight of the matter of simple physical survival, freedom from attack and assassination, I may find myself playing this game with a dead marker: you. Then what will I gain? For myself or for anyone else?"

Jahna pursed her lips, refusing to give his argument the affirmation it demanded. They reached mockdirad compound in silence. The walls were shadowed with moss and darkness. Jahna trailed her fingers down a rough log. Mockdirad had taken other quarters, surrendering his compound to StarMother's party for the interval.

Inside, a single torch lit the compound area. Dimness seemed appropriate as Jahna drifted from Beck's silent escort to her own private stall. Its floor was spread with dry moss. Her cases stood against its back wall, separated from the earthen reality of their surroundings by incongruity. Jahna laid Hurak's grandfather across one case. There were reedcloth blankets tossed in one corner, a concession to Jahna's dearth of natural pelt. Knees buckling, Jahna settled on the springy moss. Across the compound, one of the babies wailed, a night-song of infantile despair. Even though she knew the babe would be attended immediately, Jahna's eyes filled with emphathic tears. There were, after all, other needs, other hungers, that inspired silent inward wails, never voiced, never answered.

If she molded these six babes and their successors, what birthright would she be granting them? Hypocrisy, doubt, perhaps even torturing half-buried memories of a blue-sky world they could never attain? And if something should remove Beck from the scene prematurely, if the dozen babes were left under the dubious guardianship of the pelts, what would they become with maturity? Playthings, ornaments, subjects of bloodthirsty contention.

Jahna lay on her back staring into darkness. She had told Beck she had reached no decision. That much was true. The decision had reached itself. Since the fire it had been slowly precipitating from the fogged interior of her mind. Now it presented itself, solid, final.

She had only to follow it. Still she did not fall asleep easily. Because she was forced to admit, in the privacy of her stall, that the motives behind her decision were neither noble nor altruistic. All the reasoned considerations she had reviewed these past two days were no more than rationalizations. All she could credit herself with was a species of personal honesty. And somehow that was not enough.

Much later she wakened with a startled gasp, her eyes flaring open. In the dimness of her stall, a face bent near, gnomish, twisted, topped by a shock of flashing white hair. Quickly Jahna struggled to a sitting position. "What is it?"

The gnome removed his hand from her arm. Despite his terrible face, his voice was wispy as a night breeze. "You want the babe, StarMother?"

"I—what? What babe?" Jahna instinctively kept her voice a whisper between them.

"Yuba-bull, she has one calf, Mother. But it will die without milk."

Jahna's mind struggled fully awake. "Yuba has a baby? With her?"

He nodded. "You want it?"

"Then you know where she is? You've seen her? You—"

"So she is dying, StarMother. The band of magic. But the babe, a sweet boy-babe—you come if you want it."

"I—"

Possibilities raced through Jahna's mind on a hundred swift feet. "Of course." She jumped up, her thoughts dashing ahead of her out of mockdirad compound and into the vines, where the gnome would lead her to the big woman, where she would wave her figurative wand and negate the choking spell, freeing Yuba-bull from sentence of death, freeing her babe from an orphan childhood, and freeing herself from the crushing sense of guilt she had carried since coronation eve.

The gnome sprang aside as she swirled her cape from a case and pulled it around her. "Take me."

He led way stealthily through mockdirad compound and into the grove. "We will not choose a way through the grove," he whispered, "because we do not want the people to see us, StarMother."

Jahna nodded. She followed him to the nearest

boundary of the grove and into the vines. Belatedly she remembered her light cube, packed in a case in her stall. But her eyes were adapted to darkness.

They skirted the edges of the grove silently, his white hair a moving beacon. Jahna was alert for mud sinks, for tripping vines, for moving shadows. But they met no one. They were alone in their quest. And in just two days she would be making another trek. She would be returning across the stars to Peace, as much damage as possible undone before her departure, her conscience at least minimally salved.

When they had gone a distance along the edges of the grove, they veered out into the vineland. Jahna glanced back briefly. Her anticipation precluded uneasiness.

At least it did so until the gnome held out his arm, halting her, and hissed a query at a nearby hillock. Immediately a dark shape leaped up and sprang across the vines toward them. Jahna jumped back instinctively, recognizing the girl who had boarded Nodd's wagon. Her hair was rough, her teeth sharp, bared. On a rope at her waist, Jahna saw with shock, she wore a long knife. Jahna's body rigidified. She glanced around to see her guide dissolve into darkness.

"So you want the babe, star skin?" the rough-haired girl hissed.

Jahna's vocal apparatus was momentarily paralyzed. Her mouth worked uselessly. "I—"

"So?" the other demanded, pressing near, her lips falling back like veils.

"I—yes. I want him."

"So follow."

"You—you know where she is then? You—"

"So would I say follow?"

Jahna hesitated. The girl's young body was taut, ready to spring. In her eyes was the same fierce vitality Jahna had met on that first night. But tonight it expressed itself less in hatred than in something else, some emotion Jahna couldn't readily name.

203

"So?" the girl hissed, her eyes rapacious beasts, dark, hungry.

"I'll come," Jahna agreed. After all, there was the magic Beck had bestowed upon her. It was hers for another two days, her shield and her protection. When the Nelding girl sprang away into the vines, Jahna followed.

Chapter Nineteen

LEADING WAY, Zuniin sprang across the vines with fierce exuberance, hand clutched tight on the haft of Quarl's skinning knife. She had another weapon waiting in the lakeside reeds, big muscles sweating for the kill. But the knife was a comforting symbol, a tangible promise of the violence she intended for the night. She gripped it, her thoughts racing irresistibly back to that moment when she had learned StarMother had gone to ground in Hurak's grove.

Even now the initial exhilaration gripped her again, a brilliant flash exploding inside her mind. Gusty with glee, Zuniin had slapped up palms of yellow foam from the mud sinks and smeared it across her thighs and belly. *So look down here, Moon!* she had cried, thrusting her stained hand at the heavens. *See the Mother who is going to end your sister!* Because with StarMother in the grove, Zuniin had only to dangle bait to lure StarMother the short distance from shadowrim to lakeside—and she had only to do it before Yuba-bull expired and Zuniin was left without a tool.

And faced with her determination—she recalled the moment with relish—the moon had hidden her face in cloud, craven. An omen surely, for did not StarMother walk behind Zuniin now, walk to her death? Zuniin glanced back, baring teeth, and then her thoughts raced irresistibly from the imminent moment of death to the days and weeks beyond.

For when order was restored to the groves, when pelt

and tangling realized the vicious thrall in which Sky-Mother had held them, what form would their gratitude take? Images of power crowded the air; herself one of the order, victorious in pelts, flinging herself in dance, losing herself in cry; herself as powerful as StarMother, commander of an army of moldings, subject of tangling worship, object of mockdirad rivalry. Gaudy victories flashed before her. She snatched them out of air and devoured them. She had waited long enough for this feast! Insane to consider that she was this moment a dishonored exile. Because once StarMother was dead. . . .

Once . . . And that would not be long. Zuniin turned to watch the lagging Mother pick her way through the vines. Not one hour and she would sprawl in muck, her golden hair dishonored, her pale eyes open in a last staring agony, pleading with death.

Pleading uselessly. Her magic would avenge her, but upon a dead woman. Zuniin chuckled at that joke, Star-Mother slain by the very woman her magic had already brought to the point of death. Then Zuniin turned and scampered ahead, daring StarMother to race her to the death-tryst.

When the sulphur-stink of the lake tinged the air, Zuniin halted near a small hillock and sampled the night. It was empty of life, a vast muddy barrenness. Overhead the sky was sodden with cloud. Before her, occasional clumps of reed thrust from the mud, rustling in the breeze. Here and there a lone tree grew, exile from the groves like herself.

StarMother straggled to where Zuniin waited. "Aren't we near yet?" Her voice was breathy.

Zuniin unveiled her teeth, her eyes glittering. "She is beside the lake in a stand of reed. So are your legs weak, star skin?"

StarMother did not honor the disparagement. "And the baby—how long has it been since she was able to feed it?"

"Oh, no worry," Zuniin assured her breezily, flicking her rough hair across her shoulders. "You will receive a sound babe because I have tapped trees to feed it two days now." It gave her an airy sense of power to nourish the imaginary babe so generously.

Unexpectedly StarMother's pale face waned, slipping back into night. "Then I don't understand why it was necessary to bring me out here tonight, citizen. You could have delivered the babe to the grove at any time."

Conflicting impulses moved Zuniin, one to slap Star-Mother across the face with her gullibility, with her helplessness here on Zuniin's ground, the other to oil her unease with smooth words. There was, after all, still a short distance to be covered. Zuniin's teeth set against each other. "There was a cause."

The pale face retreated again, melting back into night. "I think I'll have to know more about that cause before I go farther," StarMother pronounced stiffly.

Zuniin's hands clawed air in anger. So who did Star-Mother think she was, to demand? "So you want the babe thrown into the lake, Mother? You want it to suck its lungs full of muck? Because you have to know cause?" Zuniin sprang near to confront the other.

StarMother's eyes grew round in their shadowed sockets. "Why would anyone do a thing like that?"

Zuniin clucked. "Huh! Why would anyone hand over a helpless babe to the star witch?"

The other was very still, rigid. "Presumably because the mother wants her child to survive. I thought that was why you brought me out here."

"So come," Zuniin snapped. She glared at the other, then sprang away again. Hard legs carried her toward the lake. When she had covered meters, she turned to see if StarMother followed.

She did, unwillingly. Even at that distance, her attitude could be read.

Zuniin maintained her lead, her feet beating rhythms through the vines. *Die bag, die hag, choke witch, choke bitch! Scream Mother, cry Mother—die, die, die, Mother!*

Then she topped the knoll and halted. Below she could make out the stand of reeds where Yuba sheltered, sucking painful breaths, waiting to spring and strangle. Waiting because once StarMother was dead, Zuniin—girl-pelt, power-belt—promised to hack out StarMother's heart and StarMother's intestines, promised to spread them in a circle of very special dimensions and chant over them the spell-words she had learned from the Powers in dream last night. Then the spell uttered, she would spear the heart on the point of Quarl's knife, hold it for a moment over bull's head, over her own, then fling it into the lake. And when StarMother's heart sank, her magic would be shattered forever. Yuba-bull would breathe again. The blood on Zuniin's hands would have no power at all. She would smear it on her face, in her hair, across her breasts. It would be nothing, powerless.

At least so Zuniin had persuaded bull, leaning over her in the dark hours before dawn. Zuniin's own heart clutched now with ecstasy as she rehearsed the scene. The intensity of her emotion turned her entire body rigid. With a groan of passion she jerked around, hand on knife haft.

StarMother approached cautiously. Even in darkness Zuniin could see her pallor, her hesitancy. *So a golden crown is not everything, is it, Mother? Even star magic is not everything.*

Not tonight.

StarMother's eyes met Zuniin's wearily. "She's out here somewhere?"

"So did I say lakeside, skin?"

"You—did."

"And do you smell the mud?" She apprehended the other's reticent nod. "So she is down this slope and in that stand of reeds. You see it?"

StarMother's eyes narrowed. "I—yes."

"So go. She is waiting."

There was a pause. "You don't plan to accompany me?"

"Ah! You can't find your way into the reeds alone?" Zuniin's words were whips.

The other felt their sting. "I can manage," she snapped back.

"So manage, skin." With effort, Zuniin kept the full intensity of her victory from flashing across the surfaces of her eyes, betraying her.

StarMother hesitated briefly. Then, lifting her shoulders, she moved past Zuniin and down the slope, her golden crown paling with each successive step, her white neck glimmering in the night. *So go to death, StarMother. Walk into its arms, one step, one step, one step . . .*

But the rhythm was broken. StarMother halted, poised on the edge of darkness. Zuniin's head whipped wide, a faint rustle alerting her to something amiss. And there, lakeside to her left, she found a slight shadow moving across the deeper shadow of night, slipping almost silently, flying, its feet hardly seeming to touch ground. It seemed to be in flight from demons, so swiftly it ran. Straining, Zuniin could make out the pale of its face but nothing more.

She caught one harsh breath, body and mind paralyzed. In her mind there flashed a picture of the composition she had arranged: Yuba crouched in the reeds, herself watching from this rise, StarMother crossing the space between them, going to her death. But now a fourth element had intruded upon the scene.

It ran toward the reeds. Zuniin's frozen throat birthed an animal cry. Her hand clutched Quarl's knife, bared it. But her legs would not propel her down the slope.

StarMother turned and stared back at her. Before either could move, the small shadow plunged into the reeds. There was a throaty bellow. The reeds thrashed violently. Terrible grunts issued from them as Yuba's big body fell upon its prey.

Its mistaken prey. That prey uttered one brief shrill, truncated. Then fell the longest silence Zuniin had ever known.

By the time Zuniin was able to move, StarMother was already running toward the reeds. Zuniin flung herself down the slope, outpacing her. She was first to arrive at the death scene, first to see the slight figure in huttown garb flung lifeless in the reeds, first to see Yuba-bull's head rise, her final breath an agony in her throat. Then bull's body stretched out in a long twitching spasm fraught with groans, a rattle, and finally silence.

Bull was dead. Zuniin's weapon had destroyed itself— on the wrong victim. Bending, Zuniin rolled the huttown girl and seized her muddy hair, yanking her lifeless face up, trying to read the sense from this death. In her throat she uttered a hundred curses. Savagely she flung the dead girl back. Her cunning plan, shattered by a nameless shadow in the night.

Zuniin raised her head. StarMother's eyes were round and stunned. Her lips writhed to form question. "Wh—" Slowly she backed away, her hands raised.

The knife was still in Zuniin's hands. She raised it, stared at its blade. So there was no other way to end this witch. No other way at all. *So be it!*

StarMother, however, did not acquiesce in the decision. Instead she seized control of her muscles, turned, and began to run. With a cry, Zuniin flung herself after.

They described a zigzag course through reed and vine, each participant's muscles fueled by desperation. As she leaped after the other, Zuniin cursed viciously. Star-Mother had been so slow before; she ran like dirad now. Half a dozen times Zuniin's blade slashed out on empty air. Its prey had already dodged and taken a fresh course.

The chase rattled through the vines until Zuniin's breath was harsh, until her grinding teeth sent rays of pain through her jaws and up the back of her skull, until the curses in her throat died in impotence. Still the other evaded her.

Then, as abruptly as if signaled, StarMother dodged at a tangent and flung herself into the shelter of a pair of tall trees. With a screech, Zuniin plunged after her.

And was caught! Shadow came alive and seized her arms. Her knife was wrenched from her hand. Her victory screech became a shriek of anger. Kicking, she threw herself at restraining bodies, trying to fight free.

More hands seized her. Roughly she was hustled beyond the perimeter of the trees and pinioned against the vines. Struggling, she grimaced up into tangling faces. She bared her teeth, growling. But they laughed.

Laughed at *her*, StarMother's executioner!

Then old Dahda stepped from the trees, her sagging body supported by girdles of matriarchal anger. She approached with a steady pace and looked down upon Zuniin's helpless body. "So, mud crawler. Did you think Quarl wouldn't tell us what you put him up to tonight?"

Jerking her head, Zuniin laid eyes on the gnome. He huddled at the edge of the ring of captors, face twisted with glee. "You!"

"He," Dahda agreed. "He did what you told. But then he did more. So here we are, mud crawler. Where have you tethered the bull?"

Zuniin flattened herself against the vines, wordless.

It was StarMother who informed old Dahda of bull's end, of the huttown girl's death in the reeds. Words interspersed with deep breaths, StarMother drew the whole picture for the old Mother.

Dahda's face grew as grim as death. "So," she said softly. She studied her captive. "So. Now you have finished destroying our sister." The old Mother glimpsed around, then stepped away to retrieve Quarl's knife from a tangling. "So, Zu," she said again, returning.

Zuniin writhed under the old Mother's gaze. "No," she begged, staring helplessly at the knife. She was executioner tonight, not victim.

"You think I want to give this knife a drink of girl-blood?" Dahda teased, fingering the blade, bending near.

"No."

"You think it isn't thirsty, girl?"

"Old Mother—"

But Dahda would not listen. Abruptly she motioned to the tanglings who pinioned Zuniin. They wrestled her to her feet. She threw herself back, trying to distance herself from the knife in Dahda's hand, from certain punishment.

To her astonishment, Dahda seized not her but Star-Mother. With one hearty yank, she pulled the star skin in front of her and bared her pale arm. The knife gashed down, biting StarMother's skin, tasting her blood.

Then the flat of the bloody knife slapped Zuniin's belly, her breast, her cheek, smearing them all with star blood. She howled, lunging against her captors. She heard Dahda's barked command, but she was nonplussed nevertheless when hands fell away and she was free.

But what was freedom with star blood already burning belly and breast, its searing heat a foretaste of the agony she would know as it slowly transformed her into a single excruciating sore? She slapped at her belly with the butt of her hand. Blood smeared, but the pain in her belly did not ease. Instead her hand began to burn too. She could smell the heat generated as StarMother's magic dissolved her skin.

With a sob she flung herself back from the ring of tanglings. Old Dahda's face was fierce, StarMother's shocked. She shrieked one desperate curse at them and tore away into the vines.

She ran. She rolled. She smeared herself with mud and rubbed herself with leaves. She tore whips off trees and lashed herself. Nothing drew the pain.

She burned.

She had run forever, or perhaps only a few agony-racked minutes, when her feet realized where she must go. Her lips fell back from her teeth in a snarl. Her hard legs pounded.

She crashed through the stand of reeds where Yuba-bull and the huttown girl sprawled in mutual death. A few meters beyond she paused and then hurled herself at the bubbling surface of the mud lake. Her last cry stretched behind her like a banner, flapping wild. She stared at it and at the entirety of her short life. Then she sank into the lake. Her nostrils and mouth filled, smothering the pain of star blood, bringing another pain.

That pain was brief. Soon her limbs quit thrashing and she joined the lake, her bid for power drowned in hot sulphur mud.

Chapter Twenty

JAHNA MOVED across the vines, case bumping one leg, blue daysuit flapping lightly in the morning breeze. As she covered ground, her eyes found familiar vegetation everywhere: stalks and vines bursting from the mud, brindle squash sheltering in shadowed leaf-caves, redspear lancing, halma tunneling, in the distance the small grove from which she had watched Pengalen burn. Even the sky was a familiar face now, a dissatisfied woman, sullen with distant storm. And there was one other, more recent familiarity. That was the weight on her shoulders.

Absently she adjusted her cape. For two days now her lightweight Service cape had depended from her shoulders in layers, one her own blue cape, another a coarse woven mantle assumed from the shoulders of the nameless huttown girl, the third and fourth separate reedcloth cloaks taken up from the two dead grove women. None of the three had worn mantles to their deaths. Nevertheless Jahna was burdened with their offcast spiritual garments now. And she did not wear them light, any of them.

Pausing, she glanced back at Beck. Her eyes met hers warily. *So, Peace?* they inquired. But he was a man who carried his thoughts and his dreams silently these last days. Troubled, she walked on.

Then he spoke, his voice sharp. "The shuttle has broken cloud cover, Peace. Look up. High."

Jahna glanced up quickly, eyes eager for the flash of metal. But old Mother dulled the shuttle's metal shell just as she stifled the sun's light. The ship dropped like a lusterless metal insect, legs growing from its carapace as it scudded across the ruins of Pengalen. It came to rest in the roadway beyond.

Jahna walked faster, anxious to cover the distance that separated her from decision. But her multiple mantles slowed her, keying dark memories: Yuba's spasmic death in the reeds, the huttown girl's slight face in last repose, Zuniin's fierce cry as she threw herself into the sulphur lake. Even if she returned Peace way, Jahna knew these three would accompany her, seed of another place, of another time, always struggling to germinate and grow within her, to unfold the petals of their joint deaths in a single haunting blossom.

The shuttle opened promptly and a blue-suited male appeared upon its ramp. He held himself stiffly, his head rigid atop his spine. Two Fathers stepped from the roadway, square-cut beards righteous, deep eyes vulturous. Jahna stepped around the corner of the ruins and suddenly found herself the focus of all eyes.

"Cadet Swiss?" the shuttle pilot queried, stepping to the foot of the ramp. He was a thin man, grayed at the edges from years at space.

"Jahna Swiss, Peace Service Corps," Jahna affirmed. "I've been informed that I have free choice to return to Peace now or to remain here for two years as originally scheduled."

"That agrees with my own instructions." The pilot's eyes were as impassive as his face. "Which is your choice, Cadet?"

Jahna's eyes swept the tightening circle of faces. Panic claimed her tongue. How had she arrived at this point in time with no clear decision?

But had she? Two nights ago she had retired to mock-dirad compound and found a decision ready in her mind. Now she reached out to touch the railing of the shuttle's ramp. It was as metal-gray as the pilot's eyes, as cold as space. Grounded to the non-Nelding reality of cold metal, Jahna found another decision coiled ready in her mind.

Now it sank fangs. Jahna wore four mantles. Only one of them belonged on Peace, yet she could never divest herself of the other three by stepping aboard the shuttle now and lofting across the stars. In their separate ways, each of the three women had invested her with a responsibility. And there were other Nelding women waiting to invest her with further responsibilities. But they were not all women yet. A few were babies; most were generations unborn. One day, Jahna knew, she must walk this world in all her numbers and fulfill those responsibilities, however unsought.

"I intend to stay my two-year term," she announced, releasing the rail.

Huttown faces twisted bitterly. Black beards flapped. "You choose to spend your time with animals, trollop?"

The pilot turned a steady gray gaze upon the Fathers. "I understood the terms to be free choice."

"Those were the terms," Beck affirmed, taking Jahna's arm. "So you may relay instructions for another shuttle to land on this site at the prearranged date. We will see that landing space is cleared. You need not bother the Fathers at all."

The pilot's eyes flickered from face to face, dispassionate. He nodded. "That message will be faxed." He cast a stiff salute Jahna's way. "I will request you to step back to radius, citizens, for loft-up."

The Fathers huffed down the road, bitter in defeat. Jahna and Beck retreated to the small grove. As they watched the shuttle swallowed its multiple legs and rose to assault Old Mother's cloudy underbelly. Jahna tracked the dull metal carapace until it was lost in cloud, her eyes reluctant to leave the sky.

"Two years, StarMother," Beck reminded her, hefting her cases. "Is that so long?"

Two years? She met his quizzical gaze. "You forget. I'll be here for centuries, Beck."

He arched one brow. "But so will I. And it doesn't oppress me. Not greatly at least. Not today."

"I can see it doesn't," she replied tonelessly. Jahna took up her last case, her gaze attracted skyward again. Two years or forever? Staring up into the clouds, she wondered. Old Mother, she realized, had always waited here on her private horizon, unsuspected, unavoidable. Now, as the shuttle darted back toward the void, she wondered if any other world lay on the still unglimpsed portion of the horizon of her future, if even her own Peace lay there any longer—or if Old Mother had claimed her for all time.

Beck strode ahead of her, his eyes playing across the vines. "So shall we hunt halma, Peace? Are you hungry?"

"Um," Jahna responded distractedly, her eyes searching inward almost desperately for the slightest glimmer of blue sky, her heart heavy with the unknown.

ANDRE NORTON